We Discovered

Alien Bases On The Moon II

Eighth Edition
Updated & Revised 1997

by Fred Steckling
and Glenn Steckling

www.gafintl-adamski.com

Copyright © 1981 by
Fred Steckling P.O. Box 1722
Vista, CA 92083, USA

All rights reserved. No part of this book may be reproduced, stored in a retrieval system, or transmitted, in any form or by any means, electronic, mechanical, photocopying, recording, or otherwise, without prior permission of the author and publisher. Manufactured in the United States of America.

Library of Congress Catalog Card Number 81-90609

First printed in the United States of America. 1981
Eighth edition printed 1997

By G.A.F. International

ISBN 0-942176-00-6

I dedicate this book to all open minded people who cherish a new frontier of thought and who are willing to accept the fact that "Life" is a Cosmic manifestation, not confined to Earth alone!

"Man" is the most adaptable "creature" in the Universe.

It is not the truth which hurts.
It is the sudden realization of it!!

P.O. BOX 1722
VISTA, CA. USA
92085

Contents

			Page
Prologue			1
Introduction			12
Chapter	1	The Moon General Information	17
Chapter	2	The Apollo Lunar Mission of the United States	19
Chapter	3	Behind the Lunar Mysteries	23
Chapter	4	UFO Analysis	35
Chapter	5	Analysis of Advanced Civilization	51
Chapter	6	New Concepts Replace Old Theories	69
Chapter	7	True Colors on The Moon	81
Chapter	8	Gravity and Atmosphere on the Moon	87
Chapter	9	Water, Clouds, and Vegetation	97
Chapter	10	Photographic Analysis of Lunar Pictures	107
Chapter	11	Symbols, Signals and Markings on the Moon	131
Chapter	12	NASA Experts Reveal the Facts	143
Chapter	13	Probing Adamski's Claims	175
Chapter	14	Changes Overdue	181
Chapter	15	Why Explore Space?	185
Chapter	16	Beyond the Moon	191
Epilogue			215
References			227

Prologue

It has been several years since my father passed away in 1991, and since then, people from around the world have repeatedly asked that I expand upon the material presented in the original version of his second book <u>We Discovered Alien Bases On The Moon</u>. During this interval of time, there has been an ever increasing worldwide demand for the type of logic and reasoning, combined with scientific fact and clarity, which my father strove to represent during an involvement of over thirty five years within the arena of UFO research and extraterrestrial visitations.

Few people today could legitimately claim the sense of history, exposure, and experiences my father was privileged to be part of and contributed to. To say I feel fortunate to have shared my thirty seven years with parents and associates directly involved within this subject would be an understatement.

And it is mainly due to my first-hand knowledge, and the necessity of providing a clear and concise record of the many events which shaped those years, plus my desire to enforce the principles of integrity and truth associated with continuing both my father's and Mr. Adamski's legacy, that I have chosen to avail myself of this opportunity.

Many readers today have precious little knowledge concerning the history of UFO sightings or reports of extraterrestrial visitations. All too often, the quest for the

1

latest, greatest, most sensationalistic news has resulted in the sacrifice of logic, sensibility and science. Such logical approaches are often purposely ignored or conveniently overlooked by those seeking to confuse the entire process, and as a result, seldom is an entire or balanced picture presented to the public. Yet, even if one was to foolishly overlook the many valid publications and serious studies encompassing ancient texts, pictographs, indigenous records, etc., pertaining to flying objects and their occupants, and merely concentrate on events recorded within the last hundred years, the mountains of information would truly astound many people.

From childhood, my father was captivated with the concept of flight. In a sense, one could say that love of flying - the freedom of soaring above earthly confines - is almost a family trait. My grandfather was a military transport pilot and my father's uncle was involved with rocketry systems during that same period. Consequently resulting in his, and no doubt my, magnetism towards aviation.

Due to his early teenage association with aviation and his aptitude toward flying, he was chosen to attend a glider school located on islands bordering the German coastline. It was there he consummated his early desires to pilot aircraft.

As years passed, with growing aspirations of flying more sophisticated machines, my father passionately followed the evolution of aviation. His pursuit of a flying career also included a brief enlistment with the Air Force. However, due to enforced pilot quotas, which resulted in the military's inability to fulfill their contractual obligations, they gave him the opportunity to withdraw and pursue other possibilities.

Those years of the mid 1950's constituted exciting times in the progression of aviation development. With the refinement of both military and civilian postwar aircraft, the advent of the jet and atomic age, the exploration of the sound barrier and rocket technologies, there was much to captivate anyone's attention. More importantly, it was also during this same time period that countless reports of unidentified flying objects, objects capable of maneuvers far surpassing anything produced by terrestrial technologies, became almost common worldwide headlines.

From the skies above Europe, England, Washington D.C. and the United States, Canada, Australia, South America and countless other countries, UFO reports reverberated. Newspaper reporters, pilots, astronomers, air traffic controllers, police officers, military personnel, and ordinary citizens not only witnessed these spectacular machines in flight but some were even fortunate enough to have contact with their HUMAN occupants as well. During those years, from 1947 to 1960, there existed far less censorship concerning this phenomena. This resulted in the open curiosity of both the media and governments which in turn stimulated a greater release of factual information (i.e., Life Magazine, April 7, 1952). This situation was due to dramatically change in the not too distant years to follow.

Not only the frequency of these sightings, but also the nature of these extraterrestrial vehicles greatly aroused my father's curiosity. Already as a youth, the idea of other inhabited worlds within the unending cosmos constituted a very logical and natural concept. During his teenage years in Berlin, he collected numerous articles pertaining to UFO activities and meticulously plotted out the locations of these reports on a large global map. Recalling those early years, he told me that during a brief five year period before he and my mother immigrated to Canada, and afterwards to the United States, the map was literally covered with hundreds of position markers. After coming to the United States in 1960 and shortly thereafter relocating to Denver, Colorado in late 1960, my family witnessed several UFO sightings over the Denver area.

Dating back as far as the late 1940's, and primarily due to the atomic testing program, military projects and other specific events, such UFO sightings had become almost daily occurrences. In fact, within these western states, not only had extraterrestrial space craft been recovered, but also individuals had photographed them in flight and recorded contacts with their occupants. Yet it was in the spring of 1963, while residing in Washington D.C. and standing in the middle of downtown at 03:20 in the afternoon, that our family, a Washington Daily News newspaper reporter and some thirty other people witnessed a most memorable and spectacular UFO performance.

What was described as a bell shaped saucer craft skipped about the city's skies at approximately 600 meters altitude, hovered for 15 seconds silently overhead and then shot straight up out of sight, exhibiting inconceivable acceleration. Within days, the story appeared in the newspaper along with various other reports from neighboring areas.

With my father's familiarity of aviation development and previous experience collecting UFO data, he decided to contact the U.S. Air Force in search of their explanation concerning these recurring and substantial sightings. By this time, the United States military had determined policy and implemented strict procedures dealing with the UFO phenomena. Basically, this policy was to deny any cognizance of this matter and hopefully defer it until some undisclosed date. However, in the same breath they conceded some knowledge of this matter by repeatedly releasing the statement that *these extraterrestrial craft posed no threat to the security of our nation*. Also, it is interesting to note that a Air Force Academy text book instructed their cadets as to the existence of, and procedures relating to, UFO's. They took the UFOs quite seriously.

With a growing desire for more concrete information, my father visited the Library of Congress. There he found under the fact, NOT fiction, section a book entitled **Flying Saucers Have Landed** by George Adamski. Inside were clear, concise photographs of exactly the same type of bell-shaped craft we had witnessed both in Colorado and in Washington D.C. Straight away, he mailed off a letter to Mr. Adamski in Vista, California requesting to meet him. Shortly thereafter, we received a quick reply informing us he would be traveling out to the East Coast for lecture engagements which included an address to the Air Force reserves in the D.C. area. Instructing us to contact Mr. & Mrs. Rodeffer in Maryland, with whom he resided when visiting, we could make his acquaintance soon. In short, a great respect and friendship developed amongst Mr. Adamski, the Rodeffers and ourselves. During the following two years, we all felt extremely privileged to not only share much of Mr. Adamski's confidence, but also help arrange several of his lecture appearances in our area. This included opportunities to witness numerous close UFO sightings and contacts while in his presence. In February of 1965, George Adamski and Mrs. Rodeffer shot amazing motion picture footage of a bell-shaped craft maneuvering 25 meters away between the trees in front of her house in Maryland (see Plate 16).

Immediately after this sighting, Mr. Adamski called out family to the house. The next morning my father brought the film to Dynacolor, in Virginia, for processing and picked it up 24 hours later. Upon seeing the fantastic results, my father quickly arranged an International Press Conference at the MayFlower Hotel, just up the street from the White House. Included at the conference were representatives from most foreign embassies and correspondents from the majority of the newspaper and television networks. The entire meeting lasted well over two hours and left all involved in astonishment. This film was later analyzed by an engineer from Eastman Kodak in Rochester, New York, who confirmed it to be authentic, giving specific distances, dimensions, etc.

The wealth of knowledge, information and experiences George Adamski possessed has always amazed and annoyed both skeptics and debunkers alike. The fact that he was received and recognized by officials, royalty, religious and educational institutions during his world tours incurred a great deal of envy which continues to this day. Also, regardless of the attempts to discredit Mr. Adamski, his pictures and films, taken worldwide under a variety of conditions, have stood the test of each decade's technological analysis. His pre-space age testimonies concerning conditions in space, the moon and our neighboring worlds continues to enlighten and challenge current discoveries. And his contacts with extraterrestrial human beings, who brought messages of value and peace, can never be outdated.

Several weeks prior to Mr. Adamski's passing in April of 1965, he specifically directed and instructed my parents as to how he wanted them to continue this educational program pertaining to this work. After April, my parents increased their efforts to bring this information before all those interested. In September of 1966, we accompanied my father on a European lecture tour arranged by associates, and Adamski co-workers abroad. While flying to Germany, he filmed with his ever handy 8mm movie camera, through the Boeing 707 passenger window, a cigar shaped space craft releasing smaller saucer-shaped craft over the North Atlantic. Several days later, while on a rail trip from Schifferstadt to Mannheim, nearly everyone on the train witnessed, and my father once again filmed, a fleet of the same cigar-shaped spacecraft flying in formation alongside the train. Both events caused a sensation with the local media, and were included in a documentary shown throughout Europe the following year.

After an enthusiastic response overseas, we returned to Washington D.C. where my parents contacted both NASA and the Pentagon, inviting both agencies to review these and the Adamski films. In the spring of 1967, we accepted invitations to address Col. Freeman and his staff at the Pentagon, conversed with 22 scientists at Goddard Space Flight Center in Greenbelt Maryland, and later spoke over Radio Free Europe. Each assembly awarded great courtesy, respect and affirmation towards this UFO documentation, and, also acknowledged Mr. Adamski's work, his photographs and films. They expressed advanced knowledge of these extraterrestrial crafts, their propulsion systems and the origin of their human occupants. Rather than trying to conceal their awareness of the space visitors' interactions, they were keenly aware of, and interested in, obtaining further information pertaining to the continuous interaction between these visitors and our society. Here I stress that during these meetings, these officials supported the fact that these extraterrestrials appear just like earth people, varying in size and color as we do, and they have mingled amongst us since recorded time. Afterwards, several sympathetic scientists directed my father towards the proper channels to obtain additional NASA information in order to continue further research, the direct result of which partially includes this book.

Until the time of the first edition of <u>Alien Bases On The Moon</u> which was published in 1981, my father's continued efforts included a television appearance with Art Linkletter in 1970, numerous radio and university addresses, several European tours, plus national television and lectures in Japan. In order to correlate our own detailed lunar observations with some of the amazing photographs obtained from NASA catalogs, we also obtained a twelve and a half inch, and later, an eighteen and a half inch reflector telescope. This activity, combined with reports from a network of other amateur astronomers, helped confirm numerous observations of UFO activity, lunar constructions, and other atmospheric anomalies around the moon.

For years, my father and I meticulously examined thousands of NASA pictures, spent many late nights viewing through our telescope and worked to compile just some of the information found in the following chapters. Afterwards, we were very pleased and excited by the response to our research and efforts. In 1984, Lord Clancarty invited my parents and arranged for my father to give a presentation before a select committee of Britain's House of Lords. Once again, great amazement and respect was forwarded for presenting such quality information "in so reasonable and rational a manner." Afterwards, Lord Clancarty delivered a copy of Alien Bases On The Moon to interested parties at Balmoral Castle. Within several months of his return from England, my father was delighted to receive a personally signed acknowledgment from a member of the Royal Family acknowledging his excellent publication. During the next few remaining years, our family continued to travel in order to meet public demand; trips to Australia, Germany, and around the United States, offering our findings and data wherever requested and whenever time and our professions permitted. We consented to several documentary interviews in our home with the intention of giving the public a broader perspective into the information circulating concerning this subject today.

Since the book's initial release, the overwhelming response has carried Alien Bases on the Moon into its 8th English edition including subsequent foreign translations. And we have happily received thousands of letters from a variety of people supporting our research. We have been fortunate to converse with innumerable individuals who have witnessed similar UFO sightings; scientists, pilots, military personal, officials, teachers, and everyday people, many who have contributed to and supported this information becoming public. Not too long ago, our correspondence with a Prime Minister of a Caribbean nation, a most vocal and supportive United Nations UFO advocate, helped contribute to that country's issuance of exceptional commemorative UFO stamps.

My father had neither time nor regard for fanfare or notoriety. He was keenly aware of the pressures and restrictions placed upon public officials and therefore appreciated any of their honest efforts without accusation or prejudice. However, he did feel that in today's UFO circles far too much time and emphasis was being wasted on accusations of who is right or wrong, who has the answers and who is attempting to gain distinction for themselves. And he had little regard for those who wished to exploit or play games concerning this vital information. Ultimately, he believed each individual must be granted the right and opportunity to examine, decipher and rationally access the information for themselves. We hope this book, and our other publications, allows readers the respect and privilege of making that choice unobstructed.

Fred Steckling was a person who enjoyed the pursuit of truth, information, evidence, and the reasons behind the facts, ideas and reports as they appeared. He enjoyed not only the discovery of answers, but the questions associated with their procurement. In many ways, he considered himself a rationalist who required tangible proof in order to convince him. He, like Mr. Adamski, believed the reasons behind extraterrestrial visitations, and the benefits to mankind, far surpassed the mere knowledge of their existence. They both deeply felt we needed to collectively do far better as a people, and a planet, if we were to survive to recognize our future potential. And they both were unselfishly willing to contribute towards that potential.

Above all, I remember them both having a magnificent sense of humor; that they could enjoy a hearty laugh at themselves, and were both intently serious and stern when faced with matters concerning life, but still kind, compassionate and tolerant of the various manifestations of human understanding. Throughout these 35 years, our family obtained all the proof we could ever require, and, we are thankful for the opportunity to relay it to those willing to listen with open minds and hearts.

G. Steckling

Acknowledgments

I should like to thank the National Aeronautics and Space Administration (NASA) and the NASA Science Data Center for their cooperation and for providing the lunar photographs in this book.

This book is not intended to embarrass NASA, or any other agency of our Government. The purpose of this book is to inform and awaken the often apathetic public. The reader needs to understand that the conclusions and photographic analysis of all NASA materials by the author may not necessarily coincide with NASA's analysis of the same photographs. Most of the research and photographic analysis was conducted by the author, who recognizes that partial credit belongs to retired Major H. Petersen, of the Danish Air Force who performed some of the Lunar Orbiter analysis.

I also wish to express my deep appreciation to J. N. Stone for helping me with the orderly procedure of this manuscript.

Fred Steckling

Introduction

To many readers, my findings of UFO bases on the Moon and the published NASA photographs in this book, may come as a complete surprise. I can, however, assure you of the complete validity and authenticity of all photographic evidence.

My intentions are not to insult the intelligence of the public, nor the National Aeronautics Space Administration (NASA) where I obtained the photographs, Apollo catalogs, and microfilms. All photographic material in this book are for public release. Nothing classified or top secret may be found in this book.

Photographic analysis of all Apollo photos and most of those of the Lunar Orbiter were conducted by myself over a twelve year period. I relied heavily on my experience as a trained observer, using a large reflecting telescope. My astronomical studies, although on an amateur basis, date back to the 1960's. Furthermore, being a pilot for many years, I am well familiar with all types of flying. I feel that my qualifications are adequate to identify aerial photographs from every angle. My interest in aviation, astronomy, and outer space travel prompted my exceptional interest in the UFO phenomena.

Many pilots, civilian and those who were formerly in the military, have studied these NASA photographs. Most have responded with the same astonishment, stating: "Look at all those clouds on some of these photos!" One retired Air Force Colonel asked me, "Where did you get these fantastic photos?" My reply was, "From NASA's Science Data Center, of course. May I add that none are classified, for if they were I would not want anything to do with them".

Retired Danish Air Force Major, H. Petersen, with whom I am well acquainted, examined hundreds of NASA lunar photographs. My own investigation and analysis of over ten thousand Apollo photographs revealed overwhelming evidence to me, as well as to Major Petersen, that extraterrestrials have bases on the Moon. The outcome of my investigation, as well as my own speculation about the living conditions on the Moon, are presented in this book.

If only fifty percent of the contents and photographs of this book will be accepted, it will no doubt stir up controversy. To be honest, I hope it will.

I have faith in the American people, the Constitution, and what it purports. By presenting the findings in this book, I exercise my fundamental rights as a citizen of the United States of America. This right, I feel, obliges me to express freely, responsibly, and with respect.

The officials conducting the U. S. Lunar exploration program seem to have chosen to cloud this most important subject of our times into mystery, for reasons which are purely speculative. Perhaps the general lack of interest of the public at large in our space program has encouraged those officials. Much information concerning the Moon and outer space was released piecemeal to the press, requiring the public to read between the lines. Nevertheless, many official NASA releases were quite plain, and spoke of water, air, and volcanic activity on the Moon.

It has been generally assumed that NASA is responsible for the education of the public concerning all of their findings in space. This, of course, is erroneous. Unfortunately, NASA, as highly publicized, is understaffed, and is operating on a minimal budget. I do believe that many of my findings in regard to the lunar photographs have not been noticed by NASA because of their budgetary problems. NASA *should* be supported by every citizen of this country. Our outer space exploration program is gradually advancing Earth man to broaden his views and is enabling him to establish new frontiers in space, and on other worlds. If future generations are to survive, outer space exploration seems to be the only alternative.

I know, from personal experience, that UFOs do exist. I have sighted some of them from aircraft, through telescopes, and from the ground as well. In 1976 I managed to film thirty five feet of eight millimeter Kodacolor film of a UFO in motion over north San Diego County.

At the present retarded technological state of affairs, it would be utterly impossible to construct cigar-shaped space vehicles, several miles in length. Nonetheless, these amazing craft have been photographed, not only in our atmosphere, but also in the vicinity of the Moon.

The United States Air Force states that UFOs do not pose a threat to the security of this nation, and while there have been hostile reports of UFOs on Earth, what kind of chance would we have against just one of these gigantic spacecraft, not to mention an entire armada of them? According to my information, several nations on Earth have constructed small, free energy flying machines since 1965. They must have finally succeeded in their efforts to duplicate the small scout type craft, which visit our Earth from other worlds. Data analysis reveals that most of these small craft of extraterrestrial origin, are transported between planets, inside of the giant carrier craft. But there is also reason to believe that some of the hostile actions by UFOs, reported *after* 1965, are part of a secret terrestrial program aimed at frightening the public, and causing confusion regarding true space visitations.

I hope that this book may encourage the general public, as well as the scientific community, to not only support our space program, but also demand and request all information to which it is entitled.

Certainly it is hoped that if proper interest is shown by the public, NASA, in return, may release more information than it has concerning the Moon. As some scientists suggest, "We must lift the laughter curtain of the UFO matter, and maturely and open mindedly continue investigation."

1

The Moon - General Information

Our Moon could almost be called a double planet, because of the fact that it is much larger than any other satellite, in relation to its parent planet. The Moon's distance from Earth varies from about two hundred and twenty thousand to two hundred and fifty-two thousand miles. The difference is due to its elliptical orbit around the Earth. The Moon's diameter is some two thousand one hundred and sixty miles, while its surface area covers approximately twenty three million square miles. If we would superimpose the Moon upon the United States, it would span a distance from Las Vegas to Philadelphia.

Lunar gravity has been estimated to be about one sixth of that of Earth. It is estimated one-sixth, because gravitational attraction varies, depending upon the elevation and location. Certain areas on the visible, as well as the hidden side, show some highly concentrated masses of matter beneath the surface. We have called these phenomena "masscons". Here gravity shows noticeable changes, as has been experienced by the Apollo space flights. While the astronomy charts of the Moon state that the lunar atmosphere is very thin, nevertheless, I will endeavor to prove that the Moon's atmosphere is dense enough to support clouds and vegetation.

It is amazing how many people are still unaware of the fact that the Moon does rotate on its axis. A full rotation requires 29.9 days, or one full calendar month.

At this rate, the Moon shows approximately the same face toward the Earth for about 59% of its surface. This is caused by the libration effect.

The age of the Moon was determined to be about four and one-half billion years, indicating that both the Earth and the Moon came into existence about the same time, and probably from the same cloud of cosmic dust.

The Moon's mass has been estimated to be 1/81 of Earth's mass, its density, 0.60, the escape velocity 1.5 miles per second and the orbital velocity 2,287 miles per hour.

Concerning the moon it is interesting to note:

• A treaty of principles governing the exploration of outer space, the Moon and other celestial bodies, signed by the United States in 1967, provides that weapons of mass destruction will not be placed in space.

• The Moon is to be a demilitarized area, over which no nation may claim sovereignty.

• In 1971 the USSR responded to the United Nations subcommittee by submitting its own draft of a similar treaty, which was recognized by the U. N. General Assembly.

• This treaty was designed to establish an orderly procedure to the exploration and development of the almost unlimited resources on the Moon and other bodies in space.

2
The Apollo Lunar Missions of the United States

On May 25, 1961, President John F. Kennedy set the United States toward achieving the goal, before the end of that decade, of landing a man on the Moon and returning him safely to Earth. But, with most new ventures of mankind, some casualties were to be encountered.

On January 27, 1967, a fire on board Apollo 1 killed three U.S. astronauts. A short in the circuitry igniting the pure oxygen atmosphere in the Apollo space capsule produced enormous heat within seconds. The atmospheric mixture later was changed, and made safer. Improvements on the Apollo capsules, and several Apollo lunar orbital missions, resulted in the victorious landing of Apollo eleven on the Moon on July 20, 1969. The inscribed placard on the lunar landing module read: "Here man from the planet Earth first set foot upon the Moon, July, 1969, A.D. We came in peace for all mankind."

Since our Apollo missions were well advertised on Earth, with nearly every citizen being informed of our first landing, one can safely speculate that the placard's message was meant for someone else to read, other than Earth-man. There are those in scientific circles who indicated to me that this, in itself, is proof that other people not of this Earth, are expected to read this placard. On the Earth, placards are not placed anywhere, unless there is the assurance that they will be seen and read. The Moon certainly is no exception.

When the Apollo program ended, U.S. astronauts had spent some 160 man-hours exploring the Moon, by foot and by electrically powered Rovers. The astronauts carried out many diversified experiments and returned about 800 pounds of lunar rocks and soil from their combined missions.

The information derived from the Apollo landings has occupied the attention of scientists for many years. While it is true that much of the data was analyzed, it is also equally true that much has been ignored, because of the reduction in NASA funds and the resulting loss of personnel. There are rumors that much soil and numerous lunar rocks have mysteriously disappeared over the years. On a recent flight to Washington, D.C., I again visited the Smithsonian Museum. This time I found an extensive selection of lunar rocks, displayed in the institution's gem section. I observed these rare specimens carefully. Without much geological knowledge, I can nonetheless categorically state that any of these rocks could be replaced with the appropriate sample of an Earth rock, and no one would notice the difference.

The Apollo missions occurred as follows:

Apollo 8: December 21 to 27, 1968, which photographed the Moon from orbit. Astronauts of these missions were Borman, Lovell, and Anders. Apollo 8 returned a remarkable selection of color lunar photographs from the hidden side.

Apollo 10: May 18 to 26, 1969, which was a lunar orbital flight manned by astronauts Stafford, Young, and Cernan.

Apollo 11: July 16 to 24, 1969, the first manned lunar landing by astronauts Armstrong and Aldrin. Astronaut

Collins commanded the mother ship in lunar orbit, awaiting the first Moon-walkers' return.

Apollo 12: November 14 to 24, 1969, which was another successful lunar landing with astronauts Conrad and Bean walking on the Moon, and astronaut Gordon awaiting their return in lunar orbit.

Apollo 13: April 11 to 17, 1970, with astronauts Lovell, Swigert, and Haise on board. Apollo 13 was the ill-fated flight, which did not attempt a landing on the Moon, because of an earlier mysterious explosion of one of the oxygen tanks. Apollo 13 astronauts, however, fulfilled their photographic missions from lunar orbit.

Apollo 14: January 31 to February 9, 1971, which reached the Moon without mishap and landed safely. Astronaut Shepard and Mitchell walked on the Moon, while Astronaut Rossa piloted the mother ship in lunar orbit.

Apollo 15: July 26 to August 7, 1971, which was another successful landing mission, with astronauts Scott and Irwin conducting experiments on the Moon, while astronaut Worden awaited their return in the mother craft. It should be stated that all astronauts piloting the mother craft had their share of experiments to conduct, as well as numerous photographic missions. Furthermore, the radio messages related by the astronauts on the Moon were boosted through the mother craft to Earth. The public should understand that those astronauts who were unable to walk on the Moon deserve as much honor and credit as those who did.

Apollo 16: April 16 to 27, 1972, landed on the Moon with astronauts Young and Duke conducting the experiments on the surface. Astronaut Mattingly orbited the Moon, awaiting the return of his fellow lunar explorers.

Apollo 17: December 7 to 19, 1972. This was the last Apollo landing mission, the landing sight being at Taurus-Littrow valley. The Apollo 17 crew consisted of astronaut Cernan, scientist-astronaut Schmitt, and astronaut Evans who circled in lunar orbit. Apollo 17 also engaged in intensive lunar backside photography. The King crater area seemed to be one of their main targets.

Many serious scientists were disappointed at the discontinuation of the Apollo program which ended abruptly with the Apollo 17 flight. There was so much more which needed to be explored on the Moon and so many questions and mysteries still to be resolved. Others, like myself, who studied a great many of the NASA photographs, came to the undeniable conclusion that we found too much up there. That is the reason we stopped so abruptly.

The authors of the British Book, Alternative 3, suggest that our lunar exploration program has continued, but under complete secrecy. I feel that they are correct, and agree that we have been exploring the Moon secretly, with vehicles propelled by electromagnetism, not much different from those who come to visit us from other worlds, except in size.

If some nations on Earth have managed to duplicate just the very smallest of the UFOs which crashed on Earth over the past thirty years, they would have found unlimited means of transportation, beyond the detection of Earth surveillance equipment. Alternative 3 suggests that this is so, and that we have joined those from other worlds on the Moon, building bases and conducting studies. In our times, where so much is hushed up, distorted, and hidden, and where secrecy, fear and suspicion have mastered our lives, it seems very possible indeed, that there is some truth to all of these speculations.

3
Behind the Lunar Mysteries

Back in our high school days, we were taught a relatively complete set of facts about the Moon. We were told, and strangely, still are told today, that the Moon is incapable of supporting life, is airless, is covered with craters of extinct volcanoes, and is, plainly speaking, a globe of dead rock. The trouble is, those "facts" are no longer acceptable, since our lunar explorations by the Apollo missions have returned ample evidence to prove otherwise.

Decades ago, long before modern rocketry was developed, astronomers were puzzled by what their telescopes revealed on the Moon. "Cities that grow." Hundreds of lunar domes have now been charted. Single lights, explosions and other strange geometric shadows, unexplainable by known natural laws, have been observed by professional, as well as amateur astronomers. Let us study the record. Something is moving around up there, waving lights, cutting mountains, building domes, walls, pyramids, tunnels, and water reservoirs with reinforced walls. If the Moon has no air, it has a very good substitute; something which supports clouds, refracts light, and rubs meteors into incandescence. Science is baffled by the fact that some huge lunar craters are actually live volcanoes. During the Apollo missions, volcanic eruptions and lunar quakes have been observed and measured. Contrary to being considered dead, it can be noted that the Moon has something that grows and changes with the seasons. What else could it be but vegetation? The discoveries made by the U.S. and U.S.S.R. lunar exploration programs are so startling, so incredible, that it has virtually given many scientists sleepless nights.

One hundred and thirty years ago, astronomer Gruithuisen observed north of the crater, Schroeter, formations of crisscross lines and squares, which bear an amazing resemblance to long range aerial photographs of city blocks and streets. While astronomer Gruithuisen was branded as a crackpot at the time, his detractors could offer no better explanation of the formation. However, similar sightings were discovered later, during the 1930's, at Mr. Wilson Observatory. When the one hundred inch telescope was aimed at the Cassendi crater, a remarkable "tube system" was photographed (see plate #1). While some of these constructions were growing, others have been removed.

Astronomer Nininger discovered long ago what appeared to be a translucent tunnel twenty miles long, connecting the craters Messier and W. H. Pickering. In December of 1915, the crater Aristarchus unwrapped a Christmas surprise for observers in the form of a nice new black wall that had not been there before. It runs from the center to the rim, very much like the walls and connecting tubes in the crater Gassendi. In 1922, the lunar "mound builders" became unusually active. Three long artificial looking mounds, or objects, appeared on the floor of the crater Archimedes. Later, three more objects were discovered not far away, composed in the form of a triangle. During this period the French Astronomical Journal "L. Astronomie", reported both a long curving wall and a straight one, with arches, that bore an unbelievable resemblance to a viaduct, or some form of bridge.

During the month of November, 1970, my son and I conducted serious lunar studies of the Archimedes area. We used our twelve and one-half inch reflector. The observation elevation was seven thousand feet above sea level. One night, to our surprise, we sighted three very large cigar-shaped objects on the floor of Archimedes. All three objects were of the same size; two of them were parked in the northern area and one was in the southern area. We compared this sight with the Air Force Lunar Sectional Chart of the Archimedes area. In the chart, the crater floor was relatively flat, and no evidence of these objects was recorded. They remained in the crater for several hours. The diameter of Archimedes is approximately fifty miles. According to our measurements, these cigar-shaped objects were at least twenty miles long and about three miles wide (See plate 2).

Noted astronomer, Walter Haas, once stated that he knew of cases where well-known astronomers had observed unusual activities on the Moon, but flatly refused to report them or even discuss them. During the night of July 10, 1941, Walter Haas himself saw two meteor flashes within the space of five minutes. A group of astronomers, organized by Haas, observed a total of twelve meteor flashes across the dark disc of the Moon within one hundred seventy hours of observation. This proves that the Moon possesses an atmosphere dense enough to rub meteors into incandescence. This atmosphere produces clouds in the colors of white, gray, and red. Some are so dense that they cast visible shadows. On occasion, the crater Plato, near the lunar north pole, is clouded over much of its three thousand square miles with a white-like frost, or snow on the crater rims. Studies of the north and south polar

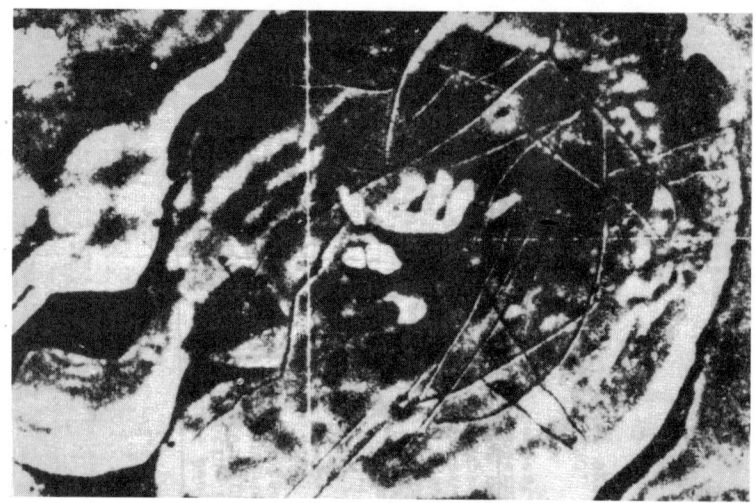

Plate 1. Gassendi Crater, taken 45 years ago with the 100 inch telescope at Mount Wilson Observatory. Notice the tube system at Gassendi Base. Also the central mountain cut into a platform presenting the letter E.

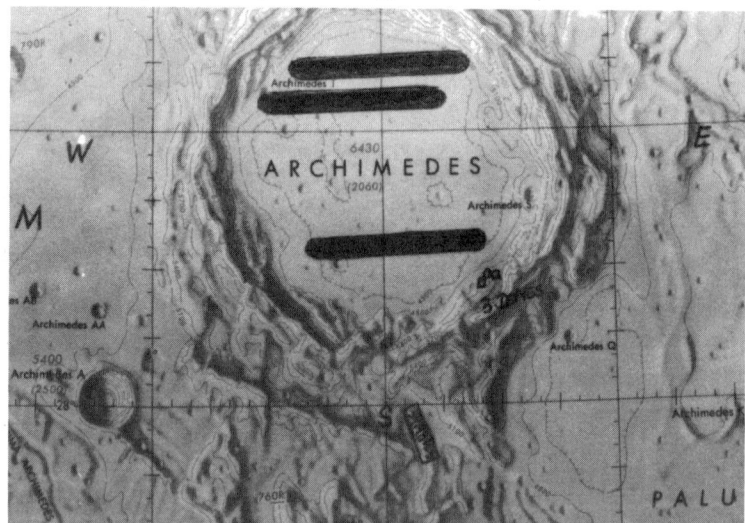

Plate 2. Gigantic objects in the crater Archimedes, as observed by the author and his son, using a 12 1/2-inch reflector telescope. (Drawing)

regions suggest a heavier concentration of clouds over these areas. This suggests that temperatures above the fiftieth latitude north and the fiftieth latitude south seem to be more moderate, because of the sun's rays striking from an angle. This places the otherwise drastic lunar temperature changes at the equator regions into a more comfortable perspective. Perhaps we could call the lunar polar regions the temperate zones.

Astronomer Patrick Moore stated in "Omni" magazine, November 1978: "In our present phase of post-Apollo enlightenment, it would be wrong to suggest that all the mysteries of the Moon have been solved." Mr. Moore speaks of the curious things seen now and then as faint glows, flashing lights, patches of mist, and active volcanoes. In other words, we could say, "The Moon is alive and well." Reddish glows have also been reported by USSR astronomers in and near the crater Alphonsus. Also mild moon quakes, as measured by Apollo instruments, do occur most frequently at the time of perigee.

In any event, the lunar industry seems to have held rather exciting conventions in the crater Plato for the past fifty years at least. Strings of moving lights have been observed there, and a triangle of light blazed in the crater for quite a period of time. Thirty brilliant lights flashed out at the crater floor, all at once, and went into a dizzy routine. While some groups would blaze up, at the same moment other groups would fade into a full glow. The British Royal Astronomical Society reported one thousand six hundred observations of a similar kind. Ever so often a bright light in the crater Aristarchus and another one at the eastern base of the lunar Alps have been observed. This has been going on for over one hundred years. In the

Mare Crisium a spectacle of dots and streaks of light were observed, while the crater Messier has blazed up on occasions with several bright lights. The crater Eudoxus displayed long lines of light.

For some twenty years, Mount Piton, in the northern section of Mare Imbrium has been sending out beacon-like beams of light. There can be no doubt, even in the most feeble minds, that many of these lights, and especially the glowing, moving objects are intelligently controlled.

Dave Darling, an amateur astronomer, with a twelve and one-half inch reflector, informed me about his recent findings on the Moon. He writes, to quote from his letter: "There is a growing belief that the Moon is a base of operations for the UFO activity that is seen in our skies." He reported the following sightings: A large cigar-shaped object on April 16, 1979, at one A.M. which was about ten miles in length, and one and one-half miles in diameter. Its color was silvery metallic, casting a distinct shadow onto the lunar surface. The location of the sighting was close to the crater Isidorus, near the Sea of Nectar. The cigar-shaped object landed about fifty miles from the sunset terminator. Again, on August 12, 1979, at 3:45 A.M., Darling reported another bright cigar-shaped object, this time beside the rim of the crater Romer. Said object was over twenty miles long, also with a silvery metallic color, bearing two wing-type appendages which protruded out of each side, one-fourth down its length. Later, the object disappeared from the flat terrace on the west side of the crater rim.

Some time ago, Mr. Darling made me aware of a large platform he observed south of the crater Archimedes. The platform is five miles long, about one mile wide, at an elevation of about five thousand feet. Approximately twenty lunar photographs, both of the Orbiter and Apollo missions, show this unusual platform which incidentally is not marked on the Air Force lunar charts of the Archimedes area (See plate #3).

I have also discovered several platforms, about thirty miles northeast of the one previously mentioned. These, however, are five in a row, perhaps having a symbolic meaning, although they appear as large letters (See plates #4 and #5).

It needs to be realized that about ninety percent of the lunar studies are conducted by amateur astronomers. The large professional instruments, such as the two hundred inch Mt. Palomar telescope, are considered too powerful for lunar observations. High-powered telescopes have a tendency to greatly magnify atmospheric particles, and are better suited for distant galaxy studies.

The late George Adamski, well-known author and amateur astronomer, photographed at least eight lunar pictures, from 1948 to 1952, showing UFO activity on, or near, the Moon. All the photos were taken through telescopes (See plates #6 to #10).

Plate 3. Large platform south of the crater Archimedes. Reported by Mr. Darling. Platform size-5 miles long, 1 mile wide, Elevation 5,000 feet AGL.

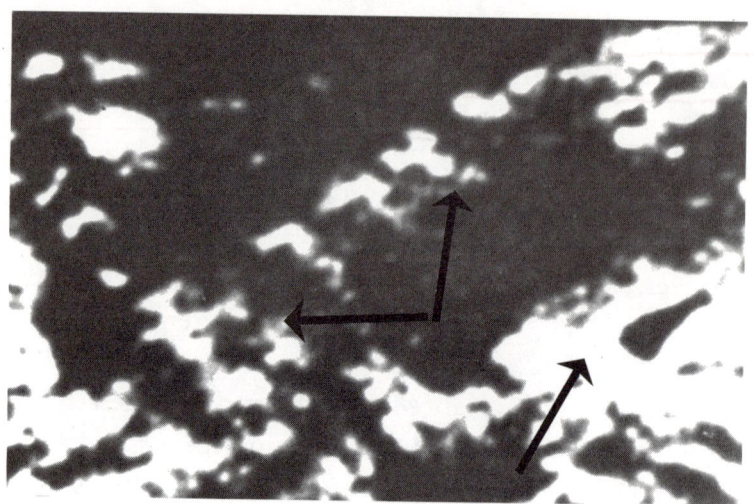

Plate 4. Thirty miles of platforms carved into the mountain top. South of Archimedes. Each platform seems to represent a letter or symbol. Also notice large construction in the valley below.

Plate 4a. Illustration of the area shown in the above photo.

Plate 5. The crater Archimedes crater wall. Note three domes inside the southeast

Plate 6. Large cigar-shaped UFO. Photographed in 1951 by G. Adamski. Telescopic photo.

Plate 7. Five UFOs leaving the moon. Telescopic photo by G. Adamski, 1951.

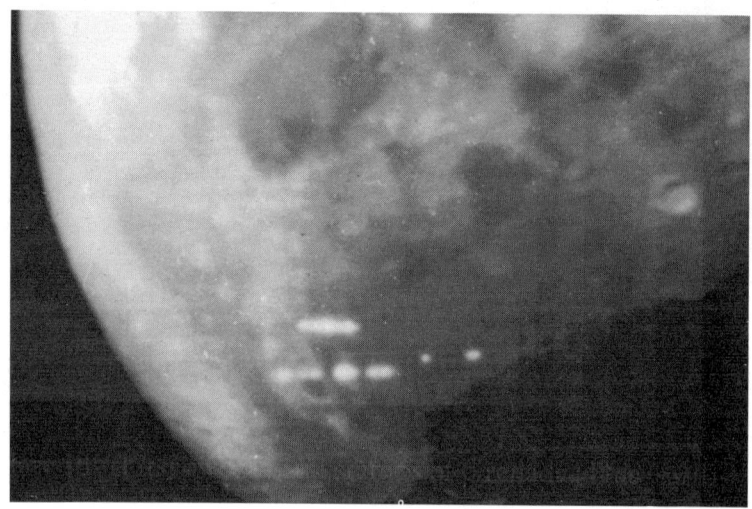

Plate 8. Fleet of seven UFOs near the moon. Telescopic photo by G. Adamski. 1951.

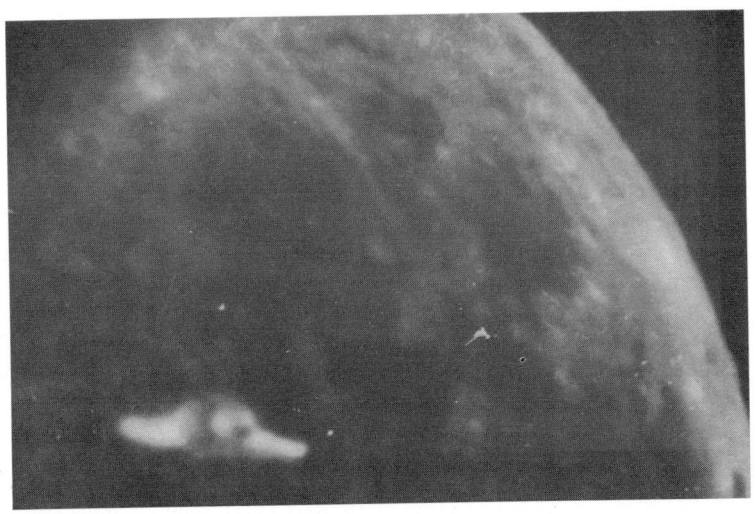

Plate 9. Bell/saucer shaped UFO near the moon. Telescopic photo by G. Adamski, 1952.

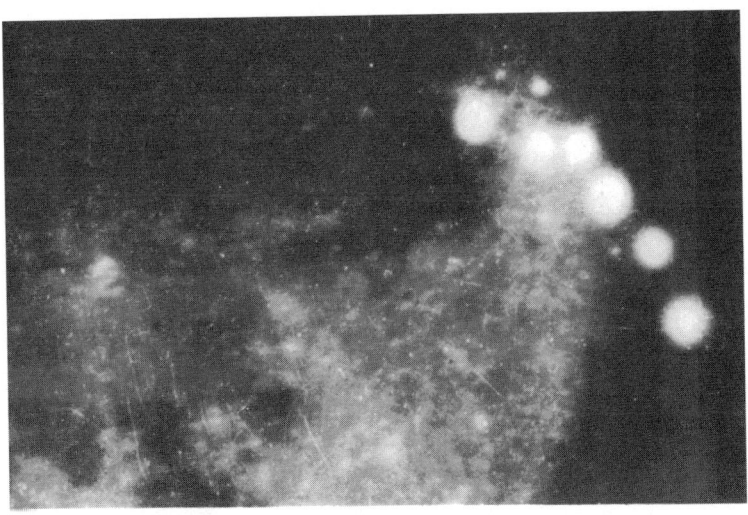

Plate 10. Cluster of six circular UFOs in formation. Telescopic photo by G. Adamski, 1952.

4
UFO Analysis

Unidentified objects have been observed around and on the Moon for many centuries. Research indicates that they seem to be propelled by electromagnetic energy. This energy provides unlimited possibilities to construct and move huge objects and to maintain life in almost any environment. The electromagnetic spacecraft emits a pulsating glow, which produces colors of the spectrum under varying conditions, such as density of atmosphere, humidity, speed and altitude of the space vehicles. Nearly all photographs of UFOs taken on Earth, in space, and in the vicinity of the Moon, show this appearance. These spacecraft are only visible as metallic objects, if the force field in which the craft is normally concealed is dissipated. Some of the best photographs in civilian hands were produced by the late George Adamski between 1950 and 1955, and by M. Rodeffer, who in the presence of Adamski, filmed a UFO with an 8-millimeter movie camera at a distance of only one hundred feet. All of these photos are used with the permission of the George Adamski Foundation, Vista, California.

Adamski not only managed to take photos of the small scout type craft, about 30 to 35 feet in diameter, but also photographed several cigar-shaped spacecraft of gigantic proportions. Some of them were many miles long (See plates #12 to #15). The very idea that someone possesses

Plate 11. (First two) Postal stamps of Grenada. This Caribbean nation investigated the UFO phenomenon under former Prime Minister Sir Eric Gairy, 1978. (Third) "Interplanetary Cooperation" 1977, Ecuatorial Guiena, Africa.

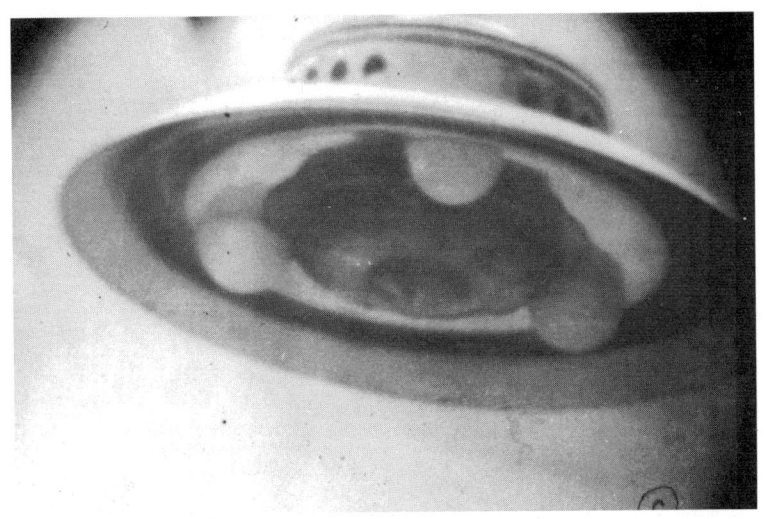

Plate 12. Interplanetary Spacecraft of extraterrestrial origin. "Scoutcraft". Photographed by George Adamski in 1952.

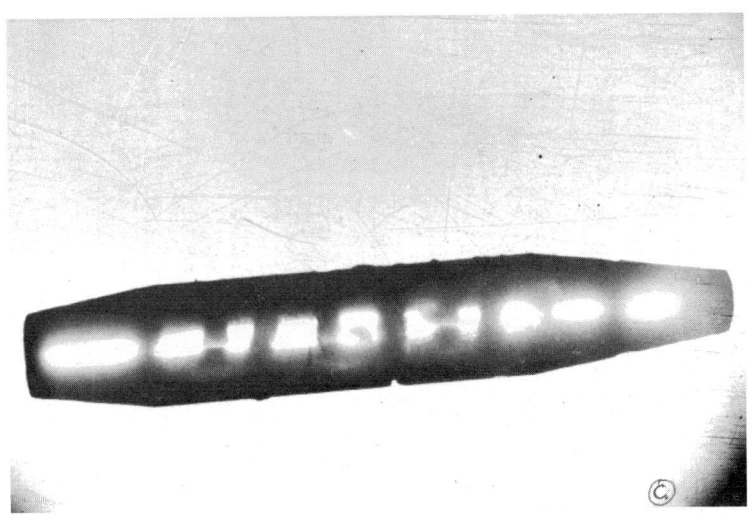

Plate 13. Gigantic Carrier Craft of extraterrestrial origin. "The Mothership." Telescopic photo 1952 by G. Adamski.

Plate 14. Carrier Craft releasing its Scoutcraft. Telescopic photo taken by G. Adamski in 1951.

Plate 15. Carrier Craft releasing its Scoutcraft. Telescopic photo taken by G. Adamski in 1951.

the knowledge to construct space vehicles of such monstrous proportions staggers the imagination. Yet, photographic evidence does prove their existence.

It would be useless to determine the cost of materials and labor involved to construct just one vehicle, several miles in length. On Earth the construction of a super aircraft carrier or a super tanker, about one thousand three hundred feet long, is in itself a superb engineering feat, and is considered to be "sinfully" expensive. In spite of this, our largest ships are puny compared to some of the UFOs observed near and on the Moon and in space. No nation on Earth could attempt to construct such a vehicle not only because of financial inability, but also because of a lack of resources and the necessary labor force. There would be insufficient funds on Earth to construct just one of these twenty-mile long gigantic carriers. This thought carried further suggests that whoever they are, living on the Moon, or using it as a base, must have solved the economic challenges of constructing such colossal vehicles long ago. This in turn suggests great cooperation and consolidation of people, talents, and experts into one genuinely cooperating labor force. This indeed is a task which, in itself, seems to be impossible for us to duplicate on such a large scale. This no doubt suggests that whoever they are up there, they are far more advanced than us.

One could speculate further, that with such great cooperation, there would result a common language and economy, with perhaps the elimination of the monetary system entirely. It is logical to assert, pursuing this same line of thought, that this seems to be the reason why the officials have chosen to ignore these inexorable truths.

Recently declassified UFO reports from several federal intelligence agencies indicate that ever since UFOs made their appearance in our skies in the 1940's, the phenomenom has aroused much serious, albeit quiet, concern in official circles. Official records, now available through the Freedom of Information Act, put to rest doubts that the governments knew more about UFOs than it claimed for the past 33 years. The fact remains, however, despite official denials, that federal agencies continue to monitor UFO activities to this very day.

The last of Adamski's contributions to the best UFO motion picture footage I have ever seen occurred on February 26, 1965, in Silver Spring, Maryland, just a short time before he passed away on April 23, 1965.

At that time he was a guest at the home of the Rodeffers. As it has been reported, M. Rodeffer and Adamski had been alerted by his contacts that a spacecraft would appear that afternoon around 2 P.M. Rodeffer was prepared and waiting with her 8 millimeter movie camera, loaded with a Dynacolor 40 ASA film.

When the amazing craft appeared, Rodeffer and Adamski, alternately filmed this bell-shaped spacecraft. The three balled vehicle was dark blue in color and emitted a low humming sound. Human type occupants were seen through the portholes. Of particular interest is the movement of one of the three spheres, acting as a gymbal type steering system for use in shifting the charge as condensers. This sphere can be seen lowering and retracting in this film, as the craft moves from side to side and up and down, causing a distortion of the appearance of the vehicle. This creates the optical illusion that the entire craft is pliable. Some scientists have conjectured that this type of UFO is powered by an electrostatic magnetic propulsion system, giving rise to this and other effects, such as a powerful gravitational field which conceivably affects the photons around the craft. The film was developed in Washington, D.C. and an analysis was carried out by a senior project development engineer for the Eastman Kodak Company in Rochester, New York. A number of tests were conducted and this film was proven to be authentic.

UFO size geometry of imagery was 27 feet in diameter. Distance from the camera was 90 feet, altitude above the ground about 75 feet. Image size and focal length, 27 feet, equals 2.7 mm's, and 90 feet equals 9 mm's. I can very much imagine that this new piece of evidence, proving once again that the Adamski type saucers are real, must have struck Adamski's critics a forceful blow.

This film was shown at the Goddard Space Flight Center (NASA headquarters in Maryland) and to the members of the House and Senate Space Committee in Washington, D.C., as well as to officials in the Pentagon.

The UFO still-frame reproductions of this famous Rodeffer/Adamski movie film are presented in this book with the kind permission of Madeleine Rodeffer of Silver Spring, Maryland, U.S.A. (See plates #16 to #19).

George Adamski described the UFO propulsion system superbly in his latest book, Flying Saucers Farewell, and the following excerpts are presented with the permission of the George Adamski Foundation of Vista, California.

"To understand more clearly the magnetic propulsion of interplanetary spacecraft, we must first consider geomagnetism, the magnetic sphere of influence which surrounds every planet and every sun, filling all space.

"We can liken Earth's geomagnetic field to the series of circular ripples created by dropping a pebble into a pond.

Plate 16. (Above) The Rodeffer-Adamski UFO. February 26, 1965, 8mm movie frame. Plate 17. (Below) Subsequent frame - same film. Notice the change of shape of this amazing craft. This is due to the revolving and radiating forcefield.

Plate 18. (Above) The Rodeffer-Adamski UFO. February 26, 1965, 8mm movie frame. Plate 19. (Below) Subsequent frame - same film. Notice the change of shape of this amazing craft. This is due to the revolving and radiating forcefield. Notice one of the three ball condensers has been retracted.

These circular ripples move outward from the center point where the pebble was dropped; expanding in size, but diminishing in force as they move.

"If we simultaneously drop two pebbles into the pond, several feet apart, two sets of expanding circular waves are created, moving outward from each central point. Where the wave fronts meet, an interference pattern is formed which extends between the two center points.

"This interference pattern assumes the shape of an extended ellipse, with its smaller ends at the points where the pebbles were dropped. Although both wave fronts have diminished in force as they traveled outward from their central points, the interference pattern has combined a portion of both forces to create a third force, which remains constant between the two central points so long as they remain active.

"The same relationship exists between the expanding spheres of magnetic influence which move into space from the sun, and from each planet or satellite. As these magnetic wave fronts expand from another source, they form a magnetic interference pattern which again assumes the general shape of an extended ellipse. Although the geomagnetic field of each planet, or sun, diminishes in strength as it moves spaceward, the elliptical magnetic fields thus created between celestial bodies by magnetic interferences, maintain a constant-strength magnetic field between the bodies.

"A planet's magnetic field is similar to 'direct current', which grows weaker as it travels from its source; however, the elliptical magnetic field shared by two planets may be likened to 'alternating current', which can be transmitted over long distances.

"These alternating elliptical fields, extending from sun to planet and from planet to planet, are the invisible bonds which balance the Solar System. They extend in similar fashion between systems, and between galaxies. They also exist between the micromagnetic fields of atoms, the 'miniature solar systems.'

"The 'end zones' of elliptical fields which influence Earth extend from about 58 degrees north latitude to 58 degrees south latitude. The axis of each elliptical field is at right angles to the magnetic polar axis, and the elliptical field axis corresponds to Earth's magnetic equator.

"The 'magnetic rivers' between planets constantly alternate or change their direction of flow, creating a two-way magnetic pulse between planets. By using only one-half of each two-way pulse, space liners move in one direction. For example, if the spacecraft uses only an outward pulse, it moves away from a planet. If the ship uses an inward pulse, it moves toward a planet. If the spacecraft allows the alternating pulse to flow through it in both directions, it can hover.

"To explain how the spaceships operate within a planet's gravitational field, we must first recognize the relationship between geomagnetism and the planet's rotation.

"On Earth many writers have referred to 'antigravity' devices, and in our scientific researches the idea has been introduced that gravity can be wrestled to a standstill. This is not an efficient approach.

"Spaceships that today are visiting our world from other planets operate on a 'pro-gravitic' principle, using the natural forces, instead of attempting to fight them. Since these ships operate on electrostatic power, it would be

useless for them to fight the geomagnetic forces, since Earth's geomagnetic field alone has an electrical potential of billions of volts.

"Planetary gravity is the natural balance between the centrifugal force of a planet's axial velocity and the centripetal attraction of its electrostatic field. Centrifugal force tries to spin an object from the planet's surface, but electrostatic attraction keeps the object from flying into space.

"The late Dr. Albert Einstein described this balance, and inseparable relationship, in his Unified Field Theory; A Flying Saucer, or 'pro-gravitic' craft, operates by generating its own gravitational field, which surrounds it in a generally spherical pattern. This field is adjusted to resonate or blend in harmony with the planet's geomagnetic field. The resonating gravitational field causes the ship to be weightless. In this weightless or balanced condition, the ship, wherever it may be, can be moved by a relatively slight thrust.

"Within its self-generated pro-gravitic field, the spacecraft can travel at a rate exceeding the speed of light! Using the forces of Nature, its movement can be the same as that of natural forces. The propelling power as produced by the generator within the spacecraft can be compared to that provided by the Van de Graaff electrostatic generators which are used in our own physics laboratories.

"Interplanetary spacecraft have often been described as 'glowing'. Such a condition is created when natural particles in space, through which a ship is moving, come into contact with its encompassing field of resonant frequency. Pulsations within this field cause a shimmering effect, like heat waves rising from pavement, which makes the craft appear to be 'alive and breathing.' This effort can also bend the light waves entirely around the craft, causing it to suddenly disappear from view, though it is actually still there, and not 'dematerialized,' as some individuals would have one believe. There is also another explanation of these sudden disappearances. As the field strength is varied, ionization may shift through every color of the spectrum. Increased energy causes the field to shift up past the visible portion of the spectrum, obscuring the craft from view, the same as a heavy cloud bank obscures a plane.

"The intense resonating field also serves as a shield to deflect space debris from the ship. At the same time a blend is automatically set up between this field and atmosphere or space through which a spacecraft may be moving, thus preventing friction from any kind. Because of this pro-gravitic nature in its operation, occupants of a spaceship are not affected by any violent maneuver, or uncomfortable atmospheric conditions.

"To travel at speeds faster than light, the ship's field is tuned to a high resonant point and the craft achieves 'prime merge.' For this, the ship is equipped with an automatic robot detector and control system, designed with provisions for manual control.

"Contrary to accepted theories, matter is not converted to pure energy under such conditions. A ship within its force field can be compared to a planet within its atmosphere, moving as a unit through space. So, when a spaceship accelerates and seems to disappear, it has merely achieved prime merge and its force field is vibrating at a speed faster than visible light. At higher frequencies it may become transparent to radar signals also.

"The 'hole' effect seen in many UFO photos is created

by a 'magnetic window.' One small portion of the ship's force field is neutralized, permitting visual and radar-type observation. At times this is necessary when the force field of the craft is at a fairly high resonance.

The three-ball undercarriage seen on most saucers serves both as a retractable landing gear and as a 'three-point electrostatic propulsion-control system.' The mother ships use a series of bands built into the framework for the same control purpose. As we use retro-rockets to steer a rocket vehicle, the UFOs use their variable three-point system to maneuver by regulating the charge.

"In horizontal flight within a planet's ionosphere, spacecraft travel along the planet's geomagnetic lines of force. They turn abruptly by shifting the ball-charge. In this way they are guided into and utilize the eddy currents found throughout space. A change of direction in the movement of a spacecraft may appear as a sudden 90 degree turn, or any of the erratic maneuvers so often ascribed to the UFOs.

"One important factor that our engineers for spacecraft will have to take into consideration is the multiple-wall construction required for safety purposes, as well as storage room for a large percentage of their propulsion equipment. There must be a minimum of two charged walls. The outer, negative wall comes in direct contact with the protective force field created around the ship. By its very nature this electrostatic force field ionizes all particles of matter near the ship's surface, and negatively charges space debris coming from within its field of influence. The greater the amount of power used, the farther this influence extends from the ship.

"A positive reference field is established in an inner wall, leaving the central portion of the ship at a neutral potential.

Important too is an automatic filtering and air-conditioning system installed between walls of a ship to purify the air and keep temperatures and pressures within the craft at a comfortable state for all persons aboard.

"Actually, there is not too much difference between extraterrestrial spacecraft and our own modern submarines which can surface on the water where outside pressures are light, or go to great depths where pressures against the ship are intense. At any depth a submarine can maneuver at will, without harm or discomfort to its occupants. So it is with a spaceship. In outer space the pressures against it are light. When it enters a planet's ionosphere and approaches the planet, pressures intensify. Yet, wherever it is, it can maneuver at will, without harm or discomfort to its occupants.

"As our submarine navigators have had to become acquainted with the many rivers flowing beneath the surface of the ocean, so our space navigators will have to learn the magnetic lanes of outer space, as well as those between a planet and its ionosphere. Temperatures, flow and currents throughout the Cosmos vary continually, in repeated patterns. These space lanes will have to be used for direction of travel, and the energy they generate will have to be converted into propulsion power if we ever hope to safely travel and enjoy interplanetary relationships with our neighbors on other planets."

5
Analysis of Advanced Civilizations

Identification of technology of an unknown superior civilization on another planetary body, such as the Moon for instance, provides us with an interesting challenge. Anything with which we are not familiar is difficult to identify, hence, we overlook many artificial objects on the lunar surface. Also, our preconceived ideas and time worn theories, taught to us for many centuries, and hammered into our minds, have materially contributed to our failure to be able to comprehend. We can say that we see it, but since it is not supposed to be there, we simply do not believe it actually exists.

Perhaps because of this fact, so many lunar photographs were released through many different publications, which do show strong evidence of life on the Moon. Not only primitive life-like moss and lichens, but also bushes and trees, grass, and even many man-made installations. Because most people are not familiar with what is in these photos, it becomes difficult to recognize these lunar anomalies. And since most top scientists do not dare to come forward for fear of endangering their positions, in some cases, these photos are all but forgotten today.

It is rather obvious to me that the artificial objects, UFOs and intelligent constructions were permitted to remain in these photos, in the event that should future development and research determine what is taking place up there, the officials can emerge guiltless, stating: "Well, we released it, but we didn't know what it was." In my view that would be saving face the clever way.

We must recognize that not all advanced machinery needs to be highly complicated. Often progressive technologies effectively simplify machines, their shape, and propulsion methods. There remains no doubt, that true mechanical progress of an advanced civilization is achieved through its unlimited aerial maneuverability. Vehicles of all shapes and sizes, for any conceivable purpose, propelled by a form of free energy, such as electromagnetic propulsion, are needed to move freight, commodities, and personnel. Roads and highways then become obsolete and as such cannot be found on the Moon. What can be found, closely resembling roads, seem to be tunnels and large tube systems, which perhaps are pressurized for use in mining operations. Tracks of vehicles rolling over the ground, up and down the hills, have been photographed. As far as I can tell, these large vehicles, some seventy-five feet across, seem to probe the soil for future mining possibilities. The tracks left behind by these vehicles show definite 'stitch-marks' by some form of belted vehicle. (See plates #20 to #24).

Even in an advanced civilization which has complete aerial maneuverability, soil samples need to be taken by vehicles making ground contact. One must also realize that, we cannot compare our technology with someone elses from another planet. Although I am sure that there exists some similarities, different devices for transportation, farming, housing, etc., may have evolved far beyond the understanding of most people on Earth.

Progress never stands still, even for an advanced civilization, which I am convinced has the same urgency as we do, to advance even higher. For instance, seventy years ago, we built aircraft from wire and cotton cloth. Today we fly machines barely resembling the early aircraft designs. The same examples can be used in other forms of transportation. In just eighty years, our world has changed completely technically speaking. We must learn to look for signs of a higher technology on the Moon, and from the photographs presented in this book, even the most conservative reader must admit that something unusual is happening up there.

Plate 20. Area blow-up. NASA photo No. 67-H-1135 LO V. Objects rolling up and down hills on craters. Large object is about 75 feet across "Inside the Crater Vitello." Smaller object to the north.

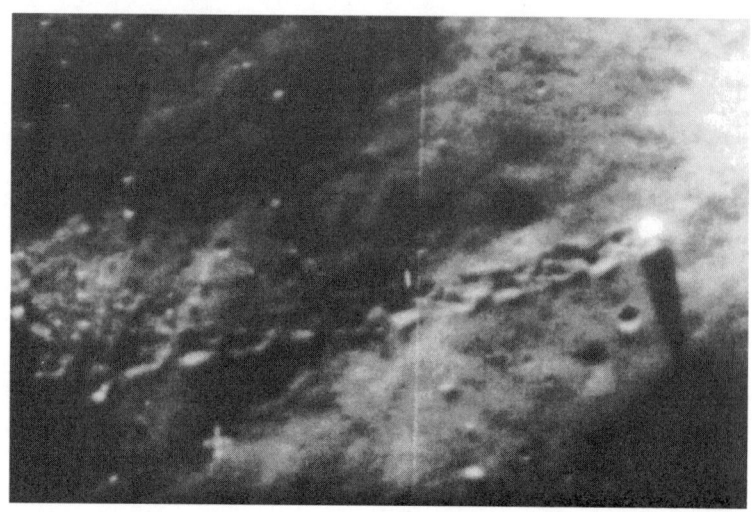

Plate 21. Area blow-up. NASA Photo LO V. No. 67-H-1135. The large object leaving behind definite "stitch-marks" by some form of belted vehicle.

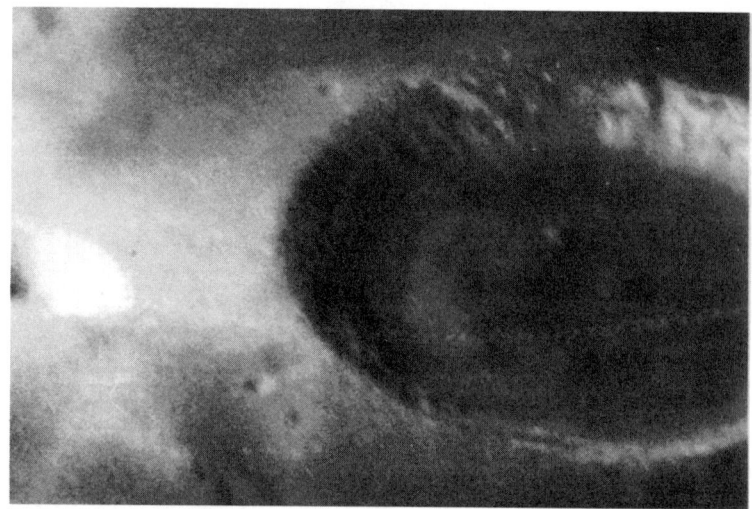

Plate 22. Area blow-up. Apollo 16 Photo No. 16-19067. Over 30 miles of straight stitch-marks up and down hill leaving tracks identical to Plate No. 23. "Lunar Backside."

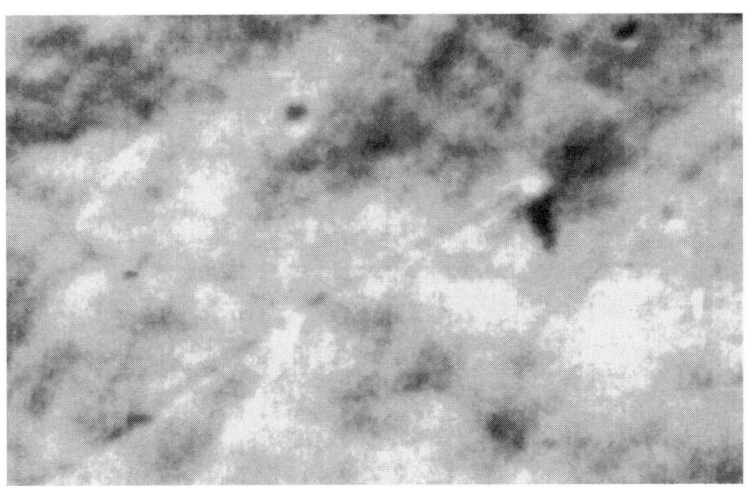

Plate 23. Area blow-up. NASA Photo LO V. No. 67-H-1135. The smaller object, 15 feet across rolled some 1200 feet up and down hill.

Plate 24. Author's conception of what rolling objects in plates 20 and 23 may look like. A type of mining vehicle or soil testing device?

It would be the height of folly to simply state, because there seems to be no lunar freeways, with its attendant miles of stalled cars, smog, and a polluted atmosphere, that no one lives there. Someone is certainly moving things around on the Moon. All we need to do is to find out 'why'. One reason might be mining. According to NASA, the Moon is very rich in minerals and metals with almost unlimited resources. Various areas on the Moon may also be used as extra-terrestrial bases to observe the Earth. I would guess that this is an excellent place for them to study our development and progress, while remaining clear of shooting range. From all appearances it can be said that the Moon is not like the Earth, and its living conditions must be very harsh in some places, but I am convinced, as many NASA photos show, some areas exist on the Moon, where life is possible, not just for plant life, but for animals and mankind.

Our assumption that man could not live in environments different than on Earth seems not to hold water. On July 31, 1952, an Italian engineer, Gianpero Monguzzi photographed high in the Italian Alps, a UFO which had landed in the snow. Monguzzi was only three hundred feet from the craft and he succeeded in taking six photographs of it. Beside the landed spacecraft a human figure walked around, dressed in a pressure suit, with backpack and antenna, quite similar in appearance to our astronauts, who walked around on the Moon just seventeen years later. (See plates #25 to #26). Logic tells us that this UFO pilot, wherever he is from, must have come from a planet with either higher or lower atmospheric pressures than we have on Earth. This proves that life as we know it is possible elsewhere, even though the environment may be different.

Earth astronauts on the Moon carried a pressure of about five pounds per square inch in their space units, which is double the pressure I speculate which exists on the Moon. If the UFO pilot photographed by Monguzzi came from the Moon, his pressure suit probably would not have contained more than two and one-half pounds of pressure per square inch. That is exactly one-sixth of Earth's pressure, or one hundred sixty-six millibars.

Plate 25. Extraterrestrial spacecraft landed high up in Italian Alps. Notice UFO pilot in left of photo wearing pressure suit, backpack, helmet, and antenna. Taken by G. Monguzzi, July 31, 1952.

Plate 26. The UFO pilot and U.S. Astronaut as a comparison. Both wear space suits and both are humans, accustomed to different environmental conditions.

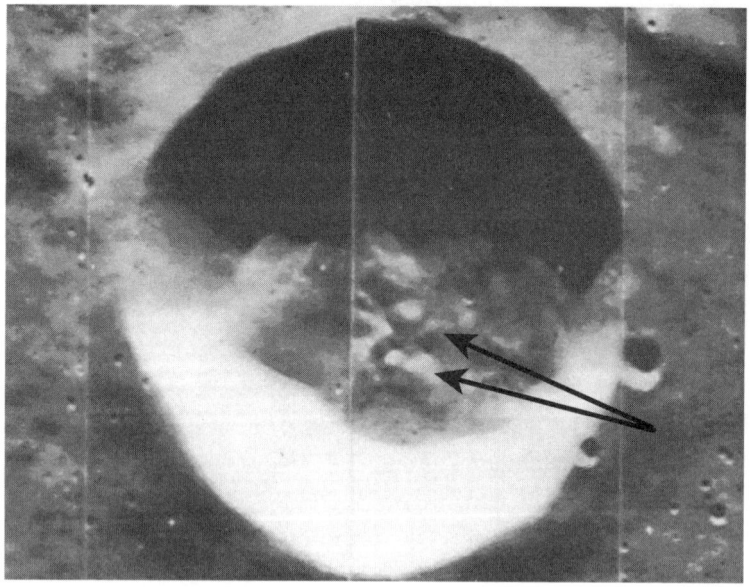

Plate 27. Area blow-up. LO IV. No. 168-H3 "Lunar Backside". Two domes on the crater floor.

In searching for large buildings and hangars on the Moon, I found predominately the dome-type there. I quickly realized that even on Earth we have recognized the efficiency and strength of dome constructions. We have built them mostly in harsh environments such as arctic stations, but also recently, for family housing. The dome can be climate controlled with much greater efficiency than any other design. Even the Eskimos know that for a fact, heating their igloos very efficiently with just one candle power. The igloo is a dome of ice and snow. On the Moon a plethora of such domes have been observed. For instance, in the crater Darwin, a whole cluster of domes are to be found, east of the crater Copernicus, and several dozens of them along the bottom of the straight wall, as well as in the center of many unnamed craters on the Moon's hidden side. (See plates #27 to #38).

One can only speculate why there are domes in some craters and not in others. The answer, of course, could be easily accessible ground water and also mining possibilities. With a few exceptions, in mountainous regions on Earth, settlements are usually constructed in the valleys. Actually, most valleys on the Moon are the crater floors, and it is here that we find all types of objects and constructions, which according to natural causes, should not be there. On the Moon's hidden side, in and near the King crater, many domes can be seen. Studies suggest that the King crater area is heavily mined. As it seems, large devices raise dust into the air as they grind up the mountain side and terraces. The domes are to be found on the crater floor, miles away from the mining activities. (See plate #38).

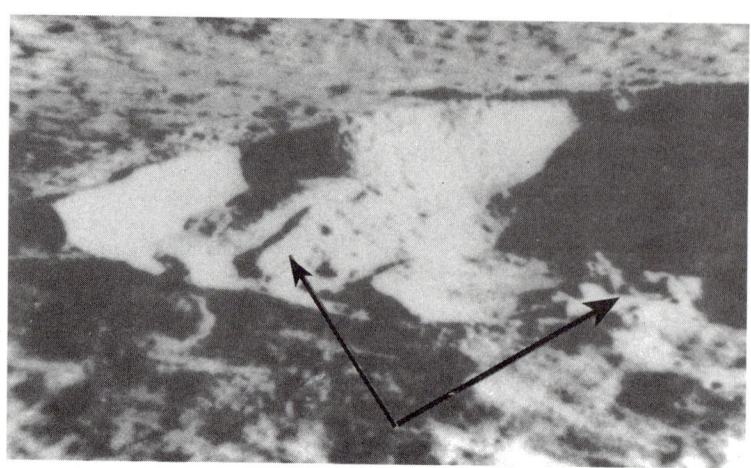

Plate 28. Area Blow-up. LO III Photo No. 67-H-201. Close up Of The Crater Kepler. Notice 3 domes located at the crater's rim to the right of photo. Also notice left crater ridge which seems to have been cut or worked on. Kepler is 20 miles in diameter.

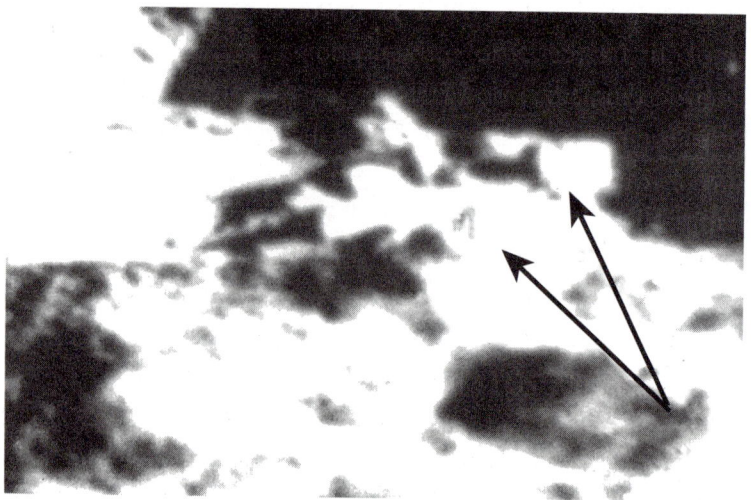

Plate 29. Area Blow-up. LO III No. 67-H-201. The Three Domes Close Up In The Center Of Kepler. Actually located on a large platform at the crater rim.

Plate 30. Area Blow-up. LO III Photo No. 162-M. Three large domes exactly spaced apart. Also notice square cut crater to the right.

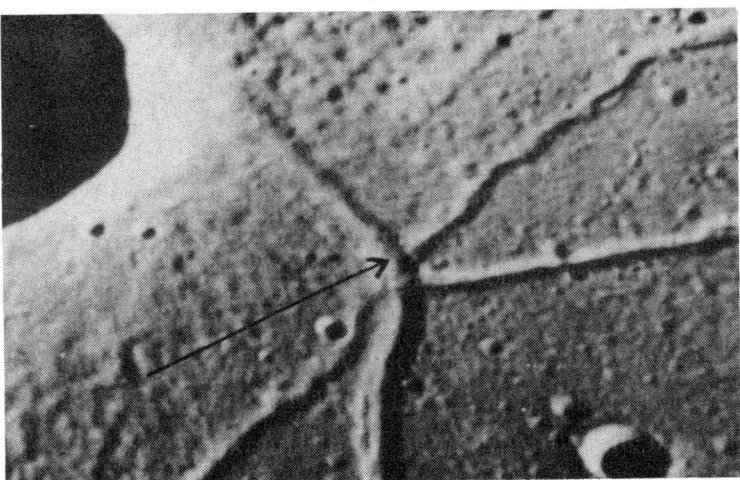

Plate 31. Area Blow-up. Apollo 10 Photo AS10-32-4810. Three domes of exact size located in the Triesneeker rilles, which look like riverbeds. The crater Triesnecker in the left of photo.

Plate 32. Apollo 10 Photo No. AS10-32-4810 northwestward oblique view of the Crater Triesnecker 3.6 degrees east longitude and 4 degrees north latitude. Triesnecker Crater (center) is about 17 statute miles in diameter. The 3 domes are located to the right of Triesnecker in the rilles.

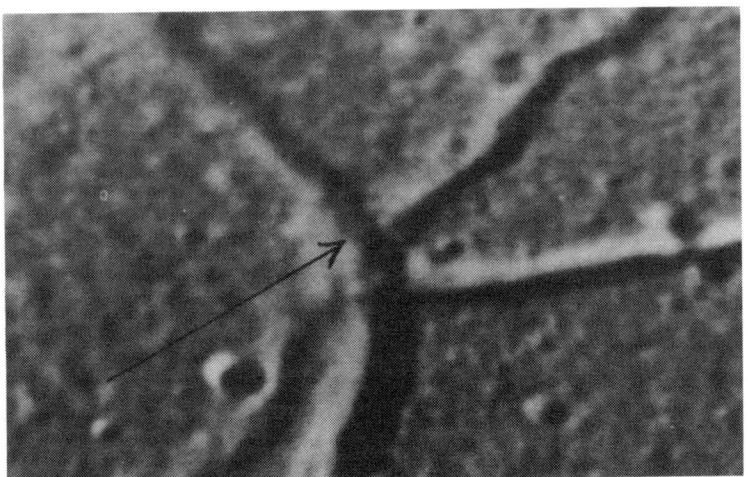

Plate 33. Area Blow-up Apollo 10 Photo No. AS10-32-48109. The Triesnecker rilles 8 times enlarged, showing the 3 domes quite clearly. No doubt an artificial construction by the Moon's inhabitants.

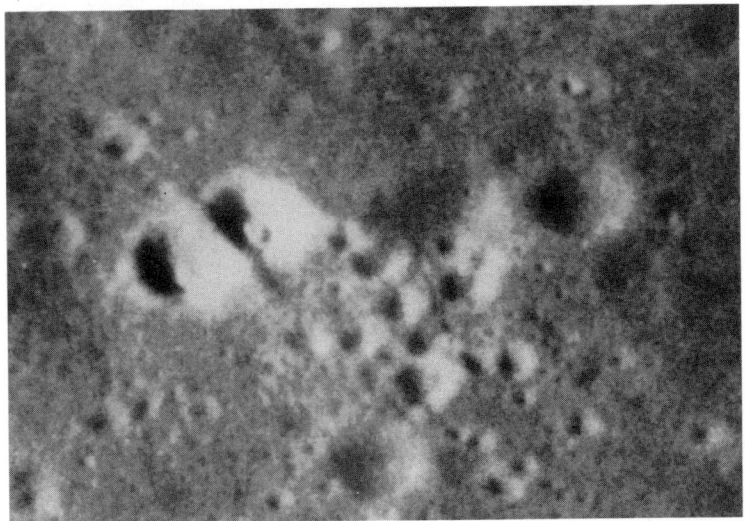

Plate 34. Area Blow-up Apollo 16 Photo, No. 16-19081. A double crater showing 2 dome-like structures or objects. Notice the long object between the craters.

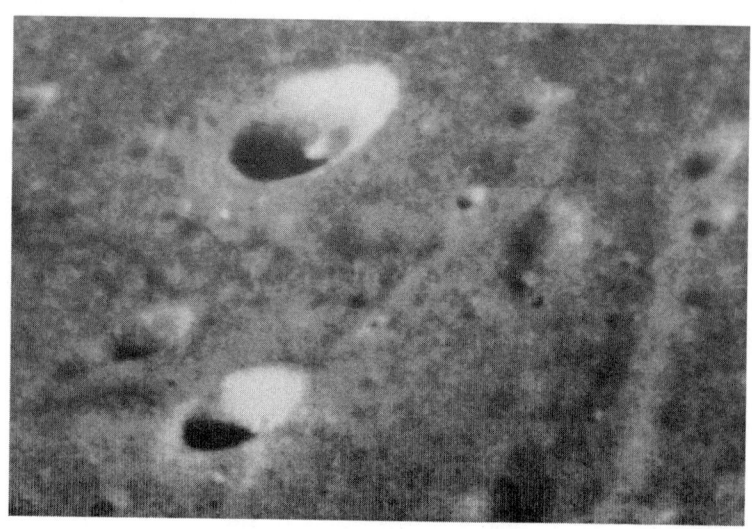

Plate 35. Area Blow-up. Apollo 14 Photo No. 14-10116 showing white dome in crater.

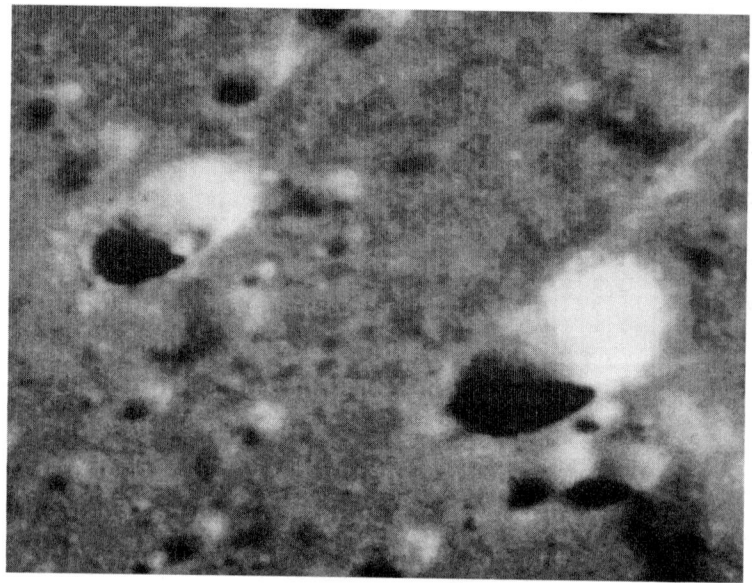

Plate 36. Area Blow-up. Apollo 14 Photo No. 14-10116 "Another Dome".

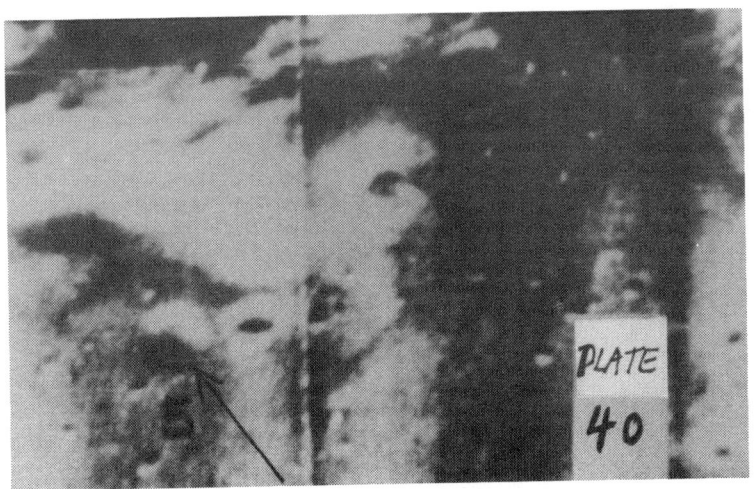

Plate 37. Area Blow-up. LO V Photo No. HR 103³. "Mare Moscovience" showing "A Very Large Dome" above the number 5.

Plate 38. Area Blow-up. "THE DOMES" as NASA calls them. The King Crater area, photographed by Apollo 16. No. 16-19229. Large dome in center seems to be a double dome (Lunar Backside).

NASA reports that the Moon's mineral wealth consists of iron, magnesium silicate, and aluminum silicate, and many other elements. The most common element is oxygen, or about forty percent of the lunar samples, by weight. The oxygen is locked in chemical combinations with other elements. Silicone accounts for twenty percent, aluminum titanium and iron combine for fifteen percent. With this wealth of lunar materials available, it should not be difficult to construct anything, from gigantic domes and hangars to machines and miles long spacecraft. Future NASA plans are to construct colonies in space. Huge twenty mile long cylinders will be built from materials mined on the Moon by Earth men. Mass drivers are the devices which will be used to shoot the containers, with minerals and metals, into lunar orbit. Here, they are to be picked up by our spacecraft for the construction of the space colony. The thought is there and so is the technology. Only the funds are lacking. But there are other problems which confront the space sociology experts. How will the people get along up there? One can only guess how far our civilization would have advanced, had it not have been for the money and wars that seem to have set us back one step for every two we have taken.

Recent hydroponic research studies conducted by the University of Arizona reveals why there seems to be little, or no evidence of open-crop growing on the Moon. It seems that some form of hydroponic farming is without question a part of an advanced civilization's technology, the method being much more efficient than conventional farming methods. The Arizona tests reveal that vegetables, grains and fruits have been grown entirely without soil, with a yield increase of five hundred percent above conventional open field farming methods.

While the open field methods of the United States are unquestionably highly efficient in comparison to other nations' productivity, unfortunately open field farming on a large scale, as conducted in the United States, is threatening with absolute certainty to turn large areas into dust bowls. Once the natural ground cover is plowed under, the bare soil is blown away by the winds. Hydroponic farming methods in controlled environments permit the highest yield production, unaffected by severe weather conditions, rain, and temperature changes. Farmers progress from field workers to highly trained scientists. Test results indicate that ten thousand people could live on only one hundred acres of hydroponic farm space. Using this method on the Moon, with the mineral rich soil that exists, there is no saying how many people can be fed, by just one hydroponic farm under a one mile diameter dome.

Author's note: In April of 1997, The Wall Street Journal printed an article concerning a major Japanese consortium's plans to build public facilities on the Moon. Several large Japanese construction companies have invested over $40 million dollars and continue to invest millions of dollars per year in feasibility studies, research and the future development of lunar colonies. The unique lunar environment has lead to the necessity for unique concepts in construction designs. From inflatable buildings, to condominiums, hotels and ten story high beehive shaped structures, the eventuality of lunar habitats with populations upwards of 10,000 people is taken very seriously. One of the companies brochures says it quite well, "The moon is the stuff of dreams - not only the kind lovers have, but also of new resources, new frontiers and a stepping stone to the stars."

6
New Concepts Replace Old Theories

The time worn assumptions that the Moon is incapable of supporting life, is airless, and is just a globe of dead rock obviously needs revision. Over the past fifteen years, through national and international press releases, the United States Space Exploration program has revealed new facts about the Moon.

The October 24, 1969, issue of Time magazine reported that a detectable magnetic field had been found on the Moon. In that same article it was admitted that the Moon possesses a thin atmosphere. Atomic powered instruments, placed on the ground by the Apollo crews, measured the atmospheric density.

The Washington Daily News on December 6, 1968, presented this article: "Is The Moon Really A Dead World?" Astronomers reported sighting geometric shaped light patterns; a moving 50 mile wide opaque object; great white domes and long bridge-like structures from the plain of Mare Crisium. The United States and U.S.S.R. scientists saw a huge glowing oval-shaped form".

Another article by the Washington Daily News reported that the Moon's surface contains material just like Earth. Plants thrive on Moon soil and seedlings of common food plants, like wheat, tomatoes, cucumbers, and limes are huskier and greener than sister plants grown in Earth soil. The Lunar Receiving Laboratory, in Houston

Texas, stated that germinations in the lunar soil indicates that it is behaving like a source of nutrients.

On October 16, 1971, a UPI press release from Houston, headlined in the world's newspapers. "Water clouds have been detected on the Moon. "The water clouds were erupting like geysers through cracks on the lunar surface, proving that the Moon is not a dead and inactive place. Both Apollo 12 and Apollo 14 detected the Moon geysers. The water cloud covered an area of more than ten square miles. Ironically, the location of these findings were on the eastern edge of the Moon's Ocean of Storms. Dr. W. Freeman stated, "The detection of moon-quakes venting gas and water means the Moon is not a dead place".

Astronaut Borman, observing the Moon through the window of his orbiting spacecraft, made this startling observation, published in the NASA publication for public release. He said, "It looks like clouds down there. "Apollo 12 astronauts Pete Conrad and Allan Bean, in a moment of lunar recreation, played frisbee with a metal cap. The astronauts exclaimed over the radio that lunar air kept the frisbee buoyed up. Former astronaut Brian O'Leary reported this frisbee incident of Apollo 12 in the Ladies Home Journal, March 1970 issue.

The next article released by NASA was of the experiences of Apollo 10. "Moon volcanoes sighted." United Press International on May 22, 1969, stated: "Orbiting at only sixty-nine miles above the Moon, Astronaut Stafford sighted two volcanoes. " One of them was white on the outside and black on the top. They also reported seeing many different colors on the Moon's back side, while the centers of some of the craters glow. "They just glow in the lunar night," stated astronaut Cernan.

In the February 1972 issue of the National Geographic Magazine a full report of the experiences of Apollo 15 were presented. On page 245 it states that the Moon has a magnetic field and it does have an atmosphere, although an exceedingly thin one. Lunar quakes and water vapors were detected by Apollo 12 and Apollo 14 instruments. On page 250 it was reported that Apollo 15 astronauts observed a whole series of small shaped volcanic cones, producing evidence of gases coming from the Moon's interior. This sighting was made in the Littrow crater. On page 252, it states that the astronauts reported unexplained haze clouds and color flashes in and around the crater Aristarchus. On page 257, there appears a magnificent photograph of a brown lunar landscape. Incidentally, many fine lunar photographs, both in color and black and white, were released in this issue. Some of them show vegetation in the color photos and also artificial installations in the center of a crater.

The far side of the Moon was reported to be smoother and more subdued. In fact, Apollo 8 returned many beautiful color photos from the Moon's hidden side, in full brown color under direct sunlight, which suggests that this brown color is true color. Apollo 8 carried out this mission from December 21 to 27, 1968. Could it be that the brown color stemmed from winter vegetation during that season? Several other Apollo 8 photographs in full color proved without a shadow of a doubt that green vegetation exists on the Moon. One can well identify the brown color of the desert like landscape with vegetation growing in shady areas of hills and craters (See color plates #39 to #42). This color photo, showing the existence of vegetation, although there are others, was released to the public in the book Footprints On The Moon, by the Associated Press. Finally, on page 260, the Geographic reports that the Apollo 11 crew, which spent three days on the Moon, found the Earth's satellite not barren or desolate, but as they worded it, "dynamic and beautiful".

Radio astronomers, studying the cool clouds of Cosmic Dust in space by microwaves, discovered clouds of complex molecules formed from many combinations of the basic atoms, such as Carbon, Oxygen, Hydrogen, Nitrogen and others.

This proves that the basic "life molecules", DNA, are already present in clouds between the stars, the clouds from which new solar systems are formed. The seeds of life or germs are already there and only need the proper conditions to develop into complex life forms according to the size, pressure and temperature of a planetary body.

The atmosphere of any planet, including our Moon, must be laced with such molecules, combining into more complex life forms when called upon by Nature's Laws.

In 1977 observations of even more complex molecules in space revealed the presence of "cyanotriacetylene." This is the biggest organic chemical molecule yet discovered in space and only slightly different from one of the amino acids, which, in turn, produce proteins, nucleic acids and genes.

This new discovery came from the well-known astronomers, Sir Fred Hoyle and his colleague Professor C. Wickramasinghe. Quoting from the book <u>Birth of a Star</u>, these two astronomers revealed their observations in these words: Quote: "The story starts with carbon grains, soot particles, coated with ice and stuck together in tiny grains of interstellar matter. This is more than mere supposition, since grains of this kind have been found in meteorites, which themselves contain organic molecules. Such tiny dust grains provide an also ideal place for the slow build-up of complex molecules.

"In a cloud of gas and dust grains in space, atoms must, from time to time, collide with a grain of dust, and such a carbon ice grain provides an ideal surface to make the atom stick in place. So, when other atoms come along and collide with the same grain, they have the opportunity to interact with one another, building up molecules.

"From time to time, collisions with other grains, or the impact of the energetic particles called cosmic rays, may knock molecules adrift to wander until they collide with another molecule encrusted grain, allowing simple molecules to build gradually up into very complex systems".

These recently discovered facts have proven to us that life, even as we think we know it, is likely to be found everywhere in the cosmos.

We see that the seeds of life are already there, and that organic molecules which are the basis of life on Earth, are found through the infinite cosmos.

In Nature there exists the urgency to express, often under conditions completely hostile to our understanding. Perhaps, with these new discoveries, we can more easily accept the thought that even our Moon is also alive and well.

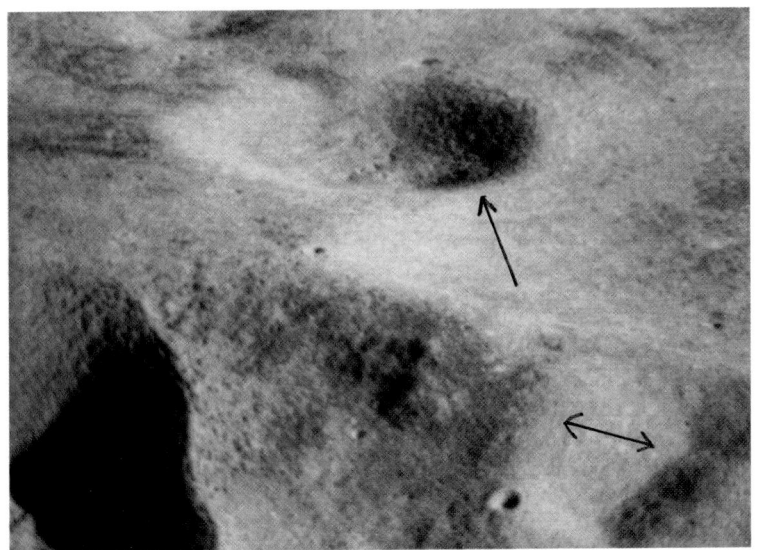

Plate 39. Area blow-up. Apollo 8 color photo of the Moon's hidden side, showing vegetation (green color).

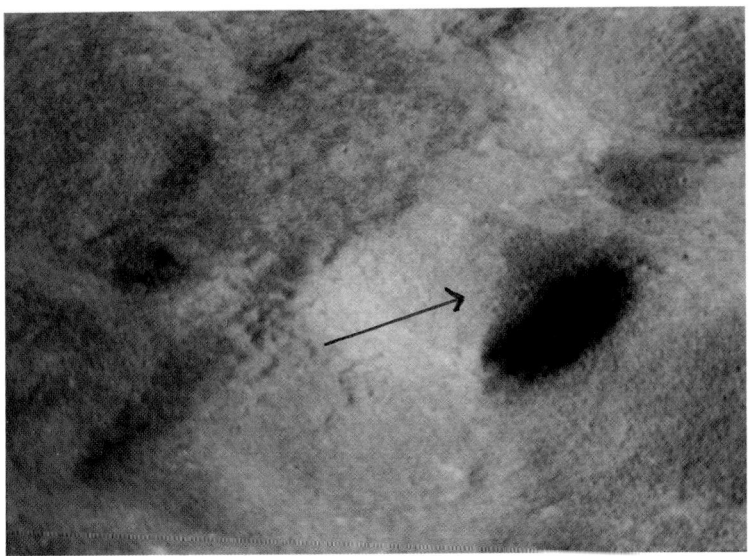

Plate 40. Area blow-up. Apollo 8 color photo of the same general vicinity of Plate 39. Here also vegetation grows in the shady areas, just like the southwest deserts in the USA.

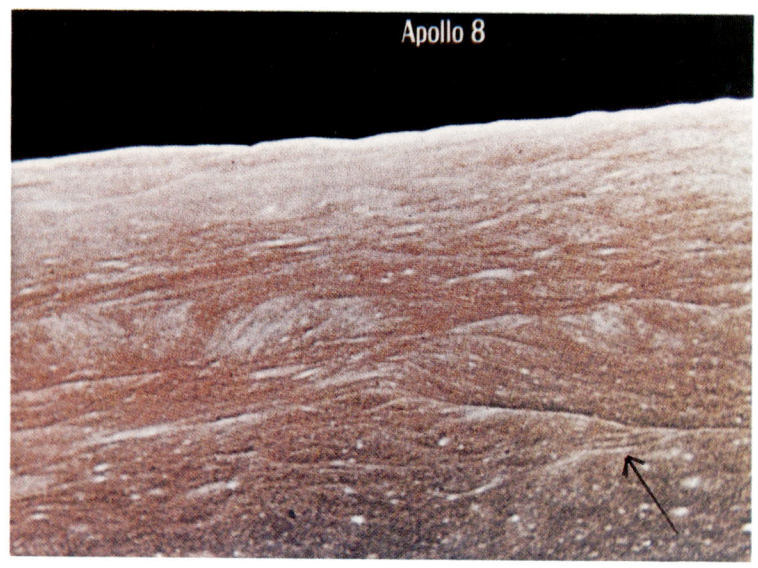

Plate 41. Area blow-up. Apollo 8 color photo. Lunar backside. "The moon in full autumn colors".

Plate 42. Area blow-up. Apollo 8 color photo. No shadows, showing true ground color of the lunar landscape below. Dry vegetation or desert brush?

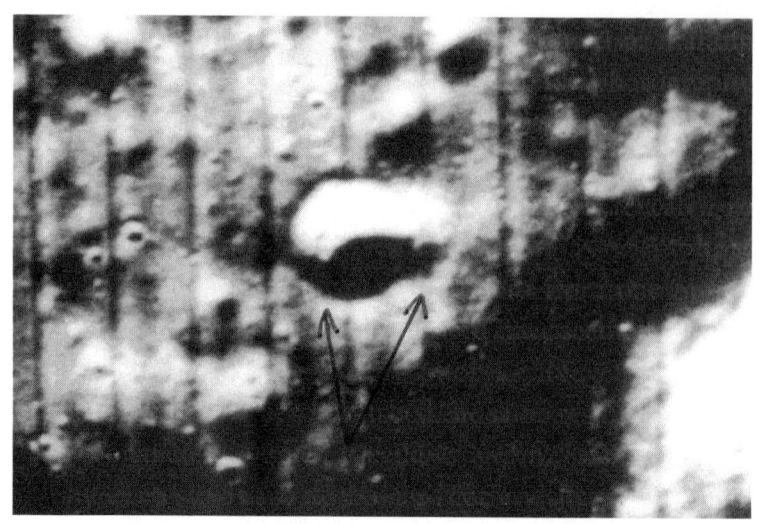

Plate 43. Area blow-up. LO III Photo showing two walls inside crater in the S.E. Mare Tranquilitatis.

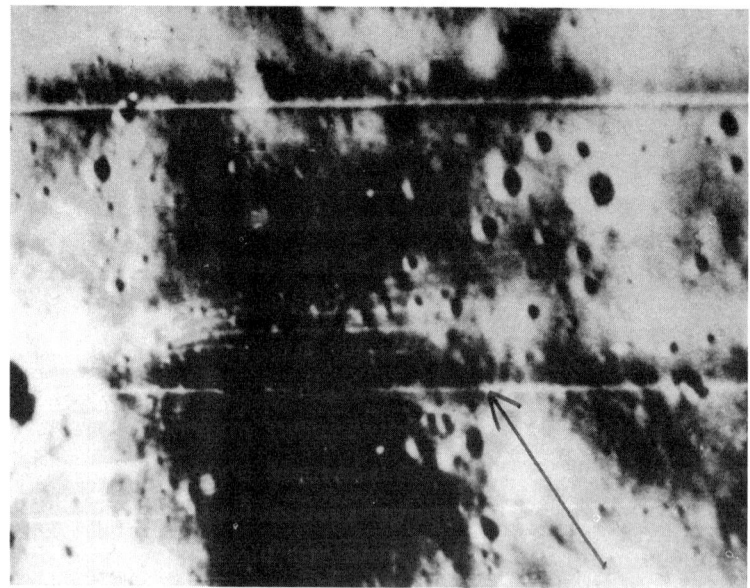

Plate 44. Area blow-up. LO III of same general vicinity as Plate 43. Notice tracks extending from crater in plate 44.

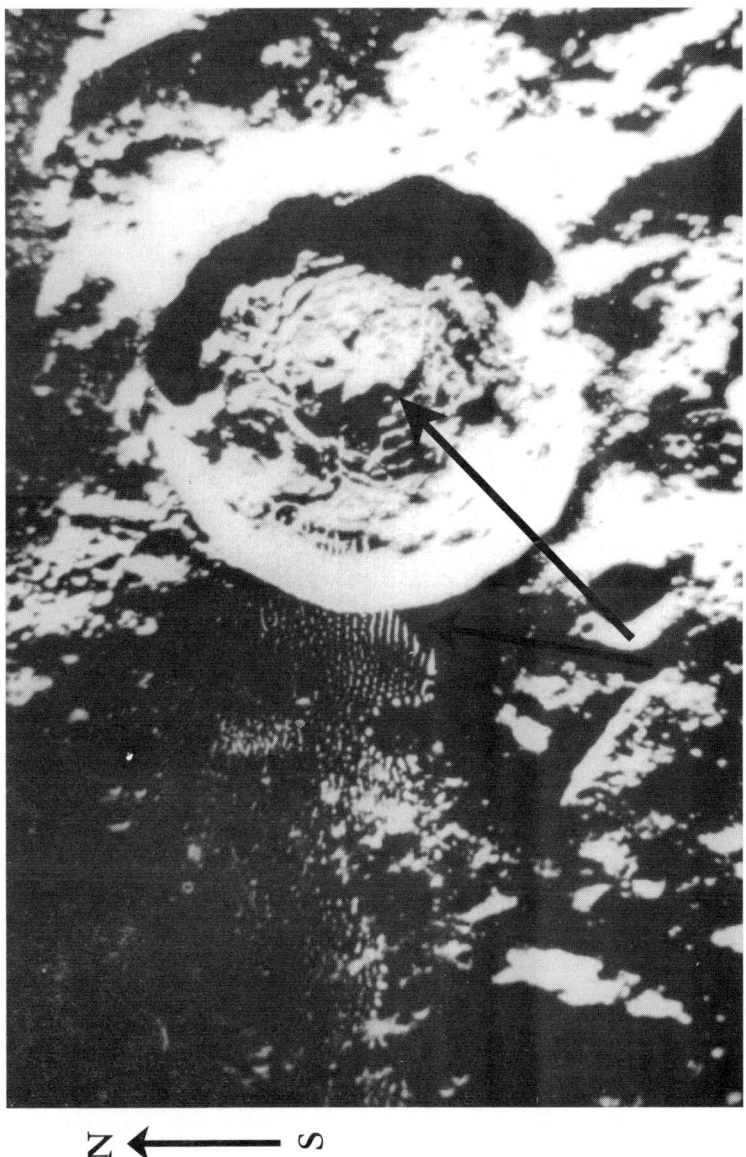

Plate 45. LO V, MR 168, the crater Vitello. Notice cirrus type clouds left of crater rim. Also notice platform in the center of the crater.

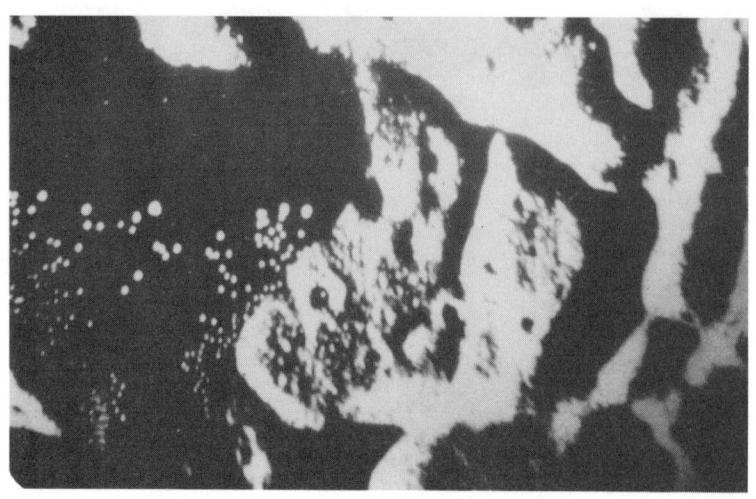

Plate 46. Area blow-up. LO V, HR 168[2.] Formation of white objects over the mountains west of the crater Vitello.

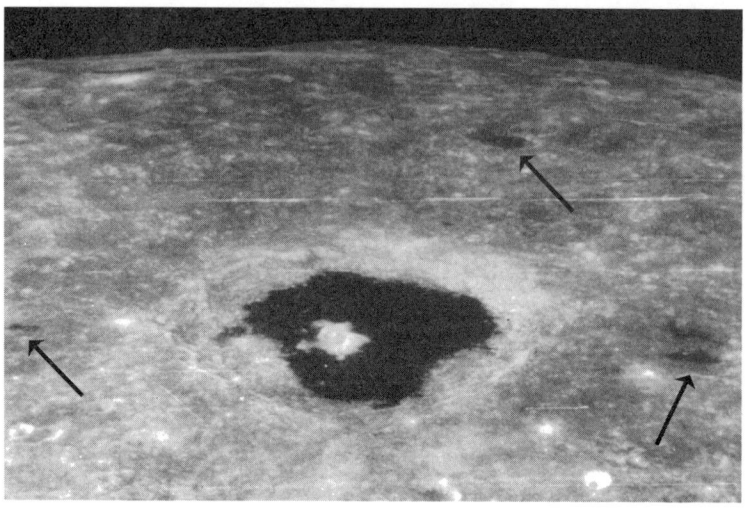

Plate 47. Apollo 8 photo of the crater Tsiolkowsky on the back side of the moon. Notice the large "lake" and the smaller ones nearby.

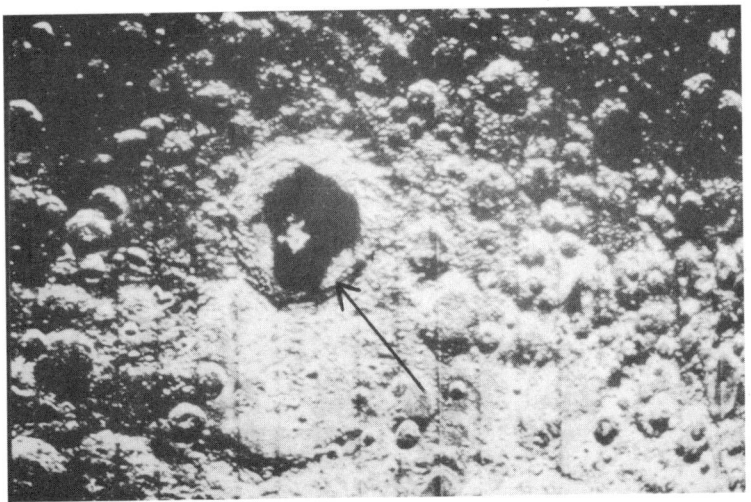

Plate 47a. Crater Tsiolkowsky (again) taken by LO V.

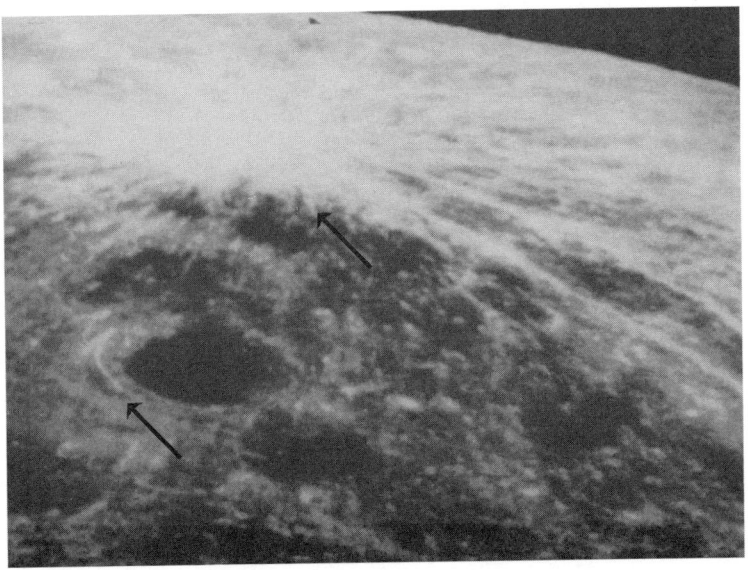

Plate 48. Apollo 8 photo of the lunar back side close to the North Pole. Notice large "lake" to the upper left. Clouds can be seen north of the lake. Objects appear to line the north west shoreline.

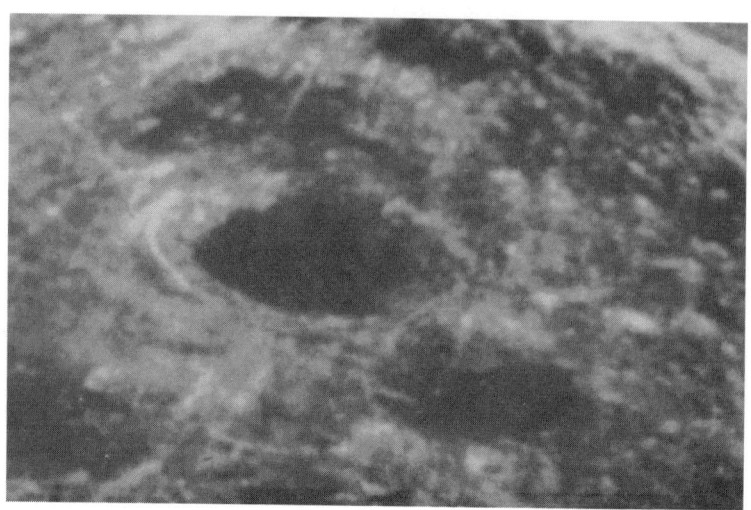

Plate 48a. Area blow-up of previous photo showing objects along shoreline.

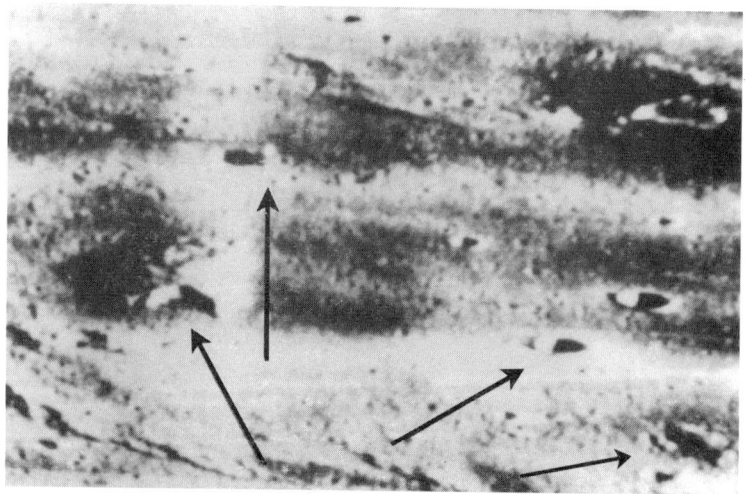

Plate 49. Area blow-up. LO II, MR 213. Notice hill, left of center, has been cut out like a piece of cake. Above the hill appears large construction casting a shadow to the left. To the right notice several perfectly cut holes or craters and two oval objects on the rim.

7
True Colors on the Moon

Analysis of many color photographs seem to show the effect of earth-shine photography. In this case, photographing the side of the Moon facing the Earth, the reflecting earthshine during the lunar night is about ten times as bright as the moon-shine reaching the Earth. Unfortunately, earth-shine on the Moon is purely a cold bluish reflection, which makes it impossible to take good color photographs, even though the light is sufficient. Also, since the rich composition of the lunar soil has a very high albedo (reflectivity), even true sunshine color photographs appeared overbright when taken vertically from the orbiting spacecraft. The true colors would be more recognizable after sunrise and before sunset, but even on Earth color photographs taken at high noon, in desert areas, seem to be faded out. There is simply too much light reflection.

Some scientists have accused the astronauts of making many photographic mistakes, but I disagree with them. Our astronauts, all of them high commissioned officers, were expertly trained in all phases of the lunar missions, especially the photographic ones, because everyone likes to see good pictures. I feel if any poor color photographs were taken during these missions, it was to conceal certain things, for reasons known only to the officials in charge. For instance, the color blue was never reported by any Apollo crew, yet several color photos in blue were released by

NASA. While the astronauts were accused of making a mistake, using an A-type film for outside photography, I again disagree. I feel that these photos were taken with a blue filter over the camera lens. Test photographs, which I have taken from the air using a blue filter, revealed very much the same effect as those blue NASA photos. Unfortunately, I could not take them from one hundred mile up, for in that case they would have seemed much the same as those blue NASA photos. Nevertheless, my photographs also accomplished the same result. The colors of brown fields, green meadows and forests all were one 'bluey' mess. It would be hard for a visitor from another planet, looking at these photos, to identify vegetation on Earth, especially if it is not supposed to be here. My thought is that all photographs taken by the astronauts were carefully planned and predetermined. Few scientists have the same trained eyes as those of professional pilots. It can be said that the astronauts just followed orders, and we should not fail to praise them for their superb jobs.

In the book <u>Footprints On The Moon</u>, the astronauts reported a very bright earth-shine, stating that the Moon seemed like a small planet. Apollo 10, from only nine miles up, advised of a landscape very much like the southwest desert and badlands in the United States. Repeatedly they spoke of brownish soil on the Moon's hidden side. Apollo 11 reported some strange white spots on the inner wall of a crater. The spots seem to have a slight amount of fluorescence. While colors in twilight were gray, in sunlight they were shades of tan and brown. Two minutes and twenty seconds before touchdown, they experienced some drift. This caused the spacecraft to drift along at a seventy-five foot altitude and it had to be landed manually. This drift seems to be the effect of a denser, not previously anticipated, lunar atmosphere.

Adapting to the one-sixth gravity was no problem, and seemed completely natural. This was recorded by all Apollo crews walking on the Moon. The lunar soil appeared similar to the color of cocoa. It almost looked wet, the astronauts reported. This seems to show evidence of much moisture in the lunar soil, as all of the astronauts' footprints were well defined. The Italian scientist, Dr. Maria, examining the lunar rocks and soil, stated that if all the water now existing on the Moon would be released to the surface, a fifty-foot deep ocean would entirely cover it.

(Left) Notice charged atmospheric field around astronaut. (Right) See atmospheric haze surrounding mountain behind rover.

Earth Rise. Notice lunar surface and atmospheric color change.

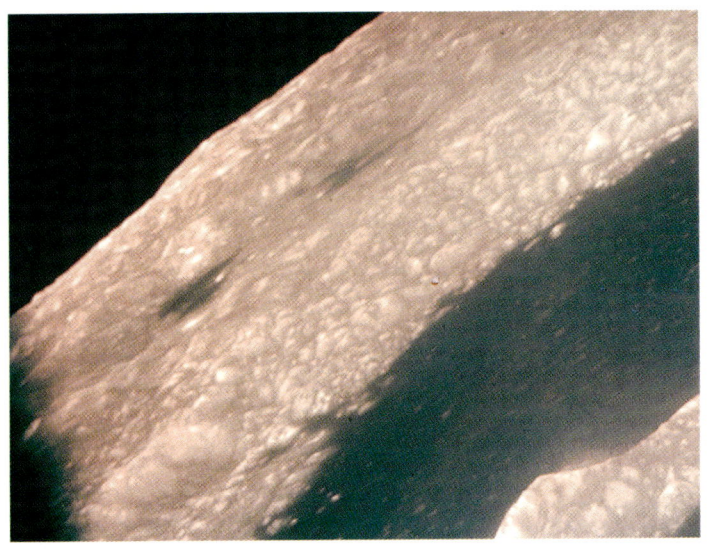

Notice dramatic colors on the lunar surface.

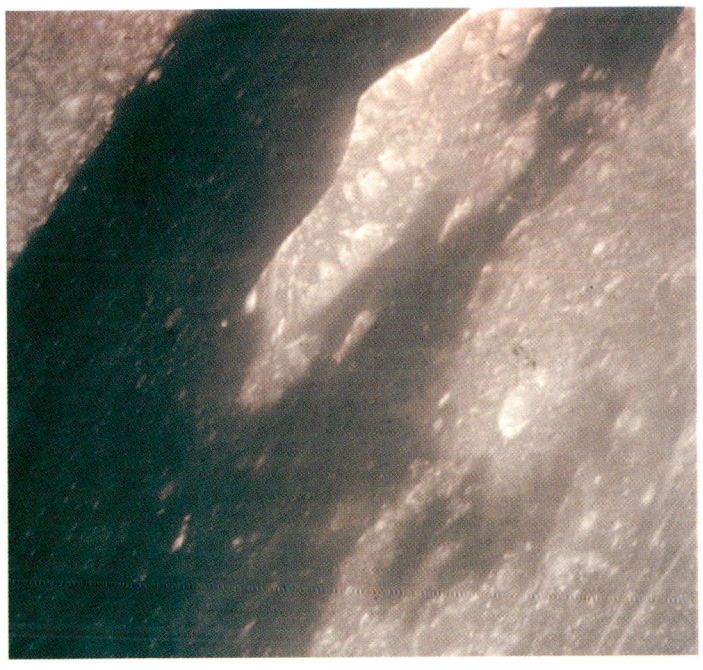

8
Gravity and Atmosphere on The Moon

Since I do not have the true data of the exact composition and density of the lunar atmosphere, I shall attempt to use logic and common sense to conduct my own analysis. We know for a fact that the Moon has a molten core, which becomes hotter the deeper we drill into it. Apollo 15 conducted this experiment. Seismic activity produces enormous pressures as well as hot gases and molten matter below the Moon's crust. If this planetary body would not possess an atmosphere, with sufficient pressure and density to act upon the outside of the Moon, thus neutralizing the pressure from within, the Moon would not be there today. This is called "natural balance".

We are told that the gravity of the Moon is about one-sixth that of the Earth. If the lunar atmosphere consists also of one-sixth of Earth pressure, it would still be about 2.5 lbs. per square inch, or 166 millibars. An atmospheric density of this pressure should be sufficient to hold the Moon together. If we use the one-sixth rule, it is not difficult to see with only one-sixth of gravity that this low pressure atmosphere would be sufficient to support life there. Another logical question arises. If a man weighs 150 lbs. on Earth, but only 25 lbs. on the Moon, he would need much less energy to move round, and probably would need an atmosphere no denser than the one that may exist there. I admit that these thoughts are not in accordance with present day thinking, just as twenty mile spaceships and vegetation on the Moon are foreign ideas, according to our commonly held ideas about the Moon.

As an example, let us use a mountain climber on Earth. A 150 lb. person, climbing through mountains with an elevation of 15,000 to 20,000 feet, without supplemental oxygen, is under severe strain. But what would happen if suddenly, 75 lbs. of his body weight would be eliminated? It would certainly ease his climbing efforts, would it not? This proves that thin air, body weight and gravity all contribute.

Man seems to be the most adaptable machine in the universe. One can only surmise under what conditions he can live if he eventually adapts himself, or better still, is born into it. Our lunar experts certainly anticipated the existence of life on the Moon. The quarantine stations set up at the Lunar Receiving Laboratories in Houston, Texas, had only one purpose, and that was to make certain that no harmful bacteria or microbes would be brought back from the Moon. I would like to remind the reader that both microbes and bacteria are living things.

Another piece of evidence that the lunar atmosphere has a pressure approximately two to two and one-half lbs. per square inch is the fact that the hatches of all Apollo landing craft were opened when the inside cabin pressure showed two and one-half lbs. If a total vacuum exists on the Moon, as we have been led to believe, the two and one-half lb. pressure inside the lander would have been sufficient to suck the astronauts right through the hatch onto the lunar surface, including all of their unsecured equipment.

The thin lunar atmosphere seems to be invisible on

most, but not all, photographs returned from the Moon. The reason for this is the possibility that the lunar atmosphere contains very little ozone gas. This would make the sky look black. On Earth, flying in an aircraft at 50,000 feet, the sky also appears black. The reason for this is that the ozone in our atmosphere, which makes the sky look blue, is now between the aircraft and the ground. I am convinced that, if the atmosphere on Earth would be reduced to only one-sixth of what it is now, our sky too, would look very black. If Earth's atmosphere was as thin as the Moon's, would it not be as difficult to detect, if one were on the Moon?

During a recent experiment simulating an atmosphere in a test tube of only one-tenth of one percent of that of Earth, mosses and lichens grew normally, and even multiplied. Even on Earth life exists at a very high altitude in the mountainous regions of Asia and South America. In Chile, there exists an immense one million acre wildlife preserve at the top of the world. Lake Chungara, at an altitude of over sixteen thousand feet above sea level, is located in this immense wildlife preserve called Lauca National Park. This lake is surrounded by lagoons, trees, green grass and rich vegetation, in which an abundance of llamas, alpacas, and exotic vicunas graze. The lake is filled with white and pink flamingos, and wild ducks take off and land with ease at this altitude.

The natives, at this altitude, produce a normal day's work, unthinkable for a lowlander, who would very quickly be gasping for breath.

Even Mt. Everest was climbed by several individuals over the past years, without the aid of supplemental oxygen. Mt. Everest is 29,000 feet above sea level. We must not overlook the marvelous adaptability of the human body under almost all conditions. As a matter of fact, all form life adheres to that road of adaptability.

Co-author's note: Shortly before my father's passing, he compiled some additional thoughts and research pertaining to the lunar gravity. They are as follows:

The exact composition and density of the existing lunar atmosphere, as well as gravitational factors other than the orthodox 1/6 rule is still kept secret by select top officials. And every effort is made to instill in the minds of the unaware public, that Newton's Law of Gravity and the airless Moon theory is nothing but the truth. (University of Chicago, Department of Physics, 1987: Determines a "discrepancy of about 15%" in Newton's gravity calculations.)

Over the years, several revealing articles and excellent books have reached my desk, some written by engineers who conducted their own investigations. Overwhelming evidence exists that the Moon's gravity on the surface is at least 64% of Earth's, which is 3 times as high as the 1/6 theory. Because of this fact, the lunar atmosphere is approximately 40% of Earth's or dense enough to support life.

In his most revealing book titled <u>Moongate</u>, containing suppressed findings of the U.S. Space Program, nuclear engineer William L. Brian II, produces the most convincing mathematical revelations of the substantial lunar gravity and atmosphere. Moongate was published in 1982, one year after my book's first edition.

Mr. Boye Petersen, editor of UFO Contact magazine in Denmark, June 1984 edition, writes:

"The stereotype slow-motion walk by the astronauts on the moon was no doubt produced by delaying the pictures before transmitting them to the television viewers on earth, to give the impression of low gravity. They must have exercised this many times before leaving the earth, but nevertheless, John Young did something which can hardly have been scheduled. He unexpectedly tried a high jump, but could only reach a height of about 14 inches, or 35 centimeters. The hop of 15 centimeters, or 8 inches on earth equals at least 3 meters, a bit over 3 yards, in a gravity of only 1/6, which is supposed to exist on the moon.

"Several times we have seen that the astronauts have been able to run rather normally on the moon. This would be impossible in a 1/6 gravity, even if they carried a load on their back equaling 200 pounds on earth. Every step would whirl them at least 3 meters, about 10 feet, upwards, and they could have, at the same time moved forward at least 45 feet before they would be ready for the next step.

"Unless you have the reflexes and physical condition of a trembling old man, you would never stumble and fall down in a 1/6 gravity, even if you were in a space suit, as did astronaut Chas. Duke.

"The presence of the solid atmosphere was evident already 5.5 kilometers above the lunar surface, for objects in the shadow were clearly visible and the sky was even more clear. On occasions, clouds were visible."

All this could not, of course, occur in a vacuum. In a vacuum, Mr. Petersen concludes, most of the equipment would cease to function, and all frictional connections would tend to freeze together, owing to lack of dividing molecules. In the same way, this would have made Apollo's moon car unfit for use if there was no air on the Moon.

Objects in the shadow would reach such low temperatures, as to make them crumble on touch. During their missions the astronauts, between themselves, talked a lot about waving flags, and flapping cables and strings of experimental instruments. Finally, Apollo 16 used a starched flag which resisted waving in the lunar breeze.

The scientist, Mr. Joseph H. Cater, made this written statement concerning the Apollo 16 mission: "This mission is now history and the usual inconsistencies were, or at least have been, obvious for the keen observer of the television screen." Through mathematical calculations of the neutral point between the center of the Earth and the center of the Moon, Mr. Cater determined that the lunar gravity is at least 60% of Earth's, contrary to the 16.7% still officially used by orthodox science.

To correlate space findings concerning the moon's gravity and atmospheric density. (Note: Air density is seldom measured directly in meteorology, because it is the combined relationship of 3 atmospheric properties; pressure, temperature, and humidity. However, pressure and density decrease regularly with altitude in the troposphere. For simple discussion, we can say that air density is a relative measurement of pressure, keeping in mind that there would be variations according to temperature and humidity in local areas. But with substantial lunar gravity and atmosphere, the variations would be slight, and density would be relevant to elevation.)

W. Brian II, in his book, <u>MoonGate - Suppressed Findings of the U.S. Space Program</u>, presented mathematical calculations indicating that the moon's gravity is 64% of Earth's. This calculation along with other data indicated a dense lunar atmosphere, but no value could be determined.

George Adamski in his book, Inside the Space Ships and in a 1965 lecture, stated that a visitor to the Moon would have to go through a 24-hour depressurization procedure to acclimatize to the moon's atmospheric density, which he said was 6 lb/in^2 (approx. 40% of Earth's). He either did not know or didn't state a gravity value.

Herbert Riehl, in Intro To The Atmosphere, tells us that in the Andes of South America and in Tibet, human habitations extend to .6 atmosphere density.

NASA and orthodox science maintains that the Moon has 1/6 gravity and no atmosphere.

Comparisons By Location
Gravity and Atmospheric Pressure

	Earth (sea level)	Andes (alt. 16,000')	Moon (craters/lowlands)
Gravity	1 g	1 g	.64 g
	32 ft/sec^2	32 ft/sec^2	20 ft/sec^2
	100 %	100 %	64 %
Atmospheric Pressure (Density)	32 ft/sec^2	32 ft/sec^2	20 ft/sec^2
	1007.	1007.	64%
	14.7 lb/in^2	8.8 lb/in^2	6 lb/in^2
	1000 mb	600 mb	400 mb
	100 %	60 %	40 %

Evaluation: We know that the natives of Tibet and the Andes live comfortably and work normally in 1g gravity and 600 mb atmospheric pressure. Consider that moon inhabitants would be living in .64g and 400 mb atmosphere pressure. Living and working in a slightly lower gravity would require less force to oppose gravity, hence less oxygen needed by humans, and the lungs would inflate normally, all things considered. Let's see if the figures are proportionately equal:

$$\frac{\text{Air Density - Moon}}{\text{Air Density - Andes}} \quad \frac{400}{600} = 66\%$$

This correlates exactly to:

$$\frac{\text{Gravity - Moon}}{\text{Gravity - Andes}} \quad \frac{.64}{100} = 64\%$$

Also, $\quad \frac{\text{Air Density - Andes}}{\text{Gravity - Andes}} \quad \frac{60}{100} = .6$

This agrees exactly:

$$\frac{\text{Air Density - Moon}}{\text{Gravity - Moon}} \quad \frac{40}{64} = .6$$

    The relationship between atmosphere density and gravity is identical for both the Andes and the Moon. If people can acclimatize to the Andes, they definitely could acclimatize to the Moon's atmosphere.

    The human lungs are able to adjust themselves to very low as well as high pressure, if changes are not done too quickly. An example with which we are most familiar is deep sea divers who slowly depressurize when returning to the surface. Of course, adaptability would be true for all form life, animal and vegetation. The conditions in the temperate zones on the Moon prove to be favorable for surface water, lakes, clouds, and forests, as reported by George Adamski in 1955.

    The data also indicates that there is a natural planetary balance between the internal pressures in the Moon and the atmosphere pressure from without.

The information obtained from the book Moongate clears up many unanswered questions. It states that 7 publications and astronomy books prior to the Apollo missions reported the neutral point between the Earth and the Moon, between 22,078 miles to 25,193 miles to the Moon, using the orthodox 1/6 rule.

However, the great neutral point discrepancy started officially with the release by Time magazine, July 25, 1969. Time reported the new neutral point figures, as discovered by Apollo to be 43,495 from the Moon. Other publications quickly followed, giving similar figures.

The 1969 edition of History Of Rocketry And Space Travel also reported the neutral point to be 43,495 miles. Encyclopedia Britanica lists 39,000 miles. The book We Reached The Moon, 38,900 miles, and the book Footprints On The Moon, 38,000 miles. While the figures vary between 30,000 and 43,495 miles, there is still a vast difference of the earlier figures, using the orthodox 1/6 rule, determining the neutral point between 20,000 to 25,000 miles to the Moon.

Calculating the lunar gravity, using updated information, redefines it to be approximately 64% of earth's. There, a 100 pound person does not weigh 16.6 pounds on the Moon, as earlier believed, but at least 64 pounds. This permitted the moon cars to be driven at such high speeds, and making those tight turns at high speeds, which would have been devastating in the 1/6 gravity. Mr. Brian concludes this high gravity or 64% will hold a dense atmosphere, produce clouds, and support vegetation and life.

The reader may be interested to note that if the neutral point would be 52,000 miles from the Moon, the surface gravity would be exactly the same as on Earth.

The Moon's atmosphere is very, very clean, for it contains much less water vapor and dust particles than our own. These particles may be the greatest factor governing the diffusion of light through the atmosphere. Due to the absence of oceans which have long dried up, as well as the long days and nights, the Moon's atmosphere does very seldom produce high winds, as is common on Earth. Due to the dried up ocean basins, the densest atmospheres have filled these cavities, leaving the high elevated mountain ranges virtually airless.

Moongate concludes that the space suits worn by the astronauts were really unnecessary and only worn for show. The higher gravity on the moon means that an entirely new technology had to be used to return our Apollo space craft. The fuel required for lift-off from the Moon with these higher gravity figures, would have been astronomical, therefore producing a weight problem, scrapping the whole project. It is very probable that the new electromagnetic technology was utilized since its discovery in 1965. From this appearance, the whole Apollo program was probably a cover-up for a super top secret space program.

I feel, however, that even if these new findings would have not been released, the 1/6 gravity calculation would have also worked out to support life on the Moon if this 1/6 rule would have applied to the atmospheric density as well. A 2.5 pound pressure, or 166 millibars, on the lunar surface, in combination with a lower gravity, would permit life on the Moon as well.

9
Water, Clouds, and Vegetation

The fact that water exists on the Moon has already been established by NASA's release, which reported "spraying geysers of water." From the photographic evidence in this book, the reader will find that not only natural lakes and ponds, but also artificial water reservoirs exist on the Moon (See plate #50).

From my studies I have found that much of the north pole area seems to be clouded over on occasion, and in certain locations. Clouds are the product of condensed moisture which rises up to density altitude from the warm ground below. For water clouds to exist, moisture on the ground must exist. Photographic analysis shows that the condensations of clouds take place at very low altitudes. I estimate this altitude to be between two thousand and six thousand feet above ground level. It must be strange indeed, to stand in one of the low lying lunar valleys during the bright daylight, watching patches of white clouds drift along in the black sky. It seems that the densest part of this atmosphere on the Moon is to be found in the valleys and craters close to the so-called lunar sea level. This law applies to Earth, so it should apply to the Moon. The lunar clouds formed at these very low altitudes, seem to hug the mountain side, much like the monsoon clouds over tropical islands on Earth. While heavy cloud formations are quite rare and appear to depend on the seasons, they do occur on occasion, mostly in the northern and southern hemisphere on the Moon.

There are several natural lakes on the Moon, close to the north pole. These appear on photographs with a very black surface. Photographs from outer space taken from above Earth in black and white or even color, show most lakes to be black also. Since the sky on the Moon is almost black, naturally lakes on the Moon, and in fact all water surfaces, will look black.

On the Moon's hidden side is found the crater Tsiolkowsky. Our astronauts have labeled this crater "The Lake". The astronauts stated that its black surface looks exactly like a lake with water in it. Other vertical close-up photos, taken during different missions, seem to show that the water in this lake is very shallow and very clear, for one can see the bottom through the water. The only time when water does not look black from the air is when sunlight is reflected from it, at which time it turns silvery white on the photographs. Plates #53 to #55 shows several artificial reservoirs, with the sunlight reflecting from them. Aerial photographs which I have taken over southern California show reservoirs very similar in appearance as those photographed on the Moon. In California, these reservoirs with reinforced walls are used for irrigation purposes.

The presence of surface water on the Moon seems to depend very much upon the seasons as do the southwest desert areas in the United States. However, oceans cannot be found on the Moon, and if they existed long ago, they must have dried up. It is no secret that our solar system is an old one. Under these conditions it seems that smaller planetary bodies dry up before the larger ones. In my efforts to search for vegetation on the Moon, I did not detect any

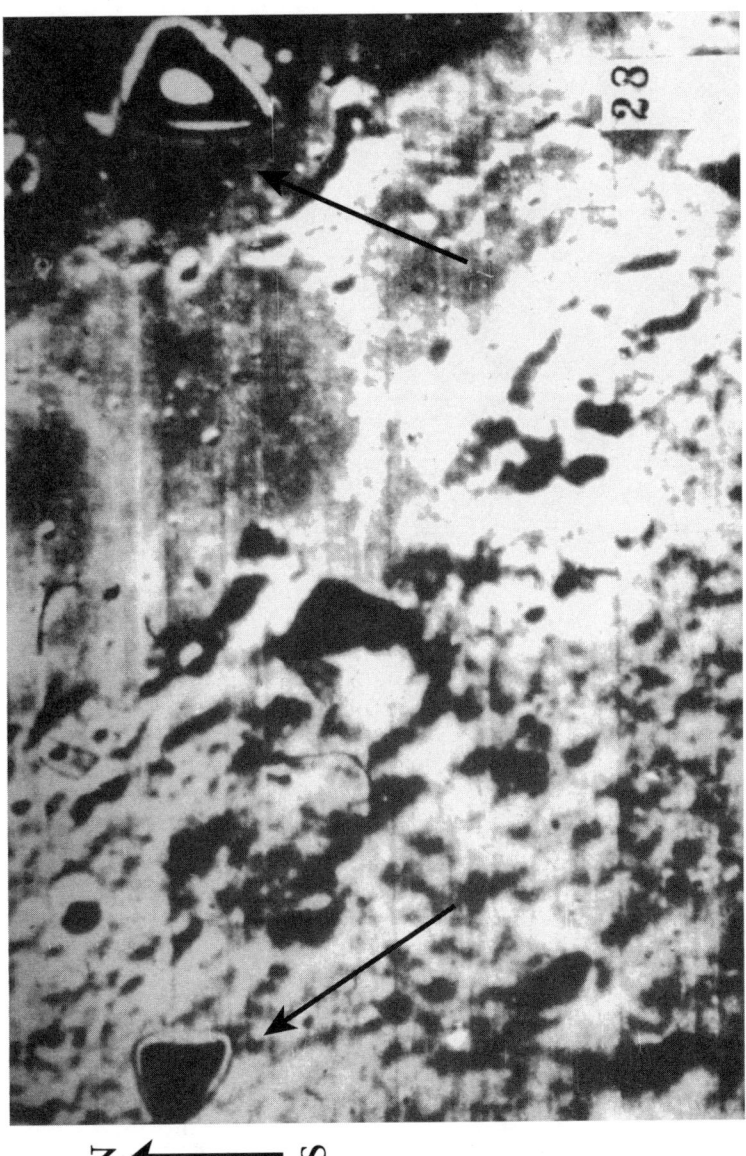

Plate 50. Area blow up. LO No. HR128, near crater Plato. Notice, two irrigation type ponds or lakes in the upper left and right of this photo. Also notice the almond shaped island in the lake to the right.

Plate 51. California USA, irrigation pond with reinforced walls. Taken by the author from his aircraft.

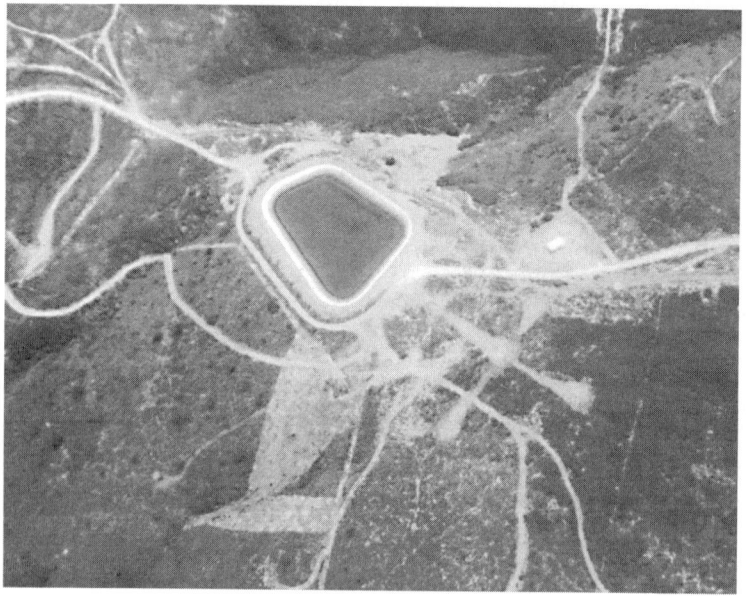

Plate 52. The same pond. Notice identical shape and appearance of those ponds on the moon on Plate 50.

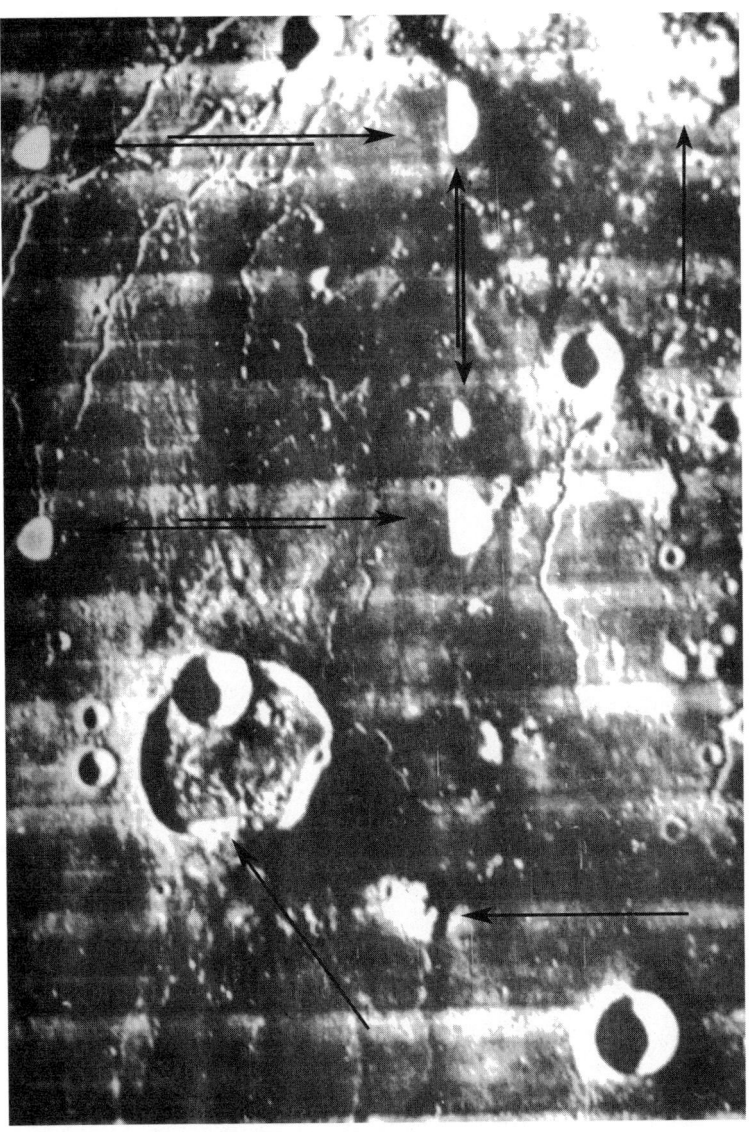

Plate 53. Area blow-up No. 151³ NASA Lunar Orbiter IV Photo of the crater Krieger and area. To the right of Krieger notice five triangular white pond-like constructions reflecting the sunlight. Also notice clouds on the edge of Krieger as well as at 50 Km. southwest of the crater.

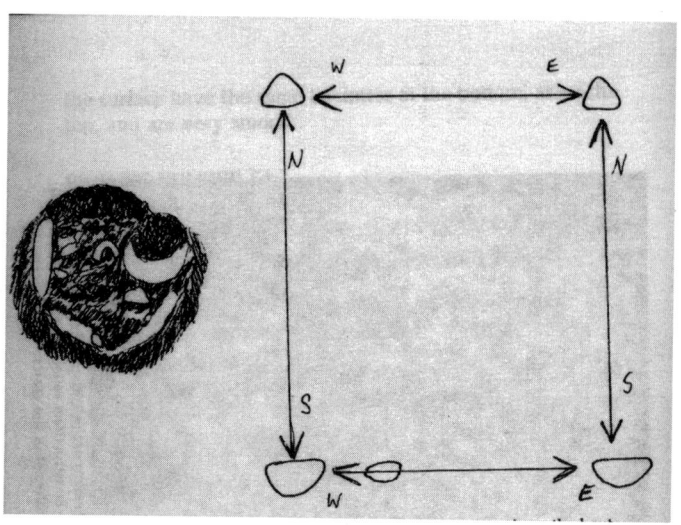

Plate 53a. Notice white objects are laid out in a square, north-south about 85 miles apart, west-east about 72 miles apart. This fact alone is proof of artificial installations.

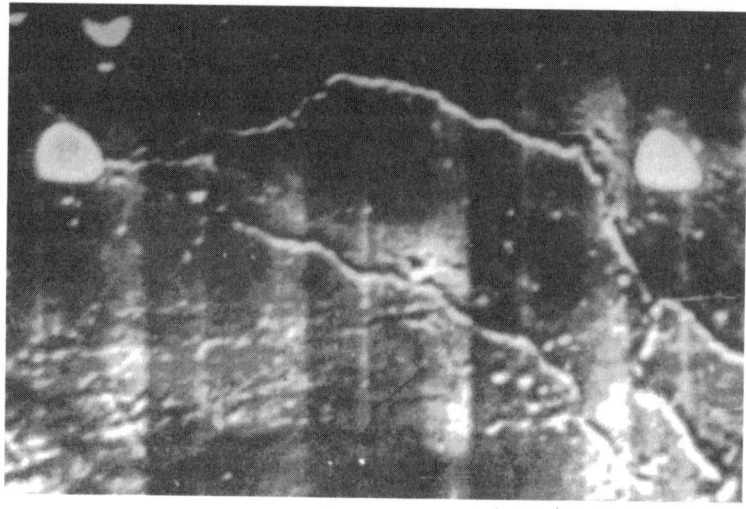

Plate 54. Area blow-up. LO IV Photo of ponds or lakes reflecting sunlight. Also notice the appearance of possible water in the riverbeds.

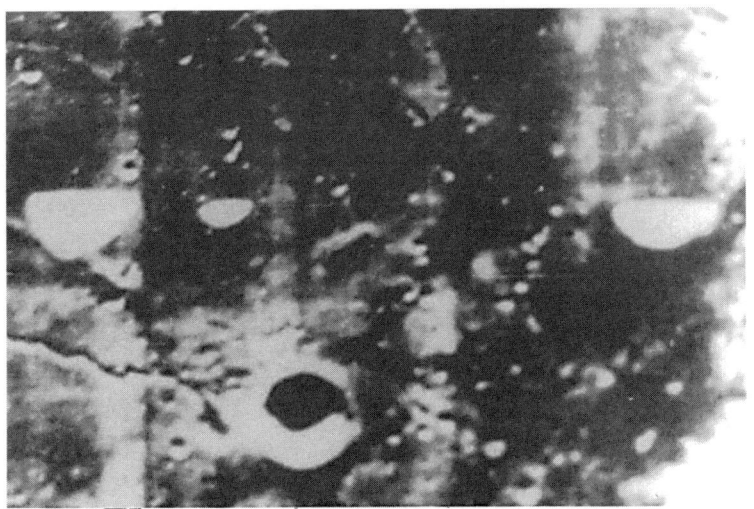

Plate 55. Area blow-up. No. 151³ LO IV of other ponds, reflecting sunlight.

Plate 56. California USA, irrigation pond reflecting sunlight. Photographed by the author from his aircraft. Notice identical appearance of this pond with others on the moon - Plates 53, 54 and 55.

plowed fields or open growing areas. As was mentioned earlier, hydroponic farming under those translucent domes would be much more productive in any event. Much ground water must exist in the lunar mountains, especially on the hidden side. Color photos clearly show the color green in the shady areas of brown colored hills and craters, very much in appearance as the southwest desert areas in the United States. While some color photos appear brown, others definitely show a green color. One can only speculate that this may be due to seasonal changes.

We must understand that even on the Moon a natural balance would take place very much like on Earth. If there are water clouds and vegetation on the Moon, it seems reasonable to assume that also some form of animal life exists there. To maintain a natural balance, some form of animal life would be necessary. One wonders how life forms would appear under different pressures. Here, some people, authors and movie makers alike, permit their imaginations free reign. I feel we can explain that life forms do not change very much in their geometrical appearances, living under higher or lower pressures, as we are familiar with on Earth. In our oceans, the fish that live close to the surface share a very common physical appearance with those fish living at great depths. Even man can safely dive several thousand feet below the sea by using air mixtures of oxygen and hydrogen. One could repeat that man is not only the most adaptable machine in the universe, but his place is the universe. Man is never confined, and to travel anywhere in the Cosmos all that is necessary is the technical knowledge.

In a recent scientific article the scientists argued that surface water could not exist on low gravity worlds, such as the Moon. They theorized that the water molecules would quickly escape into space because of the low gravity and atmospheric pressures. However, this assumption seems contradictory. Many dried out riverbeds on the Moon suggest there existed heavy run-off of water. If the surface water would have quickly disappeared into space, as suggested, then these riverbeds could not be there. It requires eons of time for water to carve these riverbeds.

10
Photographic Analysis of Lunar Pictures

This chapter is designed to identify both the location of, and provide general information relating to, many of the official NASA photographs in this book. The reader should understand that much of the Moon's hidden side is still unnamed. In this instance, of course, it is not possible to give exact locations.

Many more pictures presented in this book lack identification of name and location on the Moon, other than the Apollo Flight number. Lunar back side craters are unnamed. Nevertheless, all photos are the NASA originals with the exceptions of area blowups and enlargements. None of the photos have been tampered with, retouched, or altered in any way.

All described points of interest, such as domes, UFOs, lakes, constructions, vegetation, reservoirs, objects in craters, etc., can be found by anyone who desires to do so.

NASA has been very cooperative with me. I hope that through my investigation I have, in a small way, helped NASA to find and identify these unexplained mysteries, or at least to suggest what these objects in the air and on the ground could be.

PICTURE NUMBERS 20 to 23
LO V. No. HR 168^2
AREA: Detail from the Vitello crater. The area around the foot of the central mountain.

POSITION: 37°35, W. Longitude; 30°20, S. Latitude

DIMENSION: The original picture represents an area of 900 x 900 meters.

REMARKS: NASA explains these objects as rolling stones, the large one 75 feet in diameter, the smaller one about 15 feet in diameter. Close study of light and shadows, however, reveal that these objects are not rolling down, but on the contrary, up, coming from the lower shady area to the higher light one. It is interesting to note that the upper object clearly comes up from a crater, while the larger one is passing the slope of a crater, without turning and rolling down into it. However, what is most unusual are the tracks the larger object is leaving behind. The pattern and imprints are exactly spaced and look like stitch-marks.

PICTURE NUMBER 24
Author's conception of the larger vehicle or object.

PICTURE NUMBER 43, LO III NASA No. HR 006
AREA: South of Maskelyn F, in the S. E. Mare Tranquilitatis POSITION: 34°4' E. Longitude; 3°1' N. Latitude

DIMENSION: The whole picture represents an area of 13. 6 x 13. 6 Km.

REMARKS: In the left side one can see an area in which some strange tracks radiate. Actually they radiate from a dome in the terrain. Also notice the small crater southeast of the dome. This crater shows two objects right and left, like two walls, closing off a reservoir.

PICTURE NUMBER 44, LO III NASA No. HR 006
AREA: Same general vicinity of picture #46

REMARKS: The tracks are now clearly visible. They look

like traffic tracks in open land. These tracks all originate from the crater to the left, and are spaced so exactly apart that one can safely say they are made by some type of vehicle. The Moon is being heavily mined to test the soil for its mineral contents. Ground contact by some form of soil tester is unavoidable.

PICTURE NUMBER 45, LO V NASA No. MR 168
AREA: The crater Vitello with surroundings
POSITION: 37°35' W. Longitude; 30°20' S. Latitude
DIMENSION: The crater's diameter is about 50 Km.

REMARKS: The central mountain appears to be cut into a large platform of some kind. Vitello is the crater where astronomers have observed many strange activities. From the left, many small dots and white lines seem to float over the terrain and the left edge of Vitello. Speaking as a pilot, these dots and lines look somewhat like mackerel type clouds on Earth when flying high over them.

PICTURE NUMBER 46, LO V No. ER 168^2
AREA: Vitello again, to the west

REMARKS: Again the white objects, floating over the rugged mountains surrounding Vitello.

PICTURE NUMBER 47 and 47A
APOLLO 8 NASA No. 8-12-2296
AREA: Tsiolkowsky crater (The Lake)
POSITION: 128°E. Longitude; 22°5' Latitude
DIMENSION: About 240 Km.

REMARKS: NASA states the black mass in this crater is unknown, but that it must originate from the interior of the Moon. It obviously appears to be water, but since this would upset most of the scientific world, the best thing is to wait as long as possible to reveal that.

Apollo 8 astronaut Aldrin stated: "When I looked at Tsiolkowsky Crater, it reminded me of a mountain lake with a quiet surface and with a small island in the middle. "But Tsiolkowsky seems not the only mountain lake in this area, as several other lakes can easily be seen in this photo.

PICTURE NUMBER 48 and 48A
APOLLO 8 NASA No. Unknown
AREA: The back side of the Moon close to the north pole.

REMARKS: Another lake with water in it. Also notice cloud formations north of the crater.

PICTURE NUMBER 49, LOII NASA No. MR 213
AREA: South of the Marius crater
POSITION: $50^0 40$, W. Longitude; $11^0 55'$ N. Latitude
REMARKS: Notice hill, left of center, which has been cut out like a piece from a pie or cake. The cut is perfect. Also slightly above this hill is a large dome casing a shadow to the left. Furthermore, to the right of the picture are several perfectly cut holes (or craters).

PICTURE NUMBER 50 LO IV No. HR 128
AREA: The crater Plato
POSITION: 10°W. Longitude; 52°N. Latitude
DIMENSION: About 96.5 Km.

REMARKS: Plato crater and the area surrounding it is located in the northern region of the Moon, and over the last 150 years has been the place where the highest activity has been observed by professional and amateur astronomers. For instance, flashing lights, luminous triangles, luminous lines, as well as fog and clouds have been seen.

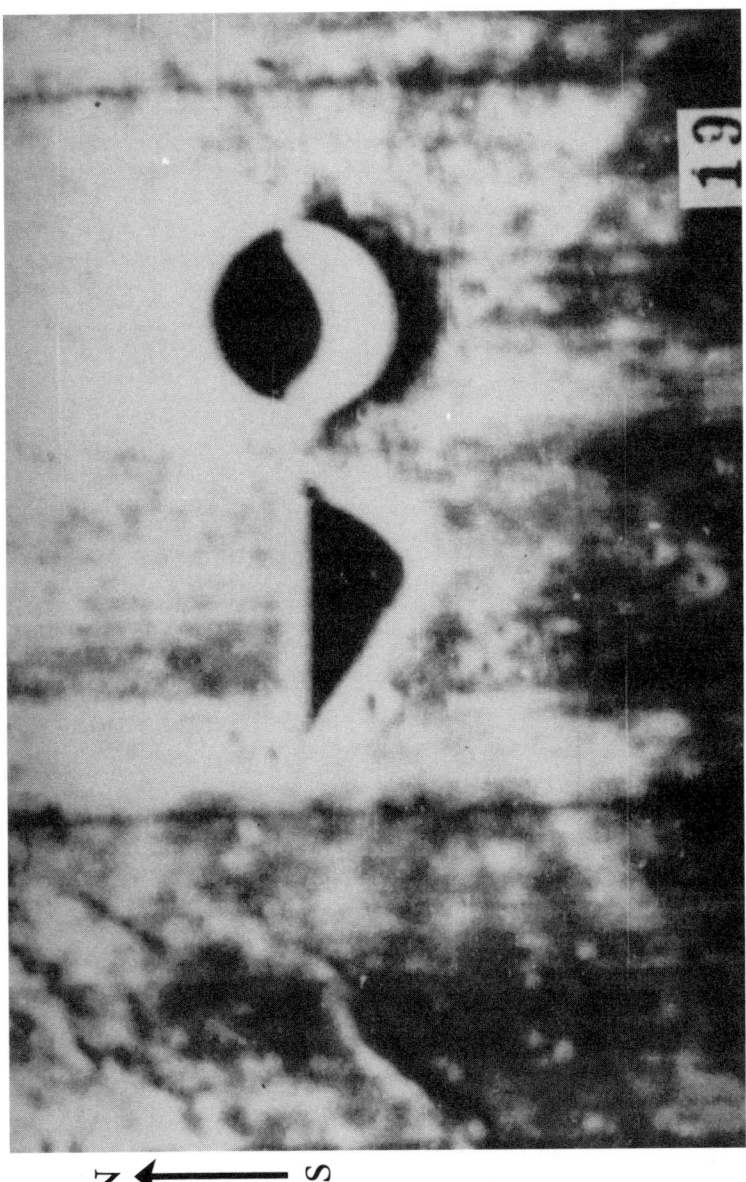

Plate 57. Area Blowup. West of crater Aristarchus. LO IV Photo No. HR157[1]. Two artificial looking installations. The perfectly shaped crater and the 25 mile cylindrical shape.

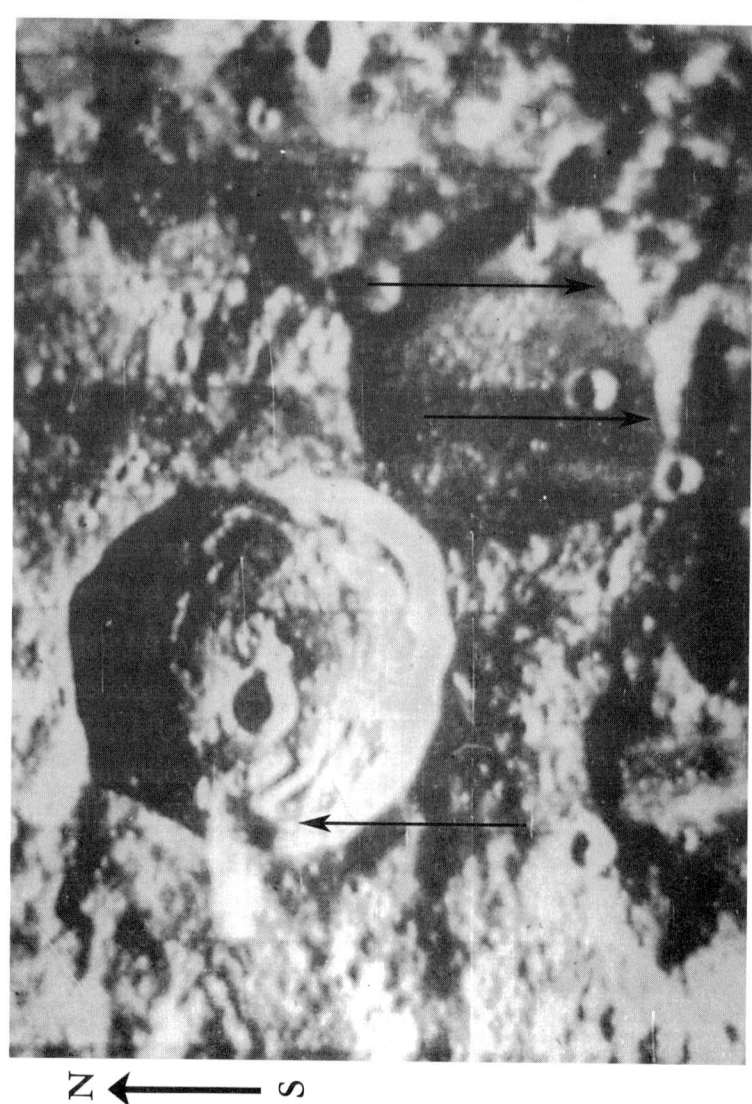

Plate 58. Area blowup. LO IV Photo No. HR161³. The crater Prosper Henry. Notice large white cloud hanging over the left wall. More clouds can be seen in the adjacent crater to the southeast including several oval objects in the center.

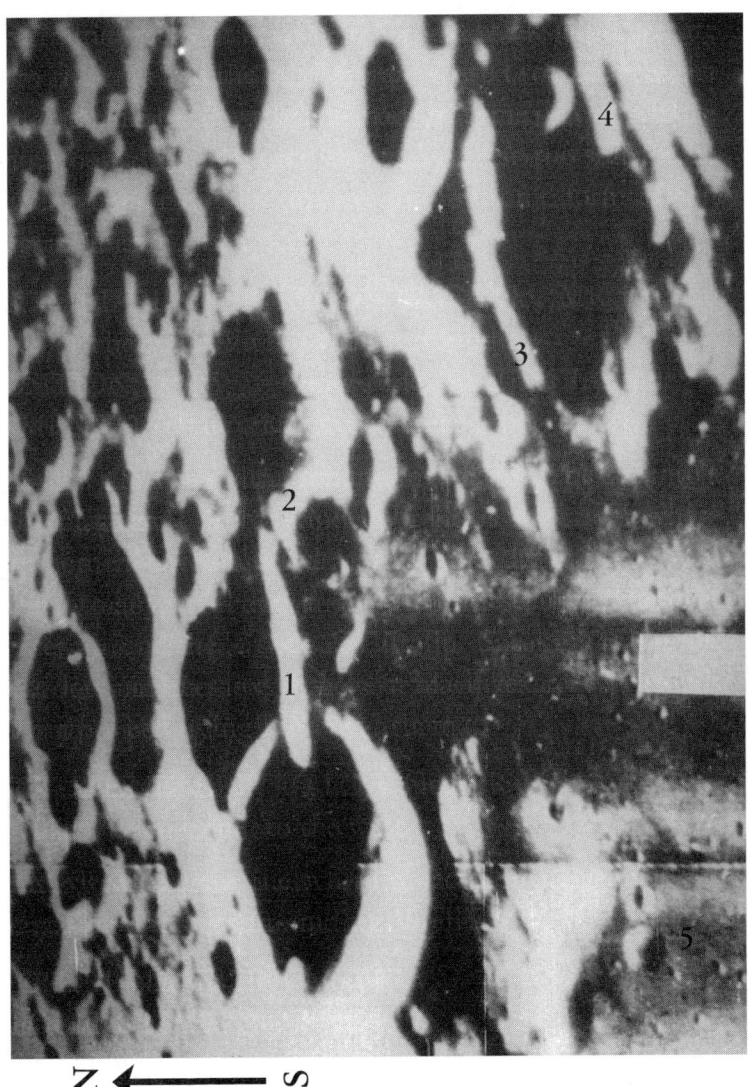

Plate 59. Area blowup. LO V Photo No. HR103³. Mare Moscovience on the back side of the moon. Notice:
1. Large cloud hanging over crater rim.
2. Oval object next to #1.
3. & 4. Airborne cigar shaped objects.
5. A very large dome.

The late American astronomer, Dr. Pickering, had seen what he himself called a storm with lightning, which raged inside of the crater Plato.

The most revealing things on this picture are the two irrigation type ponds or lakes with reinforced walls. They are triangular shaped, one on the left side of the photo, the other on the right side, with an almond shaped island (perhaps a pump station?).

The very rough terrain resembles water bearing clefts, covered with a heavy vegetation.

PICTURE NUMBER 51 and 52: Shows two aerial photos taken by the author over southern California U. S. A., showing very similar irrigation ponds with reinforced walls. The difference, however, is that these two ponds on the Moon are much larger and there are no visible surface roads, as seen in the photos of the California reservoirs. As earlier described in Chapter 5, an advanced civilization having complete air mobility, with few exceptions, does not need roads on their planet.

PICTURE NUMBER 53, 54, 55
LO IV No. HR 1513
AREA: The terrain northeast of the crater Aristarchus. The crater in the middle is called Krieger.
POSITION: 46°W. Longitude; 29°N. Latitude
DIMENSION: Krieger is about 80 Km. in diameter

REMARKS: To the right of the crater Krieger, notice five triangular shaped irrigation ponds, or reservoirs just like the ones on the previous pictures. Except here, the sun shines from the north just at the proper angle and altitude to reflect its light off the water, which shows up white in a black and white photo.

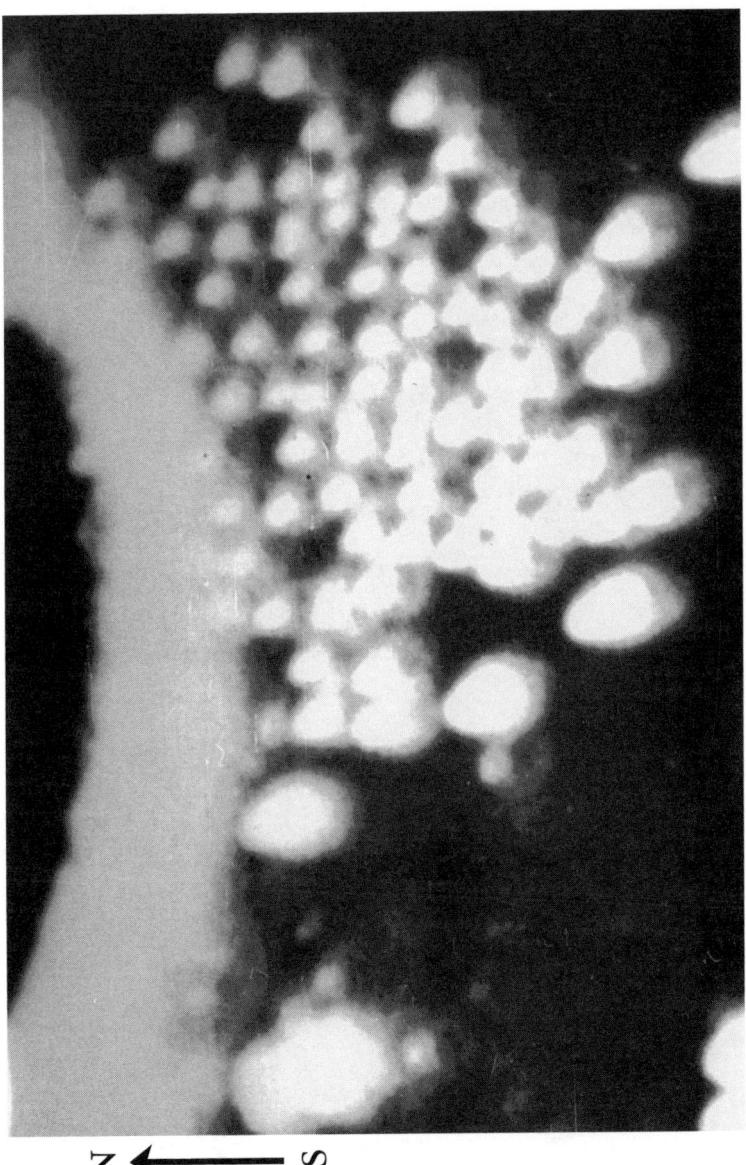

Plate 60. Area blowup. LO V Photo No. MR81. Section of the crater Ritter C. Cone shaped clouds to the right and center of this photo. Cumulus clouds in the upper and lower left.

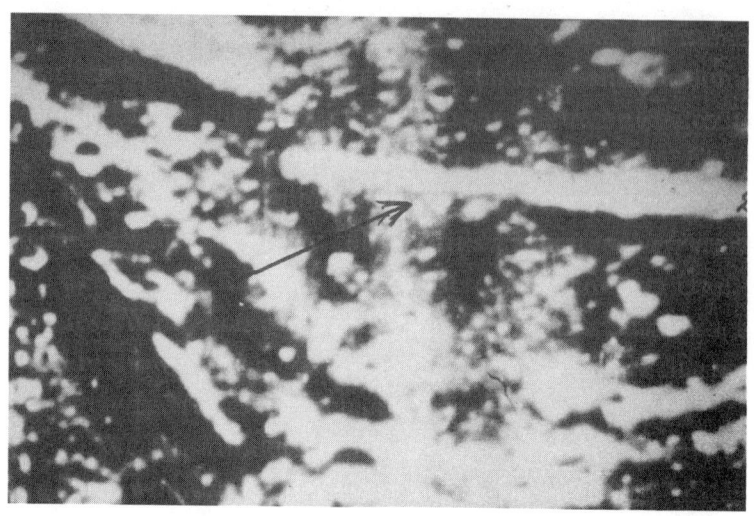

Plate 61. Area blow-up. LO IV Photo No. HR182². Smoke rising vertically out of the crater Vasco De Gama. Also notice other clouds in the center of the photo.

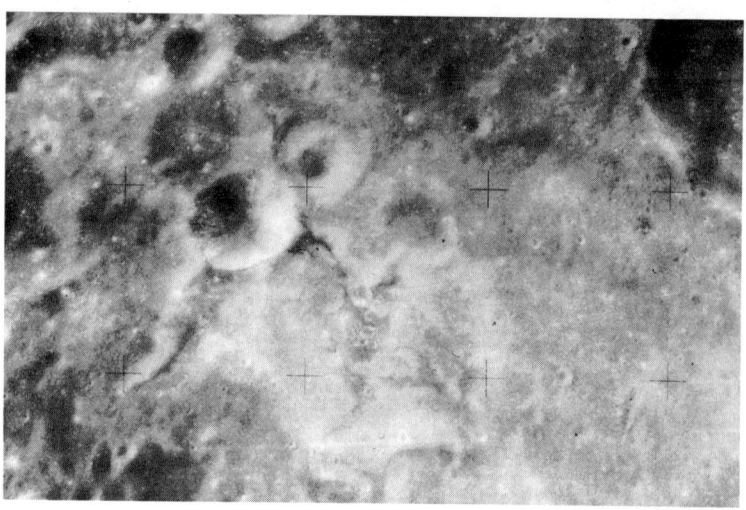

Plate 62. Area blowup. Apollo 16 Photo 16-758. Patches of fog and clouds near the crater Lobachavsky.

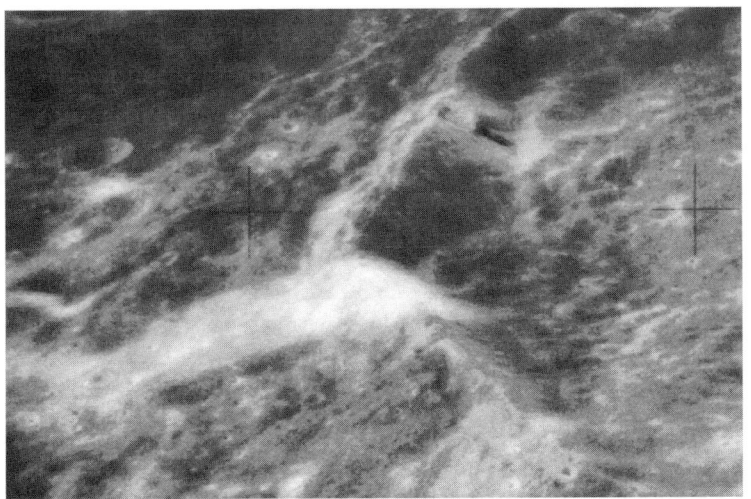

Plate #63. Area blow-up. Apollo 16 No. 16-758 photo. Large low cloud bank hugging the crater's edge of the Lobachavsky crater. Also notice large oval object on the crater's edge casing a shadow.

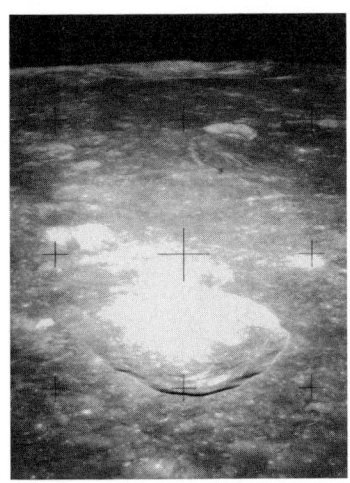 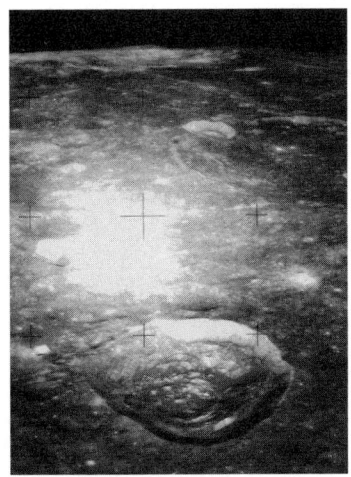

Plates #64 and #65. Apollo 14 photos No. 14-10279 and 14-10280. Notice that the large cloud or mist has moved north away from the crater it partially covered.

PICTURE NUMBER 56
LOCATION: Southern California U. S. A.

REMARKS: This is the same California irrigation pond or reservoir shown in the previous photo, number 51 and 52. But here, with the sunlight reflecting from the water, producing exactly the same effect as on Picture Number 54 and 55 on the Moon.

PICTURE NUMBER 57, LO IV No. HR 1571
AREA: The terrain west of Aristarchus
POSITION: 55°W. Longitude; 25°N. Latitude
DIMENSION: The whole picture represents an area of about 319 x 81 Km.

REMARKS: Two artificial installations. Without a doubt Nature does not produce objects positioned like the well formed crater and this perfectly straight mount or hangar, which is some 40 Km. (25 miles) long.

PICTURE NUMBER 58 LO IV No. 1613
AREA: The Prosper Henry crater
POSITION: 59°E. Longitude; 22°N. Latitude
DIMENSION: The crater's diameter is 30 Km.

REMARKS: The picture shows clearly the existence of clouds on the Moon. Notice the large white cloud hanging over the left crater wall. More clouds can be seen on the south rim of the next crater, below, right, of Prosper Henry.

PICTURE NUMBER 59 LO V No. HR 103[3]
AREA: Mare Moscovience
POSITION: 140°-150° E. Longitude; 20°-30°N. Latitude
DIMENSION: About 160 x 100 Km.

REMARKS: Again, clouds hovering over the crater's edge.

Marking   No. 1: Large long cloud
          No. 2: Tadpole shaped object
          No. 3 and 4: Cigar-shaped objects

PICTURE NUMBER 60 LO V No. HR 81
AREA: Part of the crater Ritter C
POSITION: 19°E. Longitude; 2°30' N. Latitude
DIMENSION: 10 x 8 Km.

REMARKS: These luminous objects look like cone-shaped clouds at the edge of Ritter C. These objects are definitely airborne, as they float over the edge of Ritter C.

Also notice lumpy cumulus-shaped clouds, upper and lower left of the picture.

PICTURE NUMBER 61, LO IV No. HR 1822
AREA: The Vasco de Gama crater
POSITION: 85 °W. Longitude; 15 °N. Latitude
REMARKS: A pillar of white smoke rises almost vertically out of Vasco de Gama.

The Apollo Metric 16-758 exact location not known, shows the definite evidence of fog and low clouds on the Moon, once again. Plate No. 62.

Another photo, also Apollo 16-758, but northwest of the foggy area described above, a large cloud hugging the mountain side and casting shadows, can be seen clearly on the left side of the crater. Plate #63.

Apollo photos 14-10279 and 14-10280 show some form of mist, fog, or cloud, first covering most of the large crater of 14-10280, and now, on photo 14-10279, showing the same crater clearly. The Apollo 14 spacecraft moving in closer for the next shot, must have taken just enough time for this cloud to drift in a northeasterly direction (See plates #64 and #65).

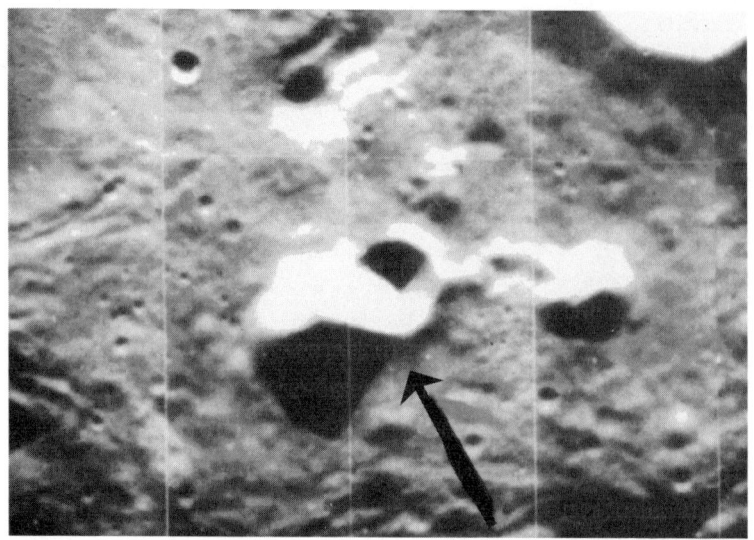

Plate 66. Area blow-up. LO IV Photo No, 187H2. The Alpine Valley area of the moon. Notice large cloud-like object covering half of the central crater.

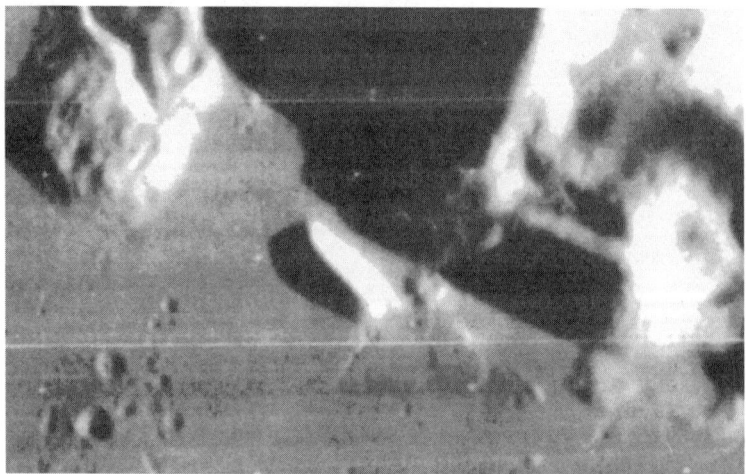

Plate 67. Area blow-up. LO IV Photo No, 187H2. Notice oval shaped object, UFO or cloud, one mile east of the large crater. More clouds are in the upper right plus three domes (two N.N.E. of the crater).

Plate 67a. LO IV Photo No, 187H2 showing large cigar-shaped object above crater floor.

The lunar orbiter 5, LO IV No. 187H2 photo, shows a large white cloud covering half of the central crater. General location of this photo is east of the Alpine Valley on the Moon.

Another large, oval-shaped cloud, just a mile to the east of the large crater, may also be a UFO, since they are known to operate within a well-outlined cloud of ionized air or force field. This photo NO LO IV 187 H2, is also located east of the Alpine Valley (See plates #66 and #67).

The next photo of the same picture NO LO IV 187H2, is a direct shot of part of the Alpine Valley, showing a large cloud in the valley (See plate #67A).

Many of these photos were shown to a retired Air Force Colonel, who independently identified these clouds, pointing them out to me on the pictures.

PICTURE NUMBER 68, LO IV No. HR 127
AREA: Western part of the crater Plato
POSITION: 10°W. Longitude; 52°N. Latitude
DIMENSION: Plato has a diameter of about 96. 5 Km.

REMARKS: Quite heavy white clouds (cumulus?) can be seen over this entire area. This is not unusual in the Plato area since there is evidence of vegetation there. Vegetation needs water to grow, while moisture evaporates and condenses into clouds when density altitude is reached.

PICTURE NUMBER 69, LO IV No. HR 128
AREA: Again, the western part of Plato
POSITION: As for picture number
REMARKS: This photograph was taken of much the same general vicinity as number 68, except that it was taken at a later time. Obviously there was enough time to show definite changes in many of the cloud shapes of the earlier photo. It is presumed that it is during the rainy season around Plato.

PICTURE NUMBER 70 to 72 LO IV No. HR 161[1]
AREA: Around the crater Damoiseau (S. E.)
POSITION: 60°W. Longitude; 4°S. Latitude
DIMENSION: The picture represents an area of 139 x 98 Km.
REMARKS: Marking
    No. 1: Damoiseau D
    No. 2: Damoiseau (30 Km. in diameter)
    No. 3: The top of a smoke pillar oozing out from the area to the left of the valley.

The valley which runs from the west along Damoiseau D crater to the southeast looks suspiciously like a riverbed.

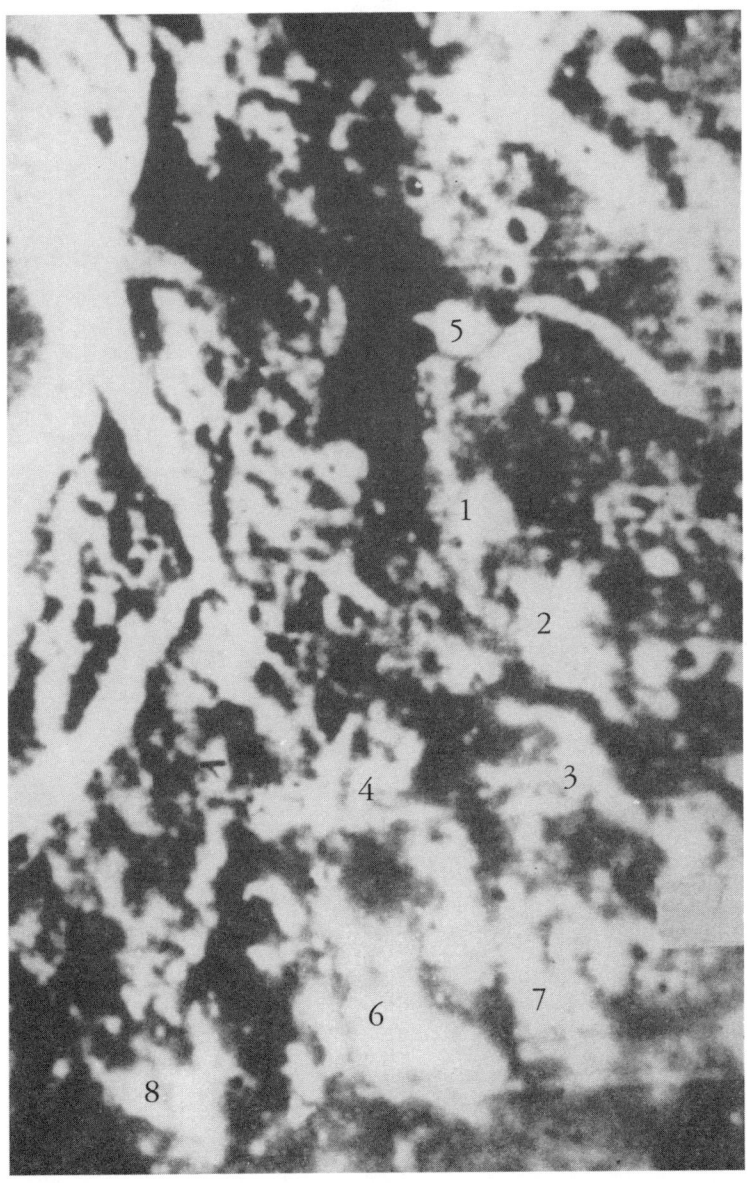

Plate 68. LO IV Photo No. HR127 south of the crater Plato. Notice cumulus cloud build ups at the center and left side of the photo numbered 1-8.

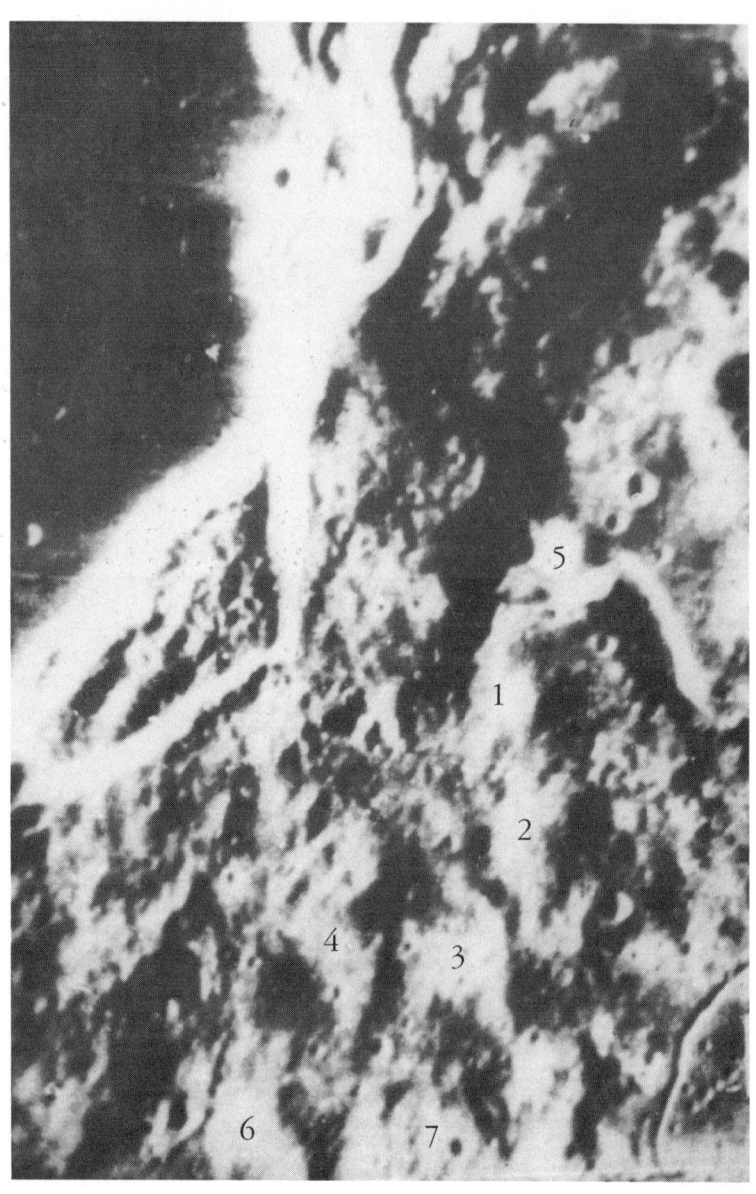

Plate 69. LO IV Photo No. HR128 southwest of the crater Plato, notice the change of shape of these clouds in comparison to Plate 68.

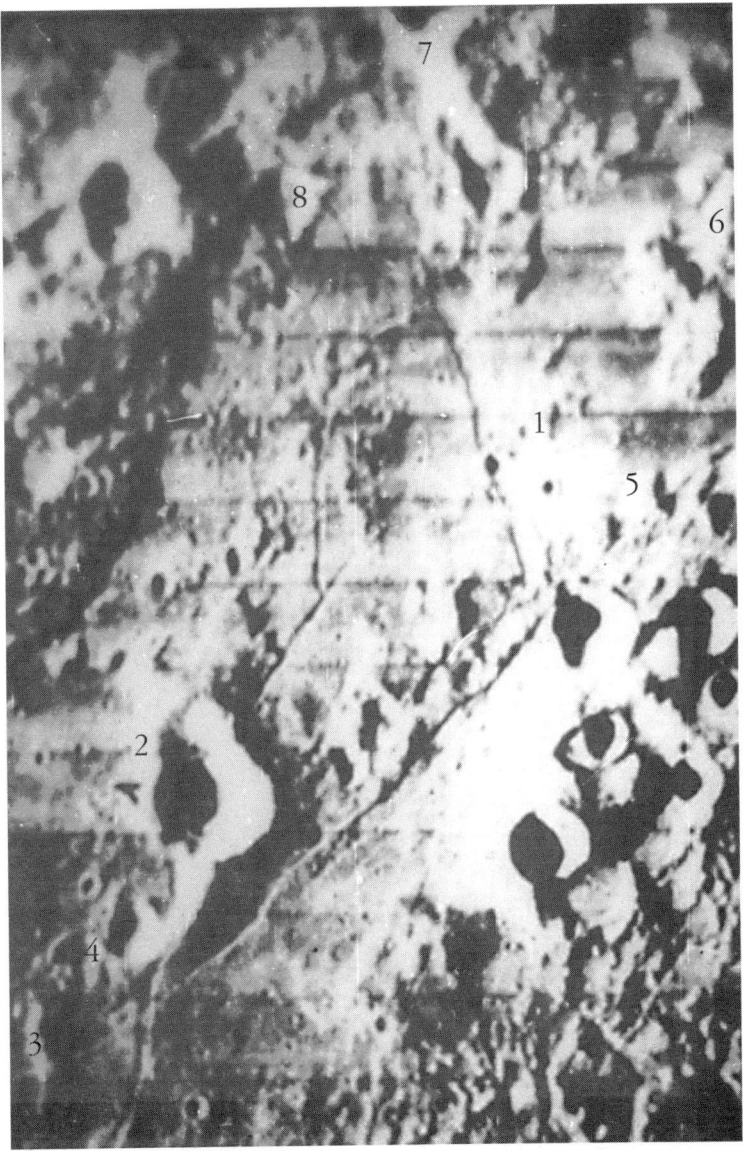

Plate 70. LO IV Photo No. HR161[1]. Southeast of the crater Damoiseau. #2, Crater Damoiseau #3. Pillar of smoke drifting from west to east. #4. Clouds over crater's edge. #5 - #8. Construction.

Plate 71. LO IV Photo No. HR161[1]. Area blow-up. Notice the double walls in the crater and riverbed flowing N.W. to S.E. Is this crater a reservoir dammed up?

Plate 72. LO IV Photo No. HR161[1]. Area blow-up of the eastern section of Plate #70. Notice: #1 Unusual formation/obscuration. #2 - #4 Construction or platforms.

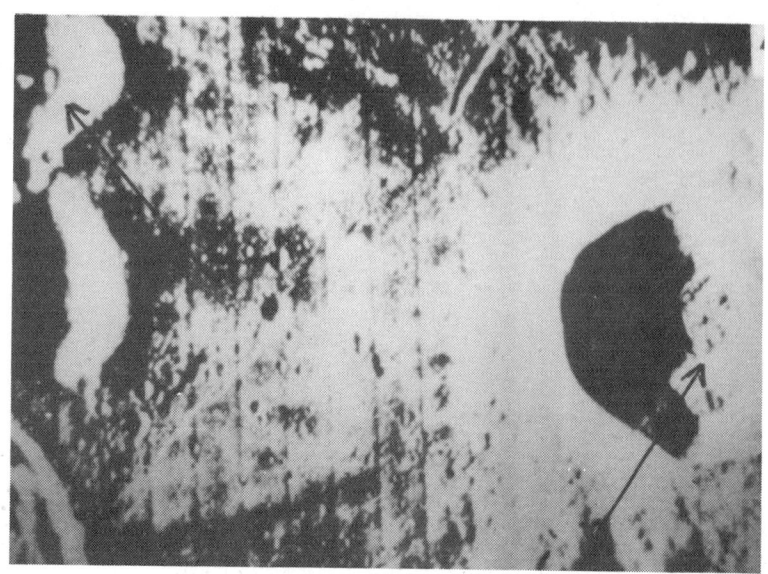

Plate 73. LO IV Photo No. MR81. Crater Ritter and Ritter C and D. Notice two dome shaped objects in Ritter and two glowing objects in Ritter C.

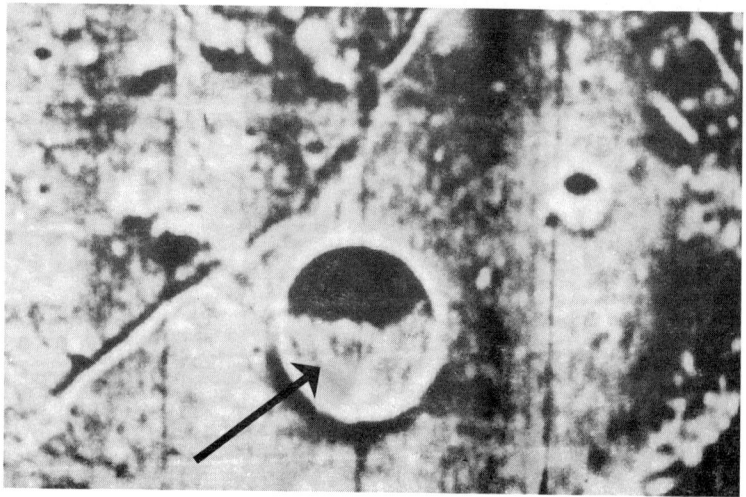

Plate 74. LO IV Photo No. HR86³. The crater Posidonius. Notice two oval shaped objects on the crater floor and clouds to the N.W. covering the canyon.

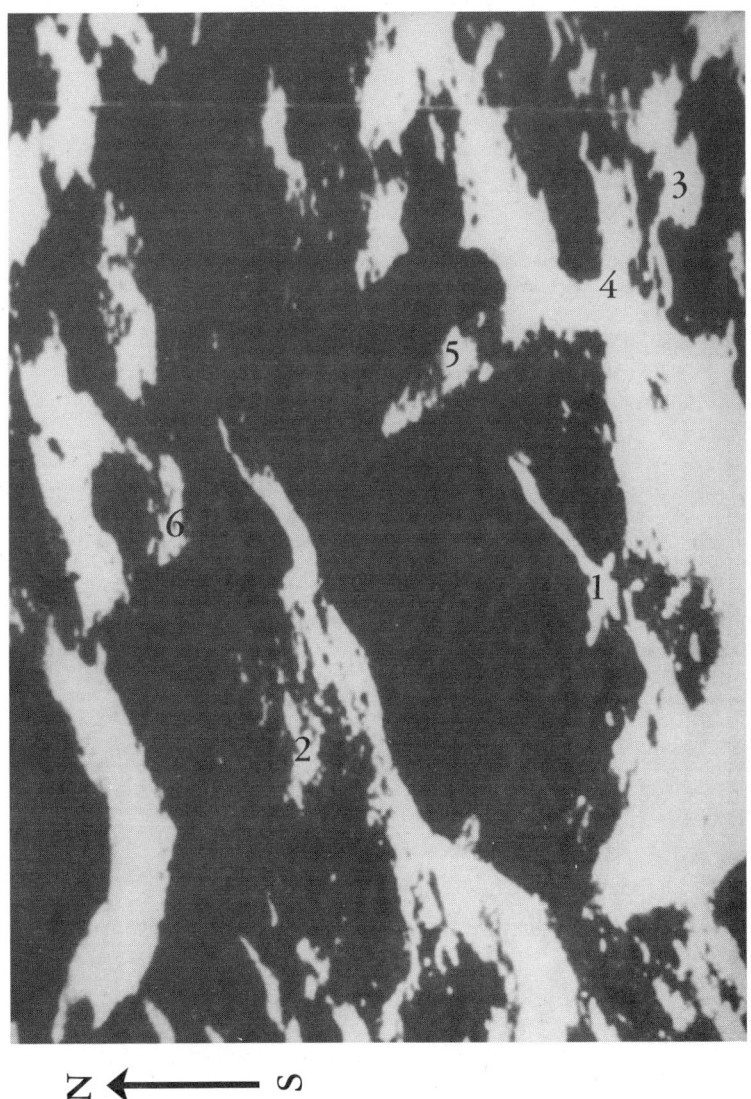

Plate 75. LO V Photo No. HR181[1]. Unnamed crater on the moon's back side. Notice in numbers 1 - 6 the appearance of construction.

Damoiseau D has two walls, left and right, closing off the crater like large dams. Is Damoiseau D. a reservoir, dammed up? It certainly appears that way.

PICTURE NUMBER 73 LO IV No. MR 81
AREA: The crater Ritter and to the left, Ritter C, D, and Dionysius
POSITION: 19°E. Longitude; 20°30' N. Latitude
DIMENSION: Diameter of Ritter about 32 Km.
REMARKS: Notice objects in Ritter and Ritter C which is very strange since these were not marked on the astronauts' chart of this area. The large luminous object in Ritter C is almond shaped, which suggests some kind of vehicle. Several objects in Ritter look like large domes or spheres.

PICTURE NUMBER 74, LO IV NASA No. HR 863[3]
AREA: Posidonius crater
POSITION: 30°E. Longitude; 32°N. Latitude
DIMENSION: The crater is about 100 Km. in diameter
REMARKS: Notice two objects in the crater, almost in the center of Posidonius. Also notice the cloud on the round crater at 10 o'clock covering the big cleft. These clefts look like riverbeds from the air.

PICTURE NUMBER 75, LO IV No. HR 181[1]
AREA: Unnamed crater on the back side of the Moon
POSITION: Unknown
DIMENSION: The crater has a diameter of 29 Km.
REMARKS: Central mountain looks as if it has been shaved off to a mesa. The area around this crater seems to be terraced. In most cases, objects, perhaps buildings, can be detected on these terraces, especially the one at one o'clock.

11
Symbols, Signals, and Markings on the Moon

Although symbology, or the art of conveying messages with symbols, has, in the main, been lost to the western civilization, nonetheless it is still practiced in other parts of the world.

There are some forms of symbols, however, which we use in our everyday lives, such as traffic signals, crosses on mountains, hospitals, churches, on airport runways, etc. A symbol can simplify a message significantly, since it is understood by many people of many nations with different language backgrounds. For instance, at the San Diego Wild Animal Park, visited by people from all over the world, a simple symbol directs the visitors to the open air bird show. The symbol consists of an eagle in flight and an arrow below, pointing to the direction of the stadium.

Many thousands of years ago, gigantic symbols of animals and runway type markings were etched or marked onto the Peruvian Highland Plains of Nasca in South America. No civilization would spend the endless hours of labor and effort to construct such mammoth markings, unless they conveyed a most important meaning. Since these markings and symbols can be totally seen and identified from at least 3000 feet in the air, they must have had aerial vehicles during those days to derive the benefits of these symbols. These symbols, no doubt, were either built by visitors from other worlds or for them by Earth people.

While the Nasca symbols have baffled almost every serious researcher into ancient history, there are many other markings that can be found over the Earth with a probable similar meaning.

From my studies of the many thousands of lunar photographs, I have detected some forms of symbols and high rise markings on dozens of these pictures. For example, southeast of the King crater, located on the Moon's dark side, some very large markings can be seen, which seem to represent the large reversed letter L, followed by a letter B, and then a third letter, another reversed L. As a matter of fact, much strange activity is to be found in and near the King crater located 120.5 degrees east longitude, and 5.5 degrees north latitude. (See plate #76).

The terrain around the large letters looks much as though it has been cut or graded, leading to the large letters to the southwest and directly below on a clearing, please notice three even sized objects, which are exactly spaced apart from each other. Studying this photo closely suggests the resemblance of large land grading vehicles from high altitude. Since we are discussing the King Crater area, I would like to mention two other very interesting findings on the enlarged NASA photo. Approximately ninety miles northeast of the King Crater smoke or dust can be seen escaping from a smaller crater about four or five miles in diameter. This suggests either volcanic activity or that the dust is blown out by some mining machines inside that crater (See plate 77).

Another unusual sighting of objects, all neatly parked in rows, can be seen in the upper highlands just a few miles east of the King Crater, located on the Moon's dark side, three objects for the first two rows, and behind those, two rows of two objects, making a total of ten (See plate #78).

I sincerely hope that these orderly parked objects are not just stones, which rolled neatly into this position and parked themselves there. I believe that even the most unyielding skeptic can agree that whatever these objects are, whether they are aerial vehicles or mining machines, or whatever else, that they were placed there by intelligent beings. The cut away crater, just to the right of these objects, looks like an entrance for an underground hangar or storage area.

I discovered another huge marking or symbol which seemed to lean against the crater wall of a small crater west of the crater Proctus, between the Sea of Crises and the Sea of Tranquility. This extremely large high rise symbol looks very much like the swastika used on Earth, denoting unity which all early civilizations recognized. While this symbol was also misused during World War II, the early civilizations, however, from whom the symbol was borrowed, greatly revered the swastika symbol which joins all men and all things in unity. One can safely say that those men who placed this gigantic symbol on the Moon were thoroughly conversant with its meaning.

Studying this crater carefully, although somewhat difficult to identify, are four even sized objects, appearing as large domes just southwest of the large symbol. To suggest that Nature casually placed them inside this crater by blind chance would indeed insult the intelligence of any serious scientist. This large symbol may still be used on the Moon, for the same principles which were long ago lost to our civilization continue to prevail there. It is about 1000 feet in size.

So many letters and numbers are to be found on so many places on the Moon. Therefore, it is obvious that they were placed there by intelligent beings. It is true that Nature sometimes produces letters and numbers by chance, because of the shadow and light effect, but not on so many occasions as to be found on the Moon. For instance, on the upper rim of the crater Tycho, the number two can be identified. This number is located some 15,000 feet above the crater floor, but other markings in the same vicinity can also be identified.

Simple crosses are also rather numerous, and they seem to have the same purposes there as on Earth. (See plate #79 to #83.)

The large letter E seems to crown the center peak of the crater Gassendi, which is the crater containing a plethora of tubes and tunnels I have heretofore discussed in this book. It appears that the crater's peak was cut into this letter E (See plate #1).

Several miles south of the crater Archimedes, a symbolic shaped platform, high on top of the mountain range, indicates several very clear letters cut into the mountain. The first symbol looks like a bird in flight, followed by the large letters Y and Z, as well as some others, not easily identifiable with our alphabet. These symbols are miles in size and extend for at least fifteen miles, if not more (See plate #4 and drawing).

Another letter, a vague but nonetheless easily recognizable R, can be detected on the upper lip of a crater. I could not identify either the name or the location of this crater, other than that it was photographed by the Apollo 8 missions. It must be understood that even though ninety-nine percent of the Moon has been photographed, most of the terrain and craters on the hidden side are as yet unnamed.

It is interesting to note that there is a white cross placed vertically on the center mountain in this crater, and just below on the crater floor, a large white construction may be recognized. This has the appearance of a joined double T. Some miles south of this crater, located in the plains, is a large raised letter S, clearly visible (See plate #84).

A huge dark cross marking can clearly be seen close to the center peak of the crater named IAU-308 by the Apollo 11 crew. This crater is forty-eight miles in diameter and located on the moon's hidden side. About five miles southwest of the cross markings are two identical sized dome-shaped objects on the crater floor, which appear to be four miles in diameter. Just south of these large domes is a large white raised platform, U-shaped, about one and one-half miles long and half as wide. Immediately behind it and somewhat lower is another circular platform on which two dark, even-sized objects are parked (See plate #85).

Maurice Chatelain, in his book <u>Our Ancestors Came From Outer Space</u>, also dwells at length on symbolism of early civilizations on Earth. He suggests that we on Earth have a common origin, and that the Earth was colonized long ago. Other authors suggested that Earth was colonized with the troublemakers from higher civilizations, who made use of the Earth very much as the British made Australia, as a dumping ground for their convicts. Should this be true, it would then be understandable why these early settlers were given nothing or very little of advanced technology so that they would be forced to solve their problems in a peaceful manner and would also be prevented from building spacecraft, which would cause them to remain Earthbound. Thus they would be incapable of retaliation.

Let us use this example: If an aircraft would crash into some lonely rugged mountains and the craft would be destroyed, but most of the passengers would survive, they would have to revert back to a caveman's existence, regardless

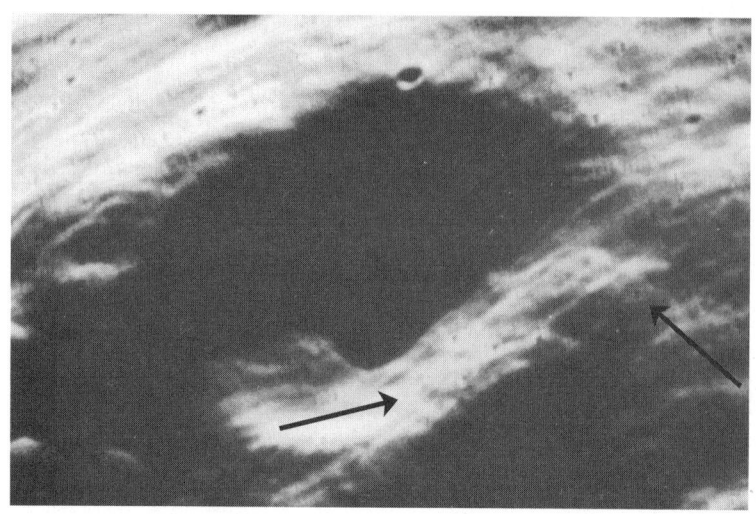

Plate 76. Area blow-up. Apollo 16 photo No. 16-19273. The 3 symbols "JBF", and 3 objects below S.W. of the crater King (bottom left corner).

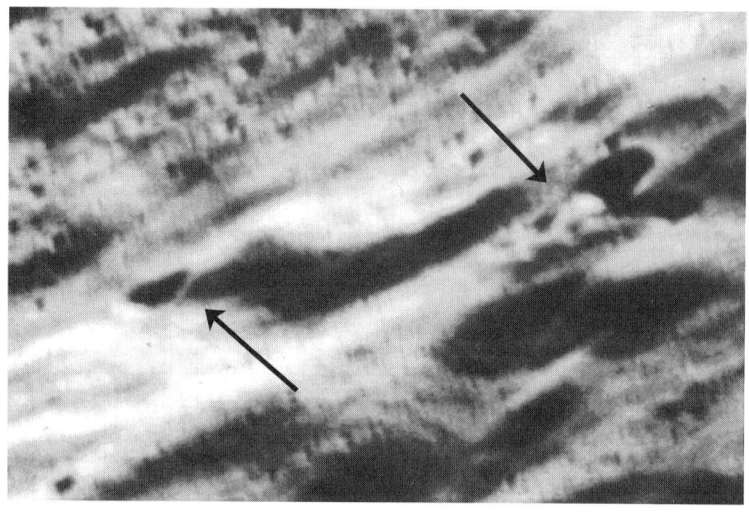

Plate 77. Area blow-up. Apollo photo 16-19273. N.E. of the crater King. Notice dust blowing out of the crater. Plus other activity . "Who is mining the moon?"

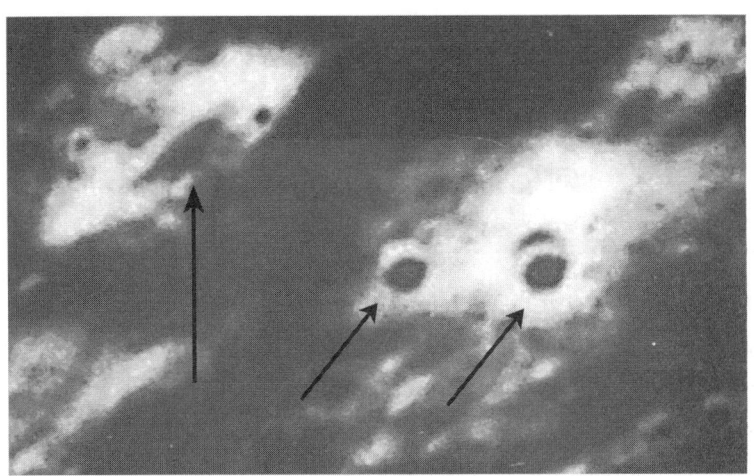

Plate 77a. LO V Photo #67-H-1651, crater Tycho.

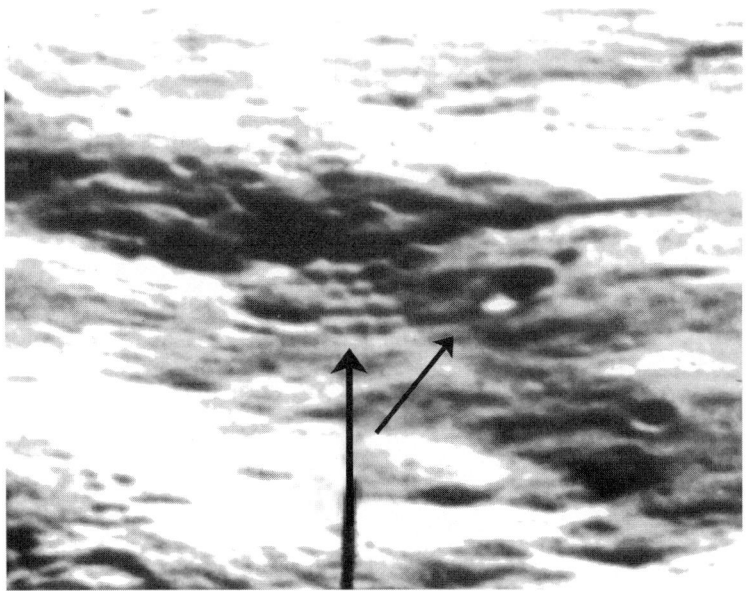

Plate 78. Aerial blow-up. Apollo 16 photo No. 16-19265. Notice 10 objects, neatly parked in rows, beside an unusually configured crater. Also see the luminescent saucer shaped object. Landing/hanger facility?

Plate 78a. Apollo 16 photo No. AS16-120-19229, crater King.

Plate 79. Apollo 8 photo of the back side of the moon. Notice white cross on the crater's bottom. This crater is unnamed.

Plate 80. Area blow-up. LO III. Photo No. 67-H-201. Large raised Latin cross near the crater Kepler.

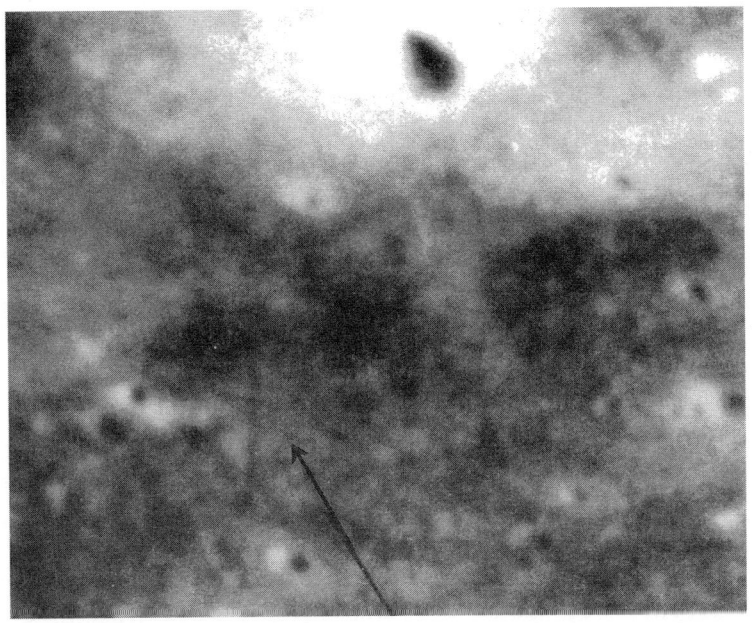

Plate 81. Area blow-up. Apollo 16 photo No. 16-19386. Latin cross.

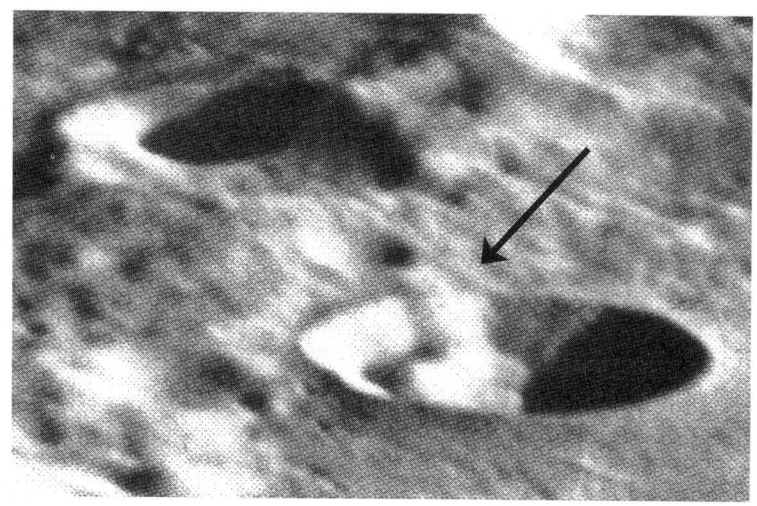

Plate 82. Material pouring from one crater to another. Evidence of mining?

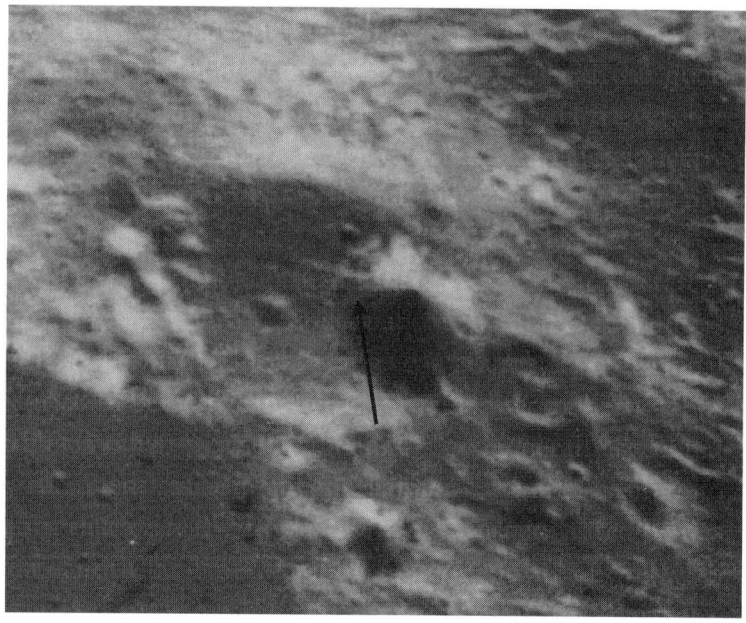

Plate 83. Area blow up. Apollo 16 Photo No. 16-19228. Crater King. Cross at the edge/base of the hill.

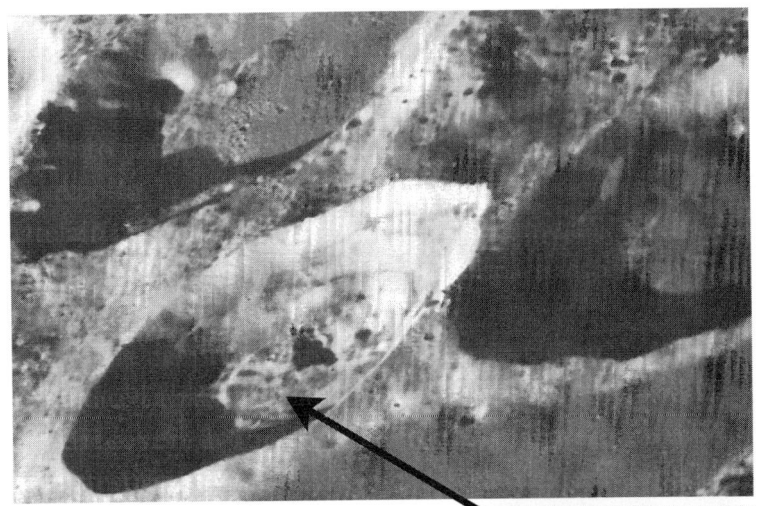

Plate 84. Apollo 8 photo. Area unknown. Notice cut crater upper left and constructions and  symbols in the other two craters left center and right.

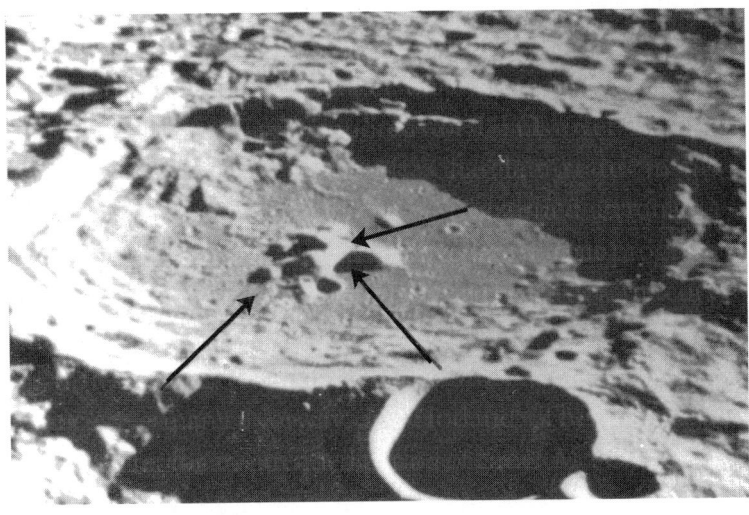

Plate 85. Apollo 11 Photo of the IAU-308. Crater, Lunar back side. Notice dark cross on center peak. Also dome-shaped objects and platforms.

of their technical background. Without the modern tools of advanced technology, even the most intelligent of men are helpless. Should these survivors never be found, their children, born in the wilderness, would not be able to comprehend what their parents tell them about their background. This example serves to portray how easily man can lose his technical capabilities.

The British Air Marshal, Lord Downing, once stated that the Earth was a penal colony, or insane asylum, for those removed from other planets long ago. While this indeed is a most accusatory statement, one wonders what provoked Lord Downing to present it so forcefully. Some religious students now speak of the evidence that the early "twelve tribes" that the Bible speaks of were races and groups of people deposited on Earth from space. Placed on different continents, they needed to learn to live together in peace. Whether this is true or not, thinking of it, the idea does have its merit. This, in essence, would be like removing the rotten apples before they spoil the barrel of good ones. This may also explain the early space visitations, of which so many authors have spoken. They would be checking up on us to see how we are doing. On the other hand, if this is true, we should not feel too despondent, because they did give us a beautiful planet on which to live, although we are striving diligently to destroy our civilization. I feel no matter where people come from, the Moon, or other planets, we are all related, and human beings are a universal manifestation.

12

NASA Experts Reveal The Facts

Maurice Chatelain was one of the top scientists under NASA contract who conceived and designed the Apollo spacecraft. He was also in charge of the Apollo communication equipment, as well as for voice and telemetric transmission from the Earth to the Moon and return.

In his previously mentioned book, Our Ancestors Came From Outer Space, he made these startling statements: "All Apollo and Gemini flights were followed by space vehicles, not of this Earth" (UFOs). Whenever the astronauts reported a sighting of a UFO in space, mission control ordered absolute silence. Astronauts of Mercury flight 8 reported UFOs next to the space capsule, as did Apollo 8 astronauts from behind the Moon, after they regained radio contact with Earth.

Gemini 7 photographed two UFOs in Earth orbit. These had the appearance of giant mushrooms with their underside glowing. Gemini 12 photographed a UFO only one-half mile from their capsule and reported seeing two more. It is known, even in the U.S.S.R. scientific circles, that our Apollo lunar missions had encounters with UFOs. One wonders where the Russians received this information. It is quite possible that they monitored our radio transmissions. The Russians believe that other civilizations picked up our radio signals and intend to visit the Moon.

Mr. Chatelain, now retired, stated to several reporters that Apollo 11 astronauts not only heard strange noises on the radio when they neared the Moon, but also had a surprise party of two UFOs watching our first lunar landing.

There is no reason to doubt the statements of this former NASA expert, and one can safely say that if anything would have gone wrong on the Moon, the astronauts would have been rescued.

Professor Dr. Oberth, the rocket specialist, came to the United States from Europe after World War II. He worked for Bell Laboratories until his retirement in the late 50's. When he retired, he made this statement to the press, "Gentlemen, we cannot take all the credit for our civilization's rapid technical advancement over the past decade. We have had help." When he was questioned about who helped us, he replied, "Those guys out there from the other planets." This statement quickly earned the good professor the honorable title of "crack-pot". However, the people responsible for his promotion never explained exactly how it is possible for a top scientist to turn crack-pot overnight.

Dr. Fred Bell, another former NASA scientist, stated, "The astronauts have kept silent about their UFO encounters because they are trained to believe it is a matter of national security." Dr. Bell admitted that he had seen photographs of UFOs taken by the astronauts. It is generally accepted by the scientists that the governments of Earth hesitate to admit that we really are defenseless against advanced beings from another planet. Many experts now believe with certainty that something is taking place on the Moon.

Mr. Chatelain stated that Apollo 10 also reported UFOs while in lunar orbit. When the Apollo 11 landed on the Moon, a UFO was seen by television viewers, moving into the television screen, from the right, for about six seconds. This was photographed from the TV screen and this photo is reproduced in this book as plate #96.

Apollo 12 had its share of UFO experiences. Mr. Chatelain also stated that many radio technicians received messages and radio signals from outer space, especially in the vicinity of the Moon.

An article printed in the San Diego Union, July 23, 1980, stated that the outstanding inventor Nikoli Tesla, who discovered the AC current, claimed he had extraterrestrial contact by radio. Tesla devices are very powerful energy signal transmitters. In the same article it was mentioned that Westinghouse and Marconi publicly made similar statements of having received signals from other planets. The article originated from the Center of Advanced Technology in La Jolla, California. Former astronaut Gordon Cooper is its president.

Astronaut Gordon Cooper once stated on national television that he chased hundreds of UFOs over Europe when he was a fighter pilot. Mr. Chatelain states in his book that Mr. Cooper, one of the best qualified astronauts to fly the Apollo missions, was removed from that program because of his encounters with UFOs on the earlier Mercury flights.

In 1928, radio signals from the Moon were picked up in France, Germany, Norway, and Holland. This discovery was kept secret for an extended period of time. Mr. Chatelain also reports that our solar system has twelve planets instead of the nine of which we are now aware. This coincides exactly with what the late George Adamski reported in his book Behind The Flying Saucer Mystery.

Recently coded messages from another solar system were received on Earth. Soviet communication experts received radio signals from planets in our own solar system. Mr. Chatelain concludes that certain legends indicate that some space visitors came to Earth from Venus. "That too is not impossible," he said. Dr. James Harder, engineering professor, Columbia University of California, reported that after very careful studies in the UFO field, he discovered from the Apollo communication tapes that several Apollo flights encountered UFOs. He also stated that from tape recording conversations between the lunar spacecraft and mission control, he discovered clear evidence of UFO sightings. He listed Apollo 11 and Apollo 12, the latter of which was trailed by a UFO on three orbits around the Moon. Harder says that because of possible public panic, these incidents have remained silent.

Donald L. Zyistra, chief of NASA's public in formation section in Washington, D.C., made this revealing statement: "During the Apollo manned flight missions, there were sightings from the spacecraft which our astronauts were unable to explain." (See plates #86 to #102).

Other NASA moon photos of interest to the reader may be found on plates #103 to #134.

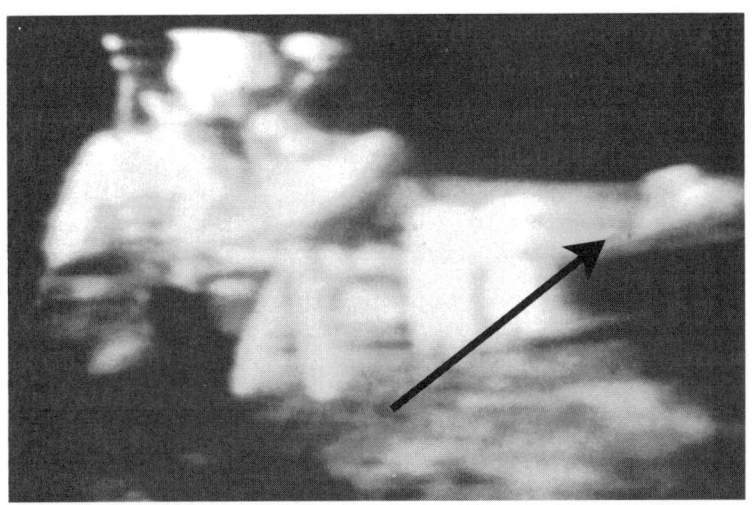

Plate 86. Apollo 11 on the moon. Photo taken from TV screen in Europe showing white bell-shaped UFO right hand photo.

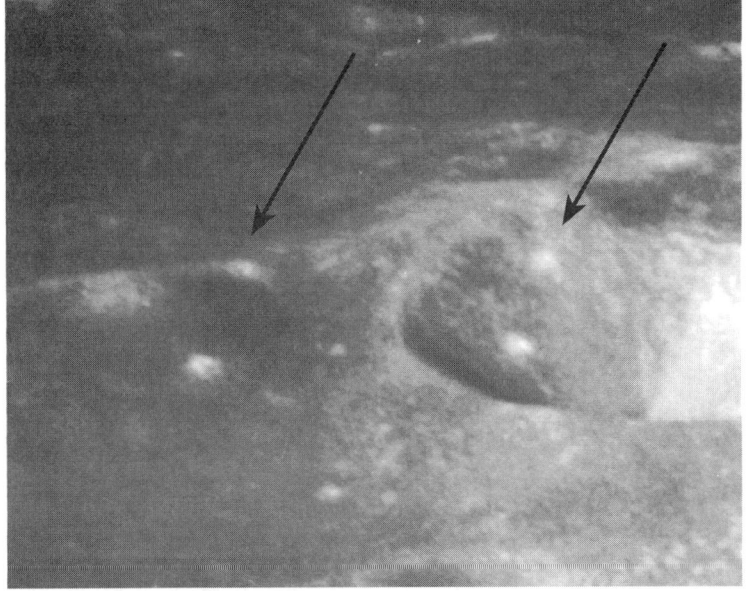

Plate 86a. Apollo 16 photo No. AS16-19376. Notice two rows of four symetrically spaced white circular objects.

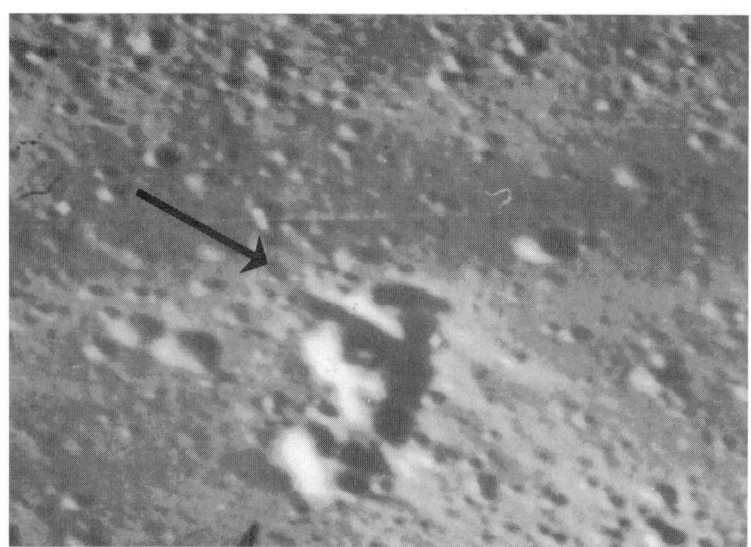

Plate 87. Area blow-up. LO III. Photo of large cigar-shaped object parked along crater edge about 200 miles S.E. of crater Kepler.

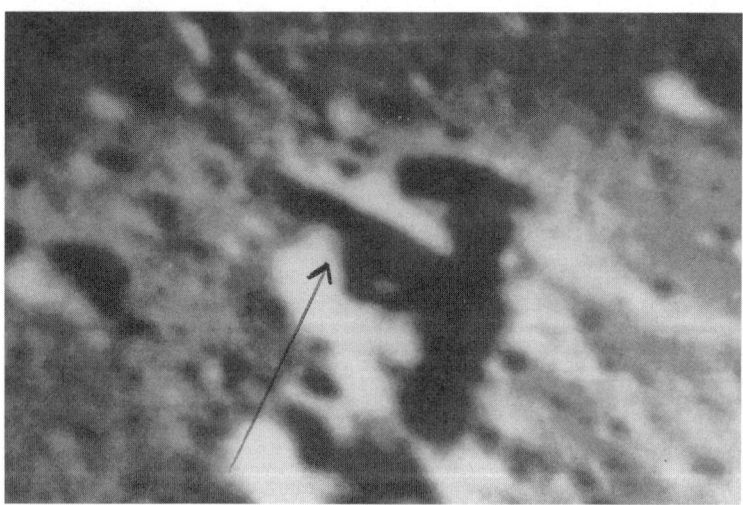

Plate 88. Area blow-up. LO III 162-M. The large cigar-shaped object enlarged 14 times. Object is about 2.5 miles long!!!

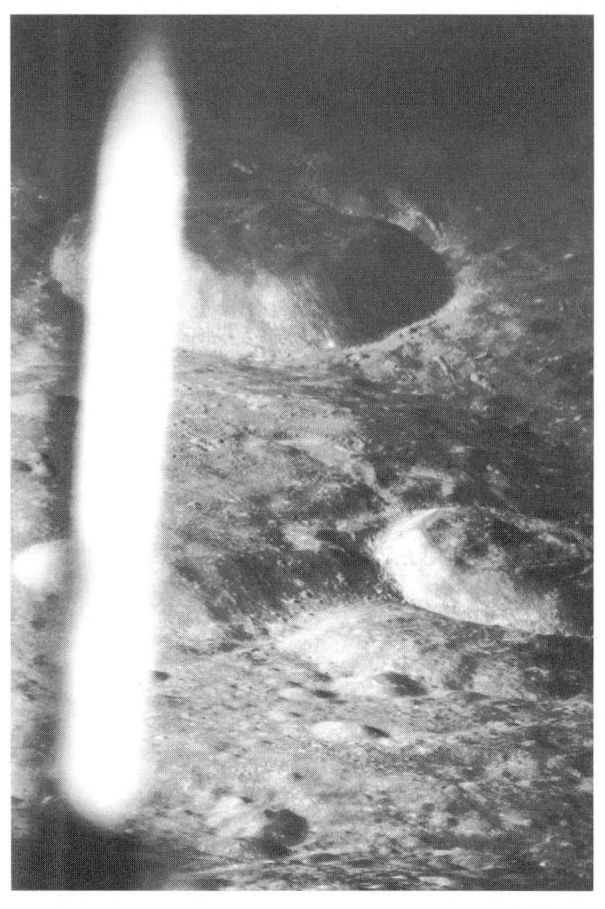

Plate 89. Apollo 16 photo No. 16-19238. Cigar shaped aerial object, hovering over the lunar surface.

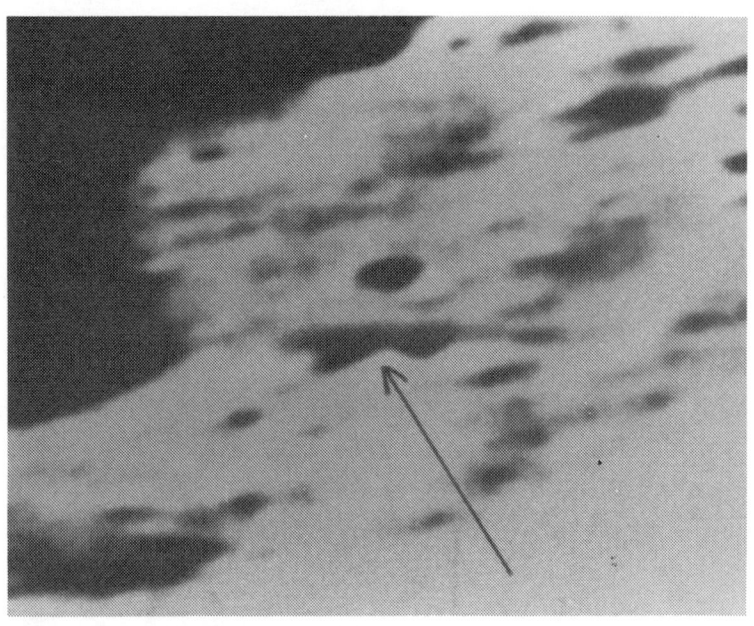

Plate 90. Area blow-up. Apollo 16 photo No. 16-18923. Large cigar shaped object on the lunar surface.

Plate 91. Apollo 13 photo No. AS 13-60-8622. Plates 91 and 92 are frames from a series of photos showing an unknown glowing object traveling toward the moon.

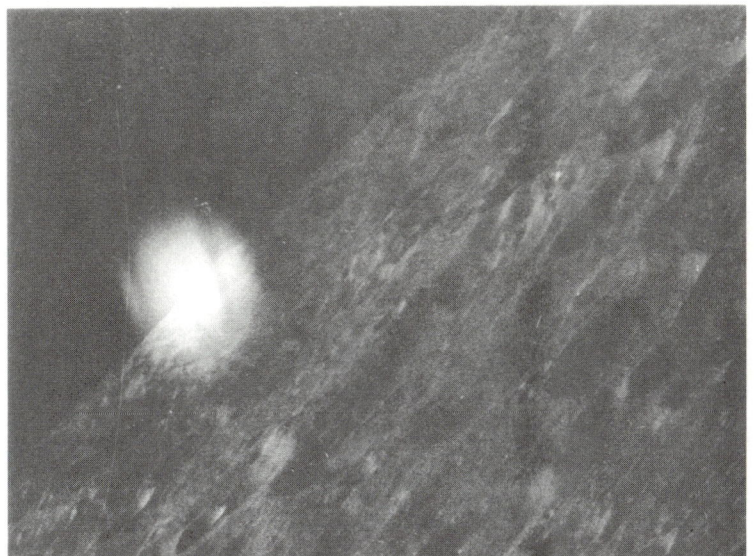

Plate 92. Apollo 13 photo No. AS 13-60-8609. UFO over the moon.

Plate 93. Apollo 12 photo No. AS 12-51-7553. Strange white aerial object high over the lunar surface.

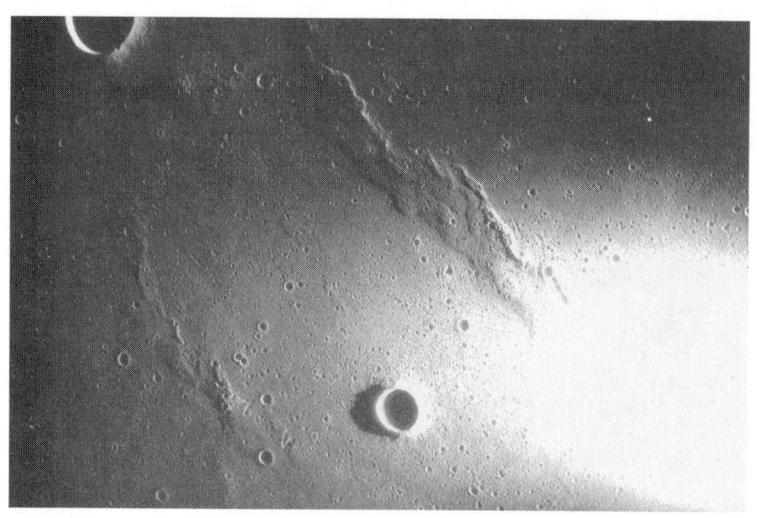

Plate 94. Apollo 11 photo No. AS 12-54-8118. White glowing object between Apollo 12 and the moon.

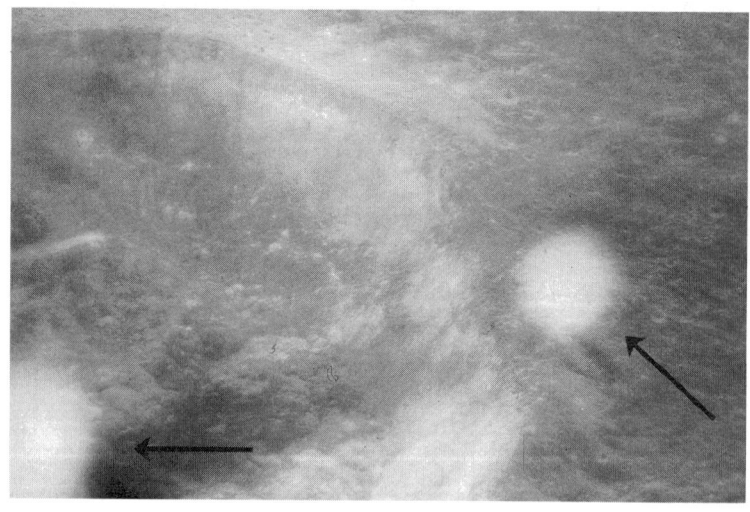

Plate 95. Apollo 11 photo No. AS 11-42-6334. Glowing objects (3) on or close to the lunar surface.

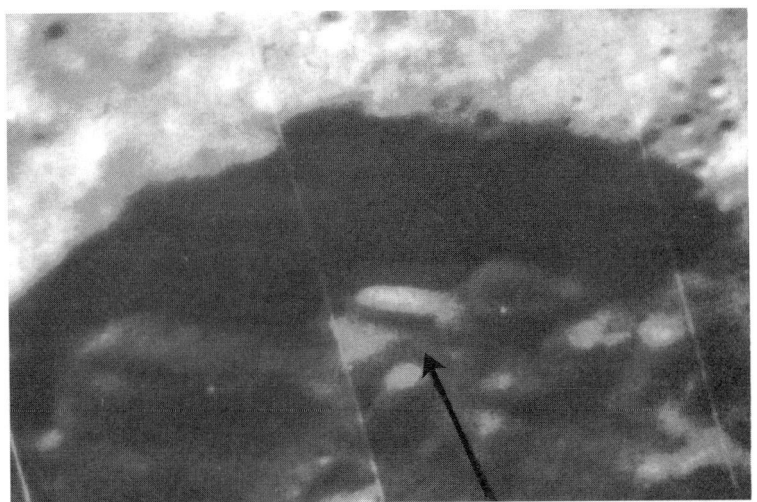

Plate 96. LO IV photo No. 89-H-3. White cigar shaped object near the crater Romer.

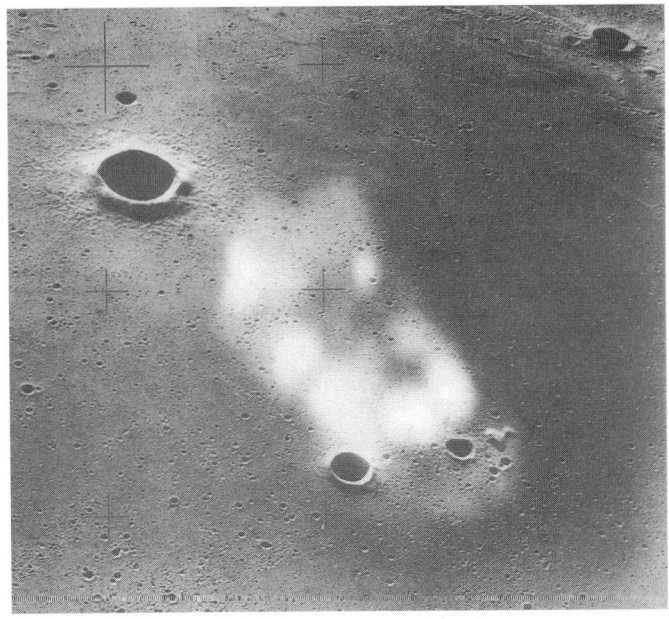

Plate 97. Apollo 14 photo No. AS 14-9837. Seven glowing objects close to the lunar surface.

Plate 98. Area blow-up. Apollo 16 Photo No. 16-19386. Elongated white object protruding from the crater.

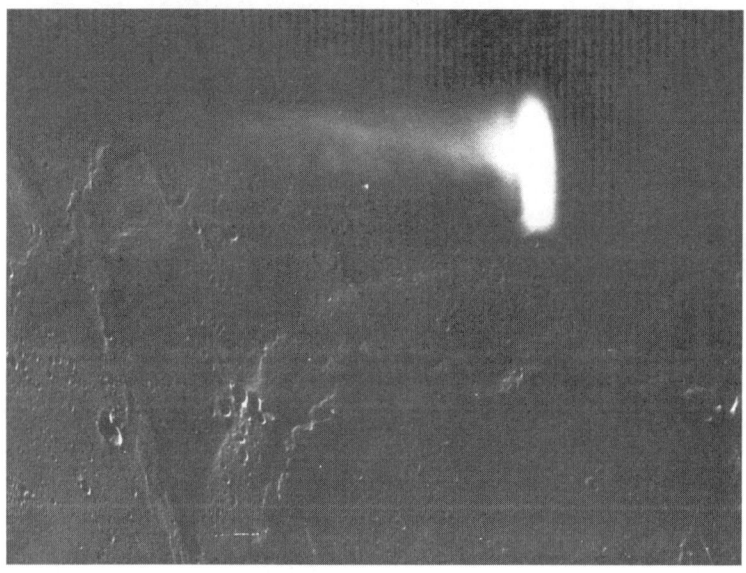

Plate 99. Apollo 11 Photo No. 11-37-5438. Glowing cigar shaped object close to the Moon.

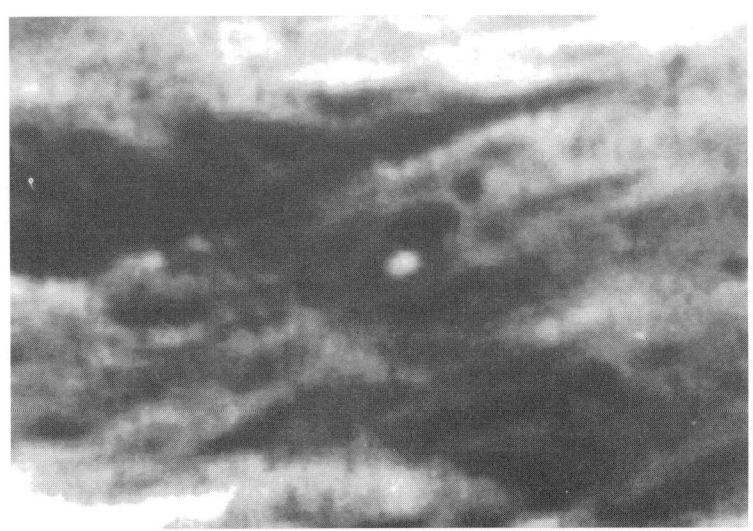

Plate 99a. Area blow-up. Apollo 16 Photo No. 16-19265. Luminescent object on lunar surface.

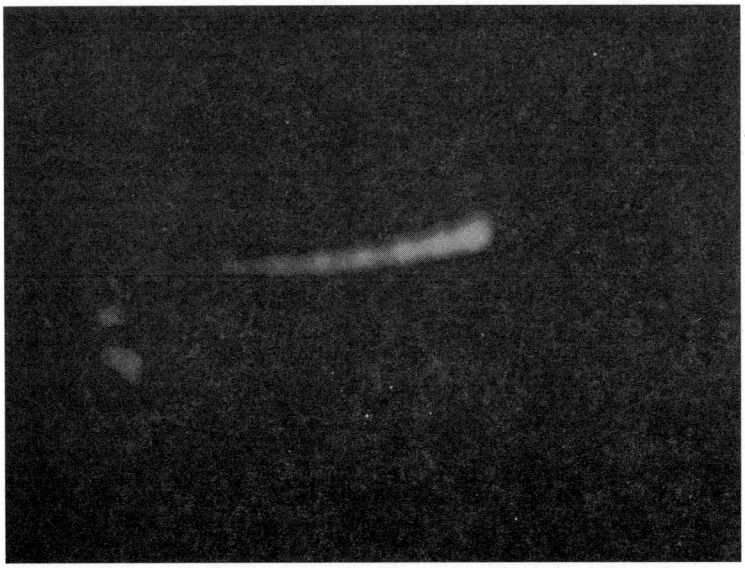

Photo 100. Apollo 11 photo No. 11-37-5436. Cigar shaped object in lunar orbit. Notice seven or more rings around this object.

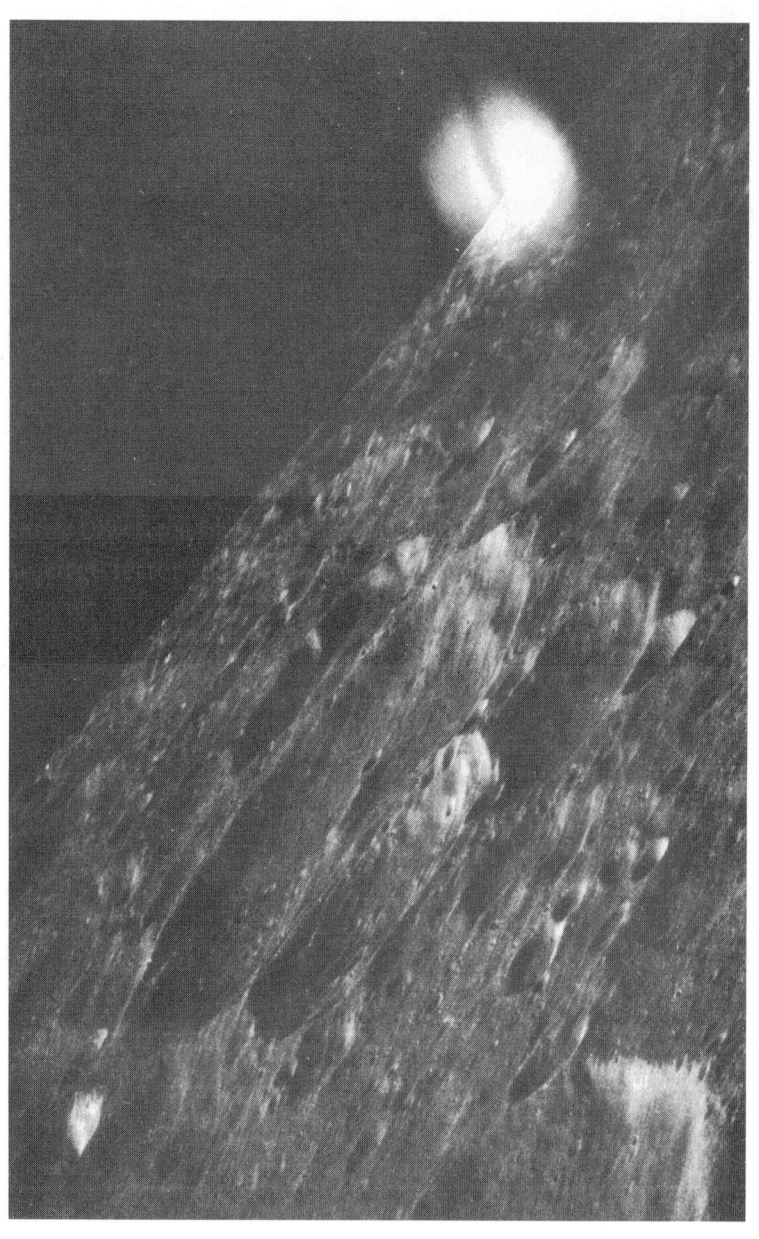

Plate 101. Apollo 13 photo No. 13-60-8609. UFO over the lunar landscape.

Plate 102. Photo No. AS-12-497319. White glowing oval object hovering over Apollo 12 Astronaut.

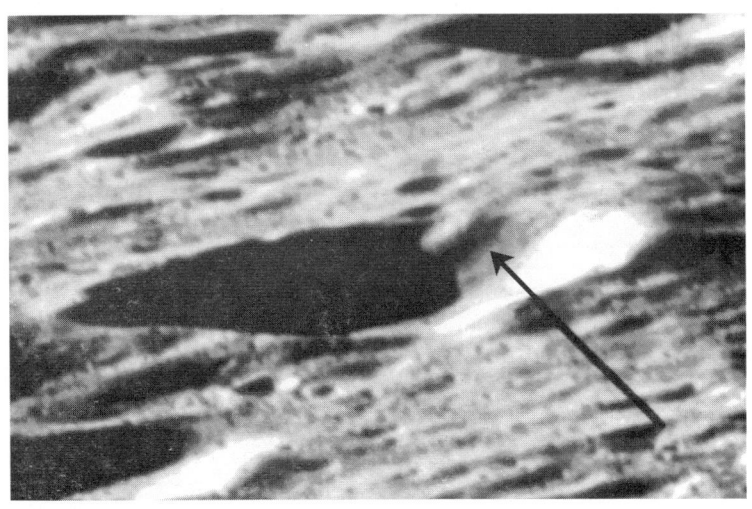

Plate 103. Area blow-up. Apollo 16 Photo No. 16-18918. Oval object inside the large crater.

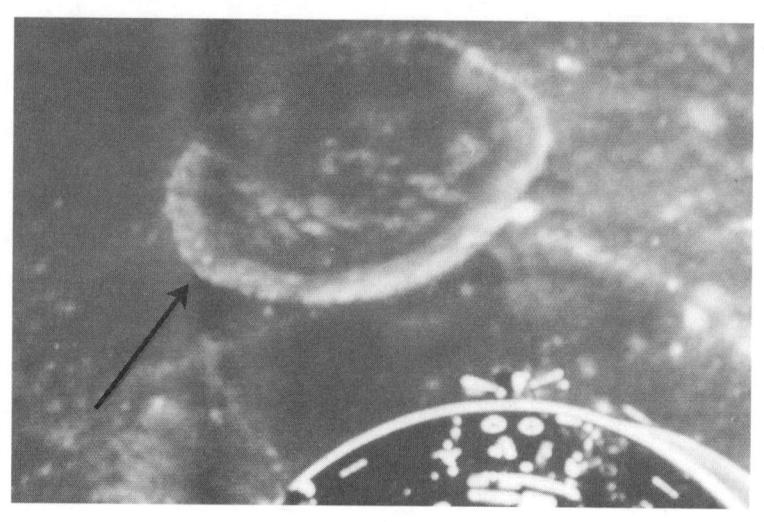

Plate 104. Apollo 10 photo, No. Unknown. Even sized oval shaped objects (8) parked along the inside crater rim.

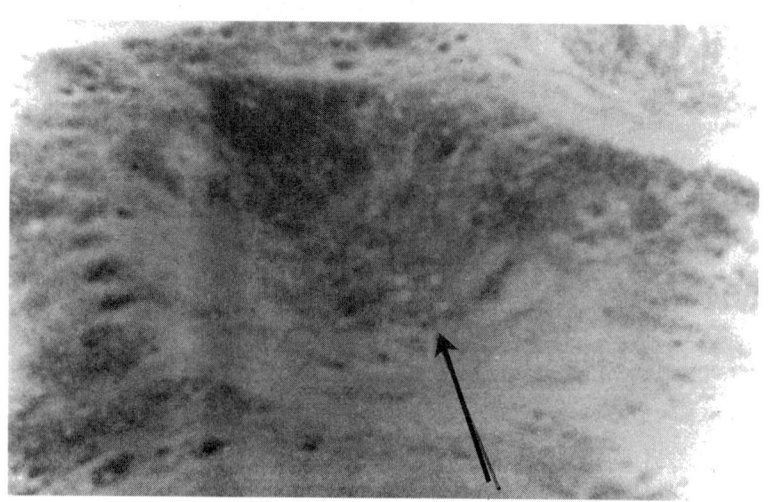

Plate 105. Apollo 10 Photo, No. Unknown. Four white oval shaped objects parked inside the large crater.

Plate 106. Area blow-up. LO III Photo No. 200H3. Objects parked inside this crater.

Plate 107. Terraced crater on the moon's back side. Also notice the "R" shaped indentation in this crater.

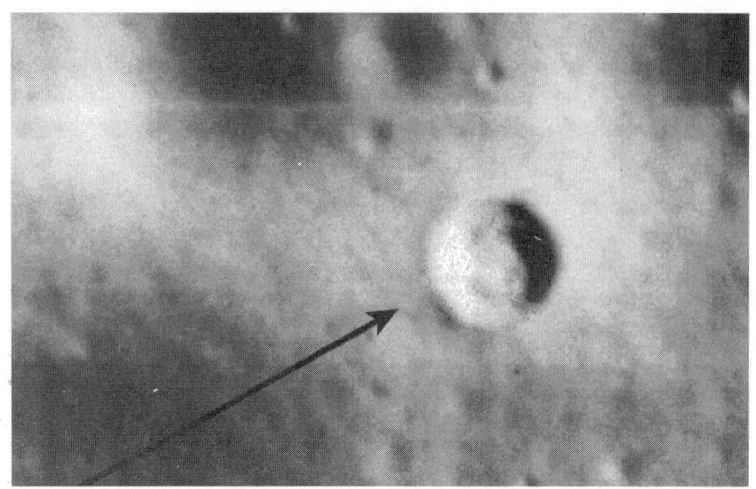

Plate 108. Area blow-up. LO III Photo No. 194H3. Notice the large letter "S" inside the crater to the right.

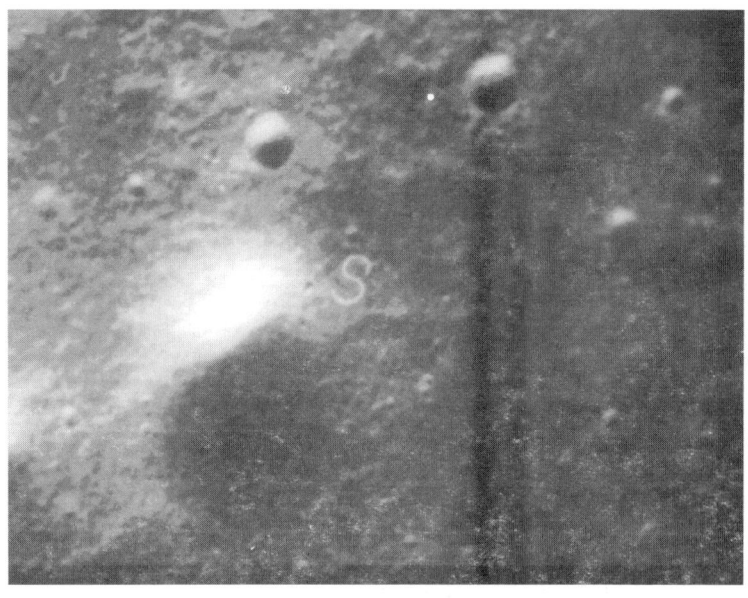

Plate 109. Apollo 14 photo No. 14-80-10439. Another letter "S". This time placed beside the crater.

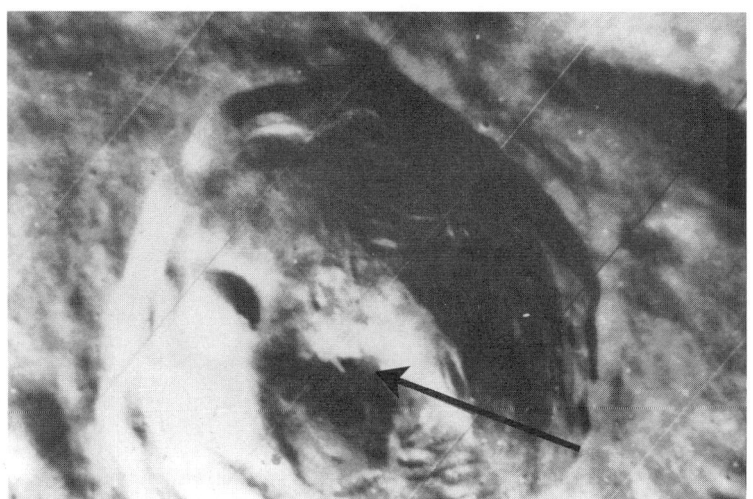

Plate 110. LO IV Photo No. LO IV 89H3. The Crater Romer. Notice large platform and long object on center mountain.

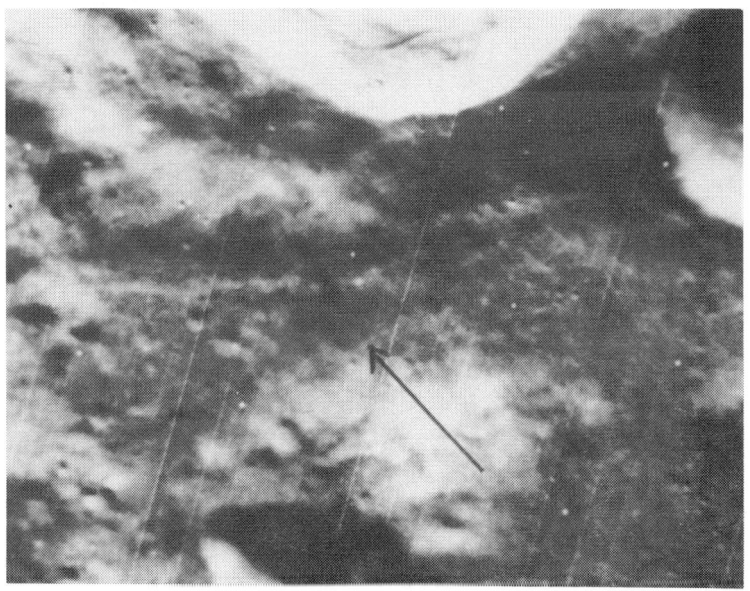

Plate 111. LO IV Photo No. 89H3. Structure bridging valley 5 miles south of crater Romer.

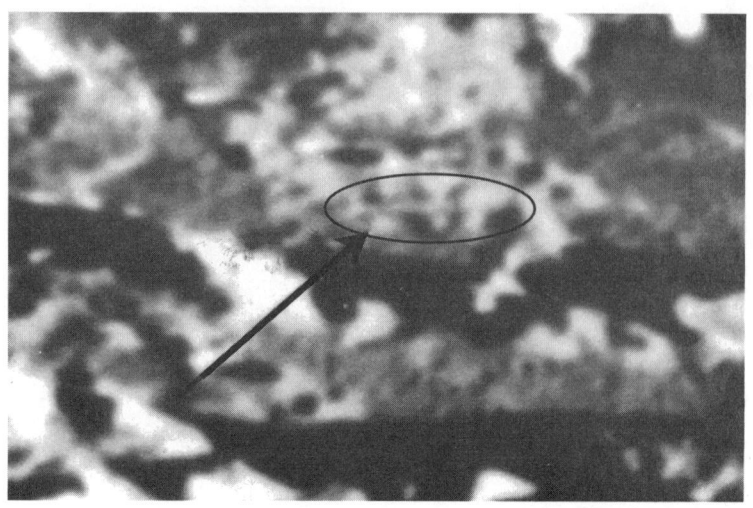

Plate 112. Area blow-up. Apollo 10 photo No. 10-32-4810. 130 miles north of the crater "Triesnecker". Notice white bridge-like structure between two mountains.

Plate 113. Area blow-up. Apollo 10 Photo No. 10-32-4810. 80 miles north of Triesnecker. Notice the cathedral-like entrance cut into this mountain.

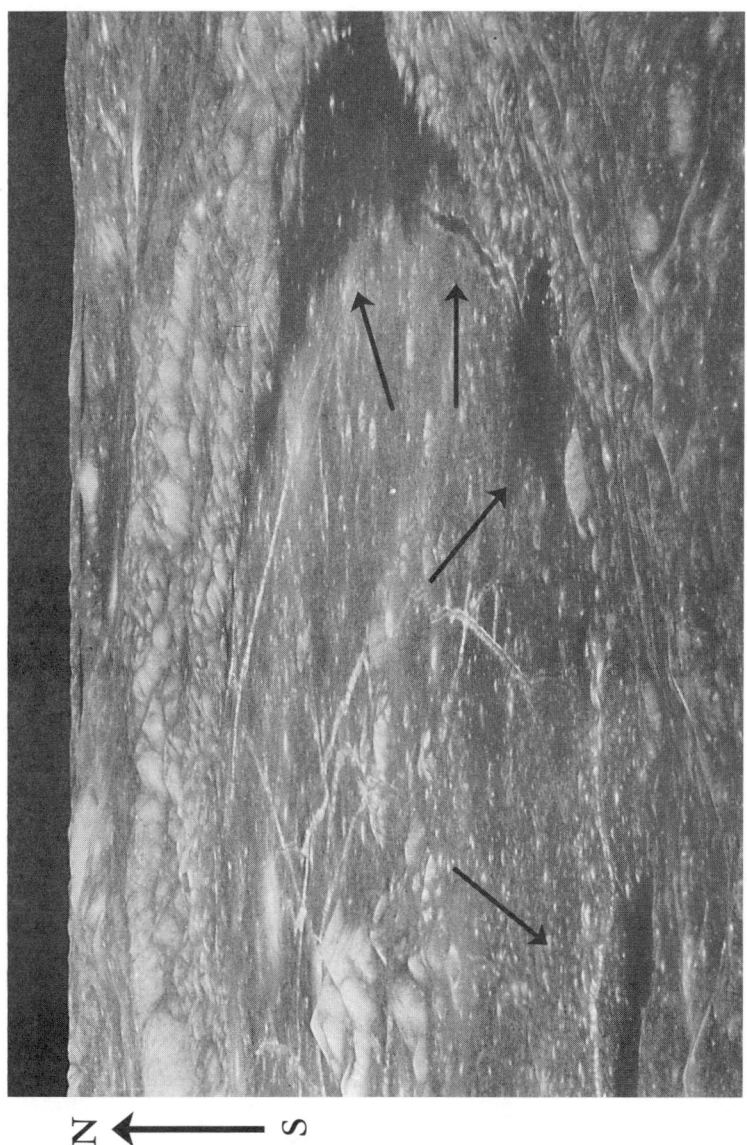

Plate 114. Apollo 12 photo No. 12-7419. The crater Humboldt and surrounding area. Notice dark patches which look much like vegetation. Also see the dark riverbeds between these patches and mountains.

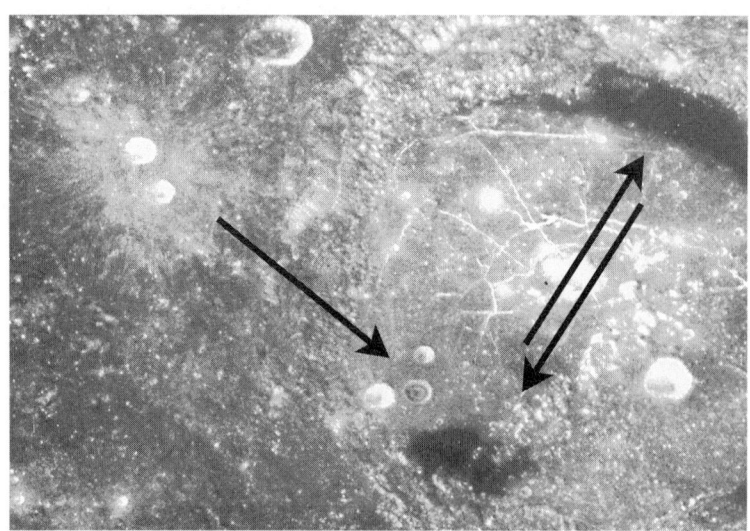

Plate 115. Area blow-up. Apollo 8 Photo of the Humboldt Crater and "Southern Sea", showing these patches of possible vegetation or moisture again. Also notice the double-ringed crater.

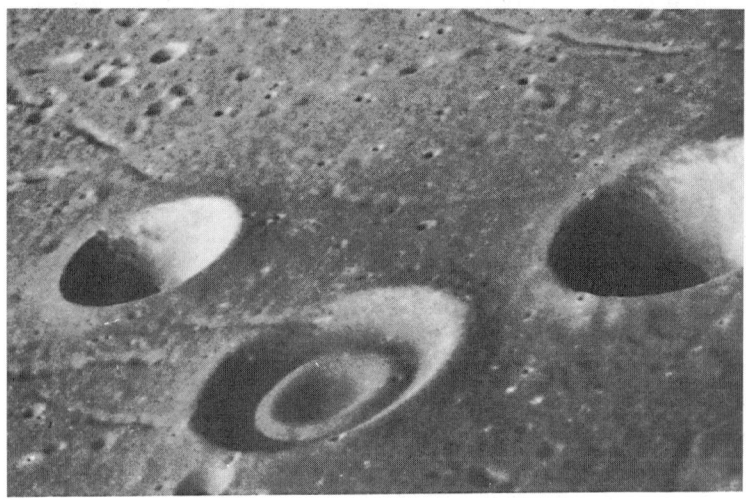

Plate 116. Area blow-up. Apollo 15 Photo No. 15-12640. See the double ringed crater in the larger Humboldt Crater. This one looks very artificial. Mining or?

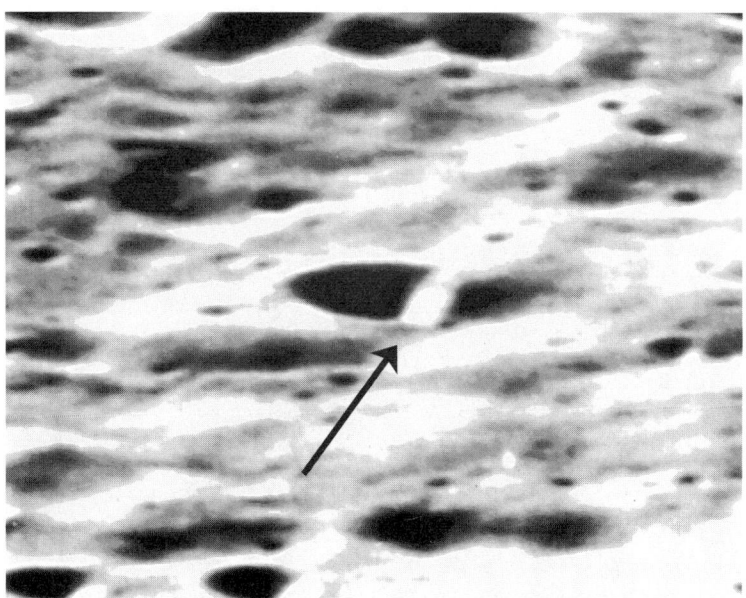

Plate 117. Area blow-up. Apollo 16 No. 16-18923. This photo shows a crater with something protruding out of it.

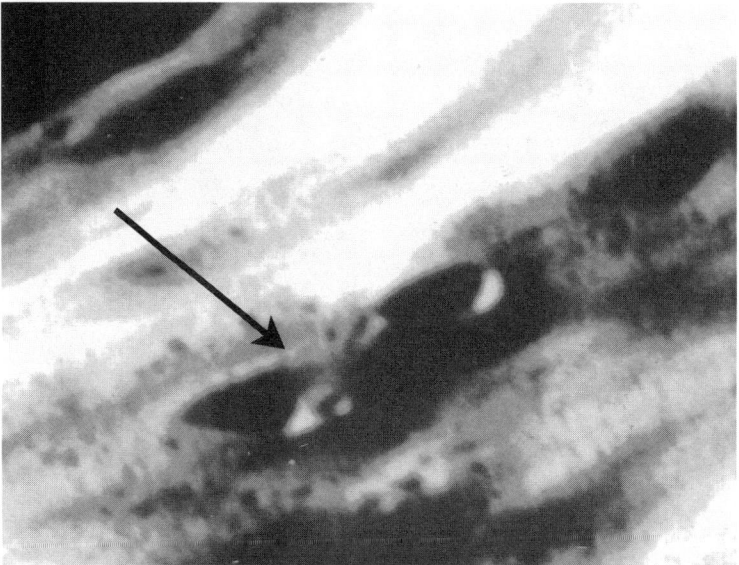

Plate 118. Area blow-up. Apollo 16 No. 16-18918. This crater also seems to show some form of activity.

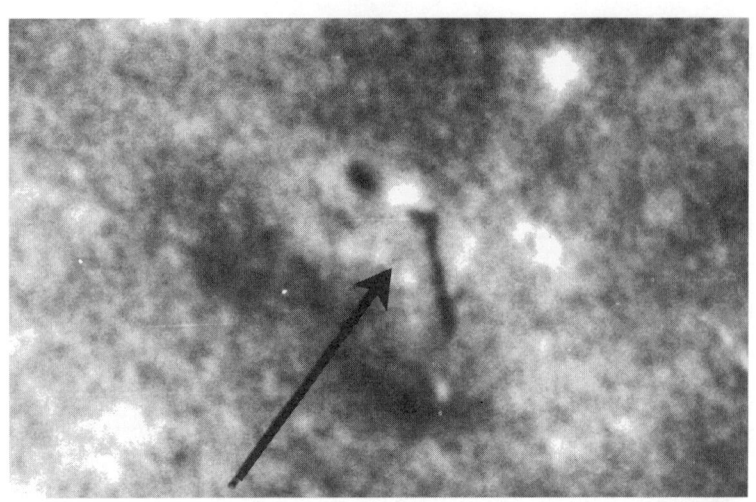

Plate 119. Area blow-up. Apollo 16 photo No. 16-19386. Notice some form of tube or pipe which looks spiraled. It leads up from the lower crater to the smaller one above.

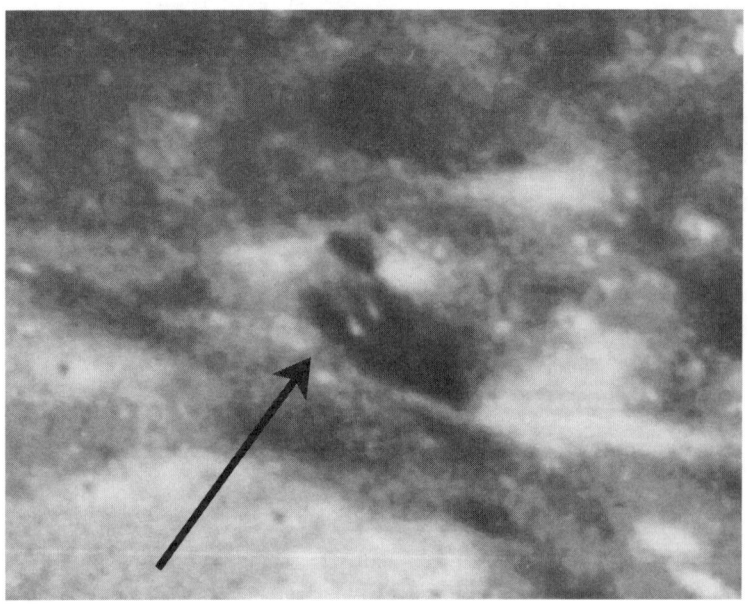

Plate 120. Area blow-up. Apollo 16 photo No. 16-19386. Two objects or constructions situated along crater wall.

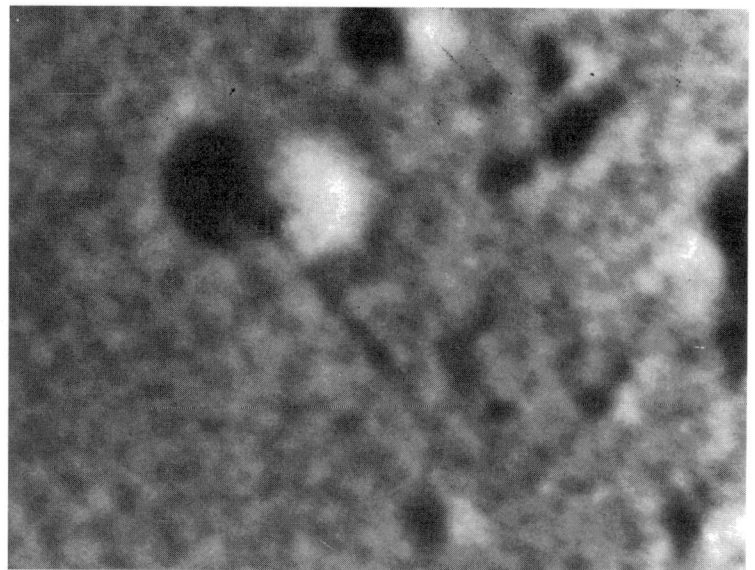

Plate 121. Area blow-up. Apollo 15 photo. Long tube extending out of a crater.

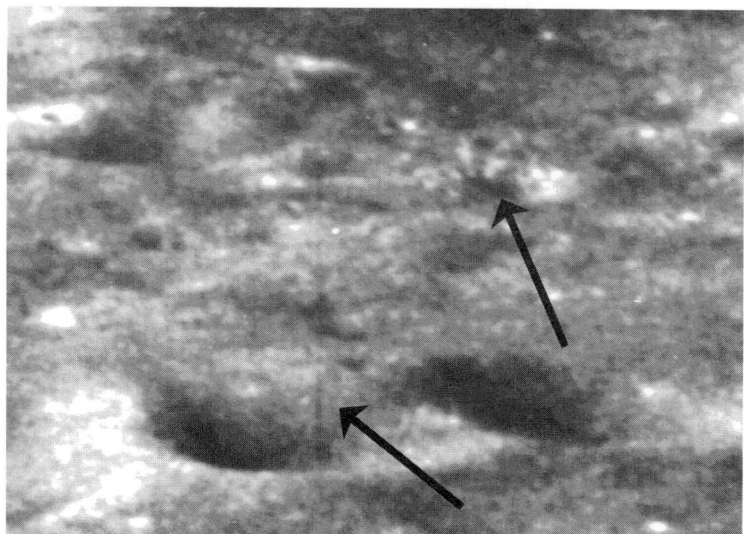

Plate 122. Area blow-up. Apollo photo No. 16-19376. Another tube or pipe between two craters. Also notice objects in the smaller crater above.

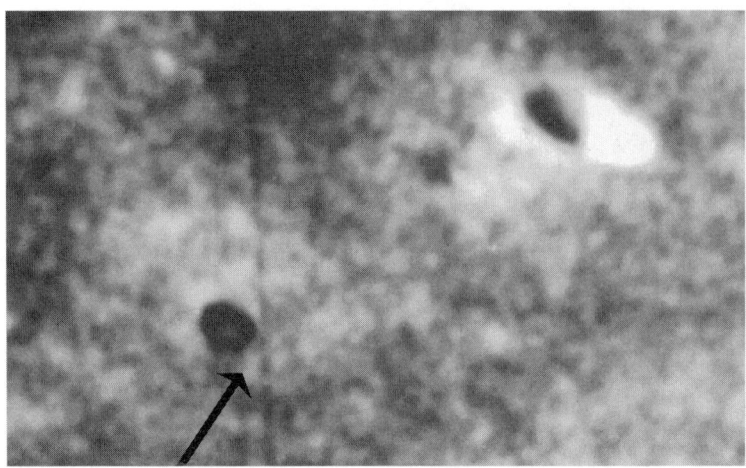

Plate 123. Area blow-up. Apollo 16 photo No. 16-19386. This photo shows a small pond with an island on the bottom of a shallow crater (see "lake" Pg. 70). Notice the long spiraled pipe-like object extending south to north close to the pond's edge. Is this an application of the Archimedes screw principle?

Plate 124. LO III Photo No. 6H showing protruding or rising substance from the bottom of a crater. Also notice a white dome inside the crater to the N.W.

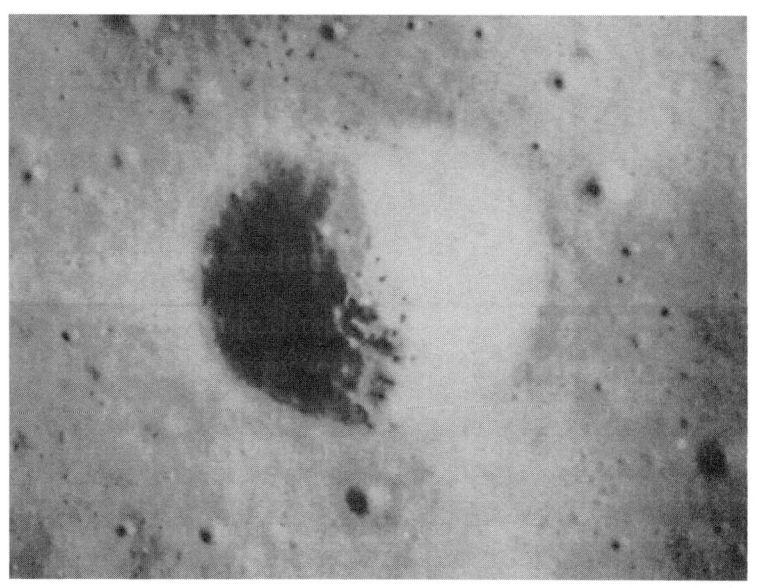

Plate 125. LO III Photo No. 133H2. This photo shows what could be a symbol, scorpion shaped engraving or construction?

Plate 127. Area blow-up. Apollo 16 photo No. 16-18923. Artificial looking structures on the moon's back side.

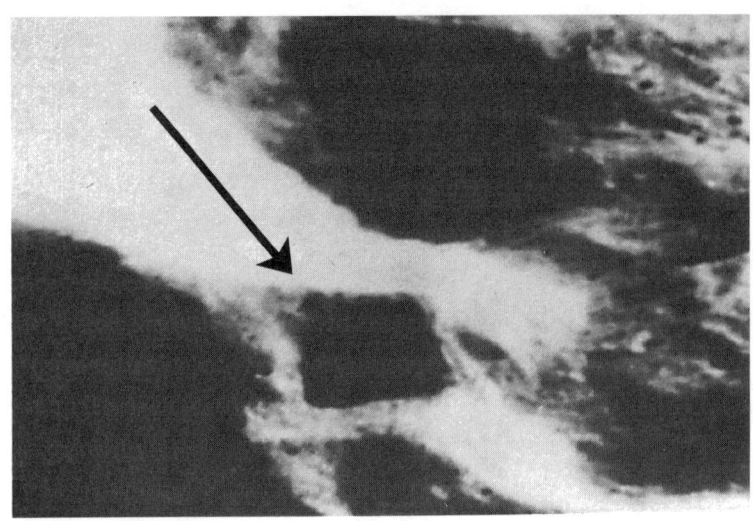

Plate 128. Area blow-up. This Apollo 16 photo shows unusually "square" shaped crater.

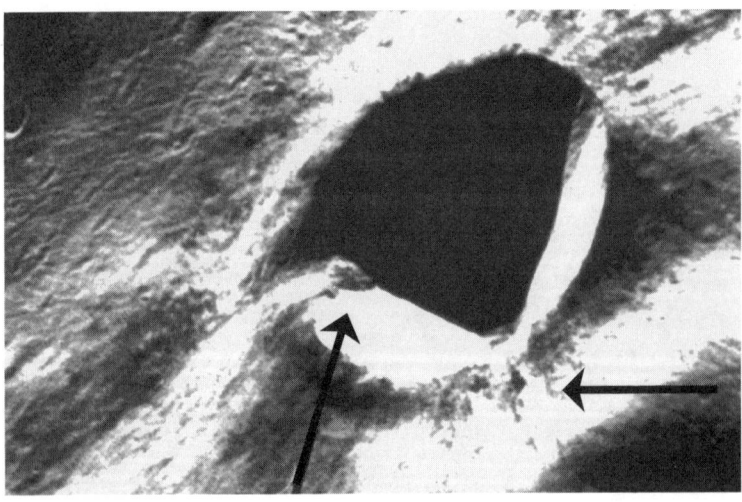

Plate 129. Area blow-up. Apollo photo No. 15-13181. Some form of spraying removal of lunar material, which looks suspiciously like a mining operation. Also notice two oval objects south on this crater's rim.

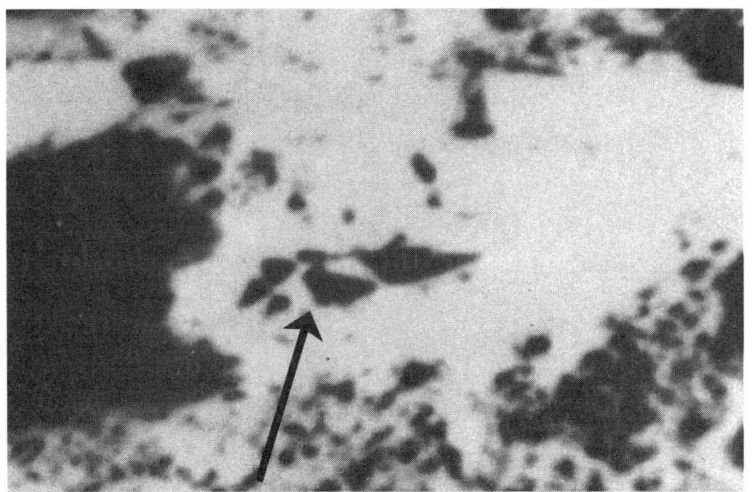

Plate 130. Area blow-up. Did Apollo 16 photograph pyramids on the Moon? On the bottom of this crater there seems to be three of them.

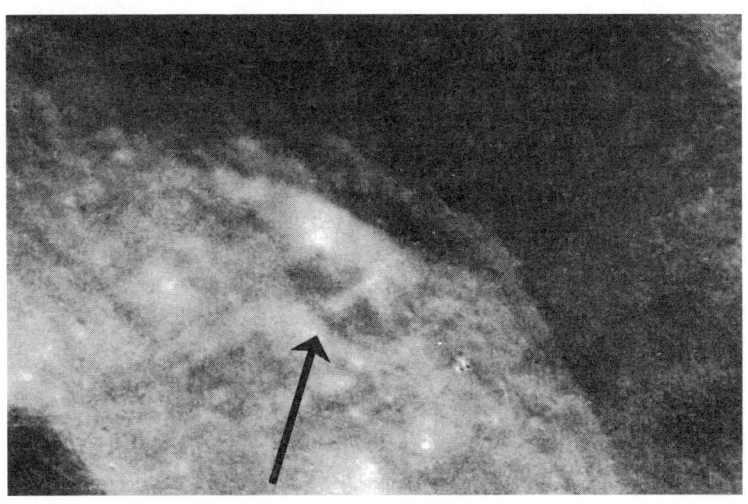

Plate 131. Area blow-up. This Apollo 8 photo No. 8-17-2704 shows two pyramid-shaped constructions on the moon.

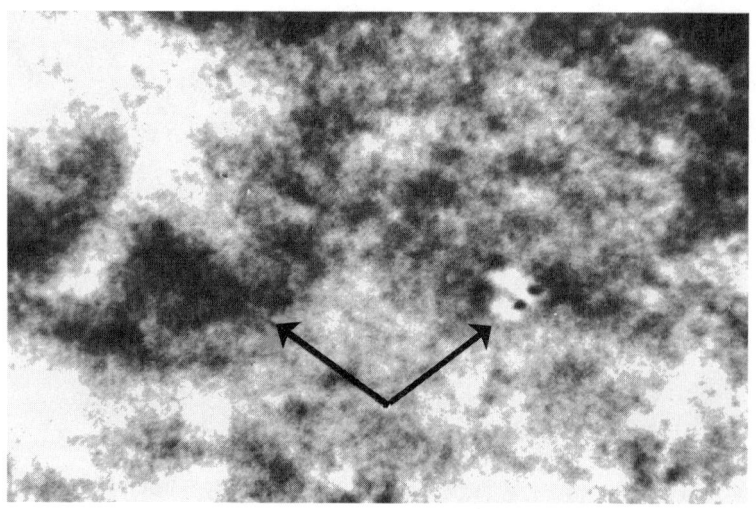

Plate 132. Area blow-up. The same three faced pyramid shaped constructions enlarged 14 times. Also notice two dark objects "parked" on the clearing.

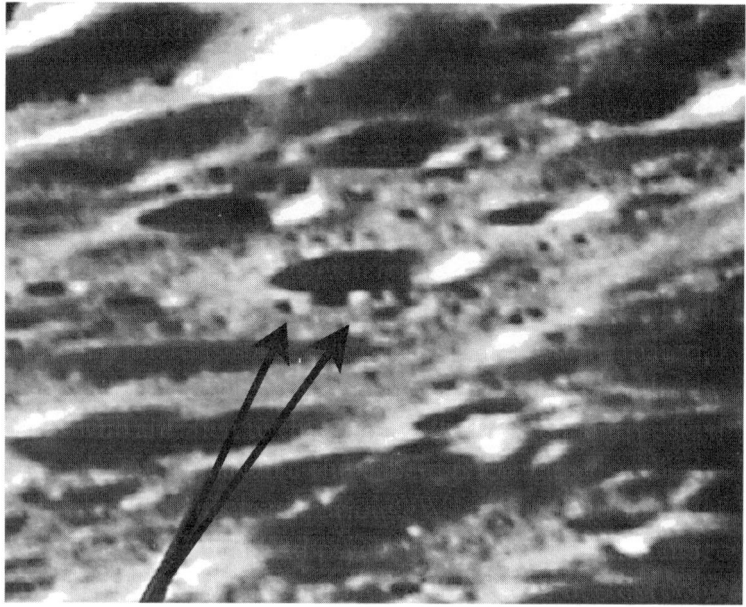

Plate 133. Area blow-up. Apollo 16 Photo No. 16-18918. Constructions much like large tanks or towers.

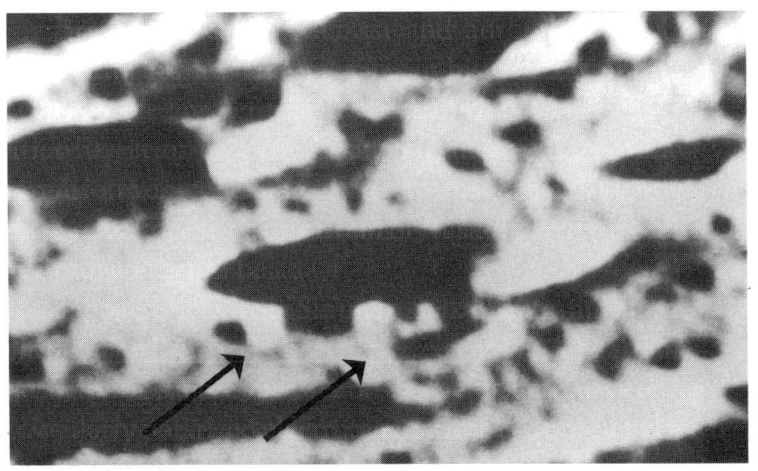

Plate 134. Apollo 16 photo No. 16-1891. 14 Times enlargement of plate 148.

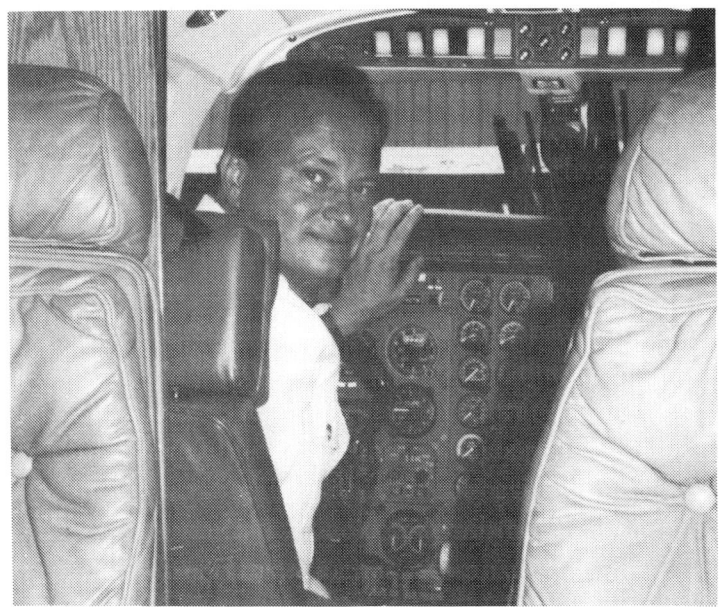

Plate 135. "The Author", Fred Steckling, pilot and amateur astronomer.

Son & Co-Author

13
Probing Adamski's Claims

George Adamski, who passed away in 1965, could truly be called the first pioneer in the UFO field. He was the author of three famous UFO books which, although highly controversial at that time, nevertheless shed some light on the following:

Where do the space visitors come from? What do they want here? Can we benefit from their knowledge? What are they doing on the Moon?

Adamski, who was also an excellent amateur astronomer, managed to photograph over a dozen UFOs through his telescopes. These UFO photographs, possibly by far the most detailed in civilian hands, became part of the great controversy of our time. While many recognized these pictures as factual, comparing them with their personal sightings and appearance of UFOs, others rejected them, with the attitude: "I have to see it to believe it," and "I saw it and I still don't believe it."

From 1948 to 1955, Adamski succeeded in taking several photographs of glowing UFOs close to the Moon. This photographic evidence, which so many other professional and amateur astronomers had sighted over the centuries, was so overwhelming that organized opposition was activated on a global basis to discredit his work. However, there were those who recognized the tremendous courage that this man possessed when he presented his findings to the public. Nevertheless, when

Adamski claimed contact with the crew of an extraterrestrial spacecraft near Desert Center, California, on November 29, 1952, the critics were beside themselves with chagrin. Adamski was labeled "crack-pot". "Impossible!" was the critic's reply. "UFOs only fly around. They don't land."

Adamski stated that UFOs come, in the main, from our solar system. The critics trumpeted "Impossible" again. "For life as we know it cannot exist elsewhere in this system."

In July of 1968, during the second session of the 90th Congress, the following questions were asked of prominent scientists by the committee members:

"Could UFOs be coming from our own solar system?" Answer: "They certainly could. We have no data from any other body in the solar system which definitely rules out the existence of advanced civilizations." These hearings were held before the committee on Science and Astronautics, United States House of Representatives behind closed doors.

Another question was asked of the scientists: "If we have been visited, why haven't they landed?" Answer: "The fact of the matter is that there are many reports of landings, at least 200 of them, which occurred in 1954 alone."

On December 25th, 1969, the Washington Daily News printed this explosive article: "Air Force Academy textbook teaches UFOs may be alien visitors." The article states that there is some evidence that UFOs are material objects, which are either manned or remotely controlled by beings who are alien to this planet. To the frequently asked question, "Why haven't these beings contacted us?" the textbook offers this explanation: "We may be the object of intensive sociological and psychological study, and contact may have already taken place secretly." The textbook concludes that the UFO phenomena has been a global entity for many thousands of years.

British aerospace scientist and author of two UFO books, Mr. Leonard Cramp, states in his recently published book, <u>A Piece For A Jigsaw</u>: "Regardless whether Adamski critics like it or not, the Adamski saucers are pro-gravity propulsion vehicles, and also electromagnetic devices."

Laboratory tests in Britain of this type of flying saucer have proven this to be a fact.

Japanese scientist, Shinichi Seike, states in his latest edition: <u>The Principles Of Ultra Relativity</u>: "The Adamski type of flying saucer operates on a G field of negative energy. A circularly polarized electromagnetic field, produced with three spherical condensers, charged by three phases current converters quantal fuel into negative energy state."

Mr. Seike, who heads the Japanese Gravity Research Laboratory, has successfully conducted experiments and tests with these types of vehicles.

British scientist John Searl has conducted experiments with inverse gravity space vehicles for years. He constructed forty research vehicles. The rotating electric field of inverse G-engine is realized by "A" charging or discharging spherical condensers set at vertices of regular N-polygon, with N-phases current or rotating electric dipole of a pair of charged spheres. The craft itself is a great electric generator. Mr. Searl and the National Space Research consortium is presently constructing a manned spacecraft with a diameter of 45.20 meters and a summit of 4.8 meters. Cabin pressure is adjustable from 5 pounds per square inch to 7 pounds which, incidentally, is identical to the pressures of the Apollo spacecraft. These craft submit a translucent glow, and glowing trails, which is accompanied by negative energy.

Adamski, in his book <u>Inside The Space Ships</u>, published in 1955, reports that the Moon has a thin atmosphere, and that there also exists surface water and vegetation. Perhaps now, with this evidence, we should examine these statements under a new light.

When living in Washington D.C. in 1963, my family and I witnessed a UFO sighting over downtown Washington. The craft looked exactly like the ones photographed by George Adamski. This sighting convinced me of the authenticity of Adamski's claims, for which he was so fiercely attacked and labeled a "crack-pot".

From my earlier studies of the slow evolution of man's progress over several thousands of years, I quickly realized that those contributing, rare individuals in our society, who have been labeled "crack-pots", were often the very ones who helped to remove this civilization from mental and scientific stagnation, and elevate it upon the higher rungs of the ladder of technological progress. Some of these people termed "crack-pots" were Archimedes, Gutenberg, Copernicus, Columbus, Galileo, Newton, Watt, Franklin, Fulton, Morse, Burbank, Bell, Edison, Pasteur, Marconi, Curie, the Wright Brothers, Ford, Einstein, Steinmetz, and many others too numerous to mention.

I came to the realization that individuals receiving such honors often possessed much knowledge and great wisdom. Only the finest people of this world who had much to give in all fields of science, unfearful of, and disregarding established theories were bestowed with such a rewarding title of "crack-pot".

What is the definition of a "crack-pot"? We could explain it in these simple terms; because of the "crack", known as a fissure, an opening is made through which may flow in ideas of universal influx. A cracked pot can also give out what it has received through this same fissure. A closed pot can do none of these things.

It is not my intention to insult anyone. My only interest is to set the record straight—to clarify that which previously was misunderstood. Because of our new findings on the Moon, may I suggest that his critics reassess their opinions of Adamski's claims and regard his viewpoints fairly, impartially, and with scientific acumen.

14
Changes Overdue

The possible detection of life on the Moon will be difficult to accept by some people, including those of the scientific community. Although it is almost impossible to discard long held theories for new thought, those open-minded people, wherever they may be found, should find the possibility quite acceptable. Many school books would have to be rewritten if all the information about the Moon were to be released. Our concept of life as we know it would necessitate changes to some extent. The attitude of being the "all-knowers" is not an easy one to release. It requires time, determination, and maturity.

From the military engineering point of view, the Moon holds great promise as a strategic area, not far from Earth. If the life there is capable of supporting Earth-man and his bases, we indeed have discovered a new frontier. It is understandable that the military is attempting to protect our country. Perhaps this is why they have kept so much information regarding the Moon secret, although I feel that when the public awakens and requests this type of information, hopefully our leaders will listen. While "protection" of the unaware public is good, in some cases, the dangers of "over-protection" can also be very detrimental to the intelligence of the people. It is also not easy to admit that a power not of this Earth could render all of our defense efforts useless.

There seems to exist a tremendous technology on the Moon, of which we could partake if we would only cooperate. Evidence has proven that they are friendly toward us, for they have permitted our astronauts to explore the Moon, photograph their spacecraft and installations and allowed them to return safely. This means that they want us to know that they are there. All we need do is to cooperate, and much knowledge would be ours, whether it be of energy improvements, or the so much needed social changes. It is not an easy decision to arrive at, even though we know "they" are good for us!

If we would accept their technology and trade with them on an interplanetary basis, it eventually would be imperative that we cooperate on Earth and create a united world. This is not an easy task as long as there is a profit to be made in our conflicts and aggressions against each other.

On the other hand, should the extraterrestrials show hostile intentions, what chances would we have against their advanced technology? We could unite and face the problems together. But, again, if we do that we would be forced to cooperate with each other, which in essence would cause us to create a united world not much different than those found on other planets.

Although the officials have not revealed everything that is going on up there, they did release some of the facts. It is imperative that we, the people, cooperate, ask questions, and demand answers in return for our hard-earned tax dollars. In this case I am convinced that some leaders would listen. One thing we have found out, surely, the Moon does not belong to us. Somebody else already has managed to reach it long ago.

Perhaps because of this overwhelming new evidence of life on the Moon, four very important scientists resigned in the wake of the Apollo 11 Moon landing. Bill Hess, the chief NASA scientist in Houston; geologist Elbert King, curator of lunar samples in the Lunar Receiving Laboratory; P. R. Bell, chief of the Lunar Receiving Laboratory; and Donald Wise. These four highly respected scientists went to Houston to start an ambitious program of scientific research in manned space flights. Why would they all resign at once, in their finest hour?

It would seem that since the evidence of life on the Moon was so overpowering they decided to resign, rather than live in secret with this stupendous knowledge. It is not easy to know so much truth without wanting to talk about it. Perhaps it is the same reason why some astronauts who went to the Moon, later changed their life-style and became very deep thinking and acting individuals.

Regardless of reasonable or unreasonable secrecies in the outer space exploration program, NASA should be supported by all citizens, morally and financially, so it may continue to explore outer space. No doubt, Earthman's survival will, in time, depend upon NASA research.

All nations on Earth should benefit from the space program. Today we are faced with problems of great magnitude which seem incapable of solution, such as pollution, energy, food shortages, unemployment, etc., etc. I would not be surprised if those living on the Moon have a positive solution for our plight. Due to the shortage of funds, I am convinced that there are still thousands of photographs which may not have been analyzed by NASA. But I also know that many close-up photos have been deposited in classified files for obvious reasons.

I personally want nothing to do with classified material, because publishing such material would embarrass the government, and this I have no intention of doing. I feel I have found all the evidence necessary from the material and photographs released to the public. Granted, most photographs in this book were never shown to the press, but they are nevertheless available for the serious investigator. The intent of this book, as I have heretofore stated, is not to insult anyone's intelligence, but merely to insert a new thought in the minds of the people, hoping that it may better our lives on Earth in time to come.

Former Apollo astronaut W. Anders, remarked, "The Earth is really not the center of the Universe. When you look at it from the Moon and it looks the size of your fist, you don't see any international boundaries. If we on this grain of sand cannot *cooperate* in space as mankind, and utilize this new medium for the benefit of all of us, then we likely won't get together on anything and we will bring about our own extinction."

15
Why Explore Space?

It is human nature to explore new frontiers. In any instance, human curiosity has driven men into regions previously thought impossible. To name just a few: the Arctic explorations, setting up bases there, some of them permanent ones; deep sea diving and charting the ocean floors; venturing deeper into the fascination of flight; and the exploration of the micro-world of cells, molecules and atoms. The research into magnetism, gravity, progravity, relativity, and ultra relativity, has given man a glimpse of a marvelous future, should he decide to travel the road of progress.

It is only logical that once we had discovered the new frontier of space, other planets and their satellites, attempting to explore them and perhaps colonize them in time, would follow.

There are many economic advantages that will benefit our civilization if we should decide to venture into this new frontier. This should be no different than the many discoveries on Earth, which previously were thought impossible. We must not overlook another factor, which is the feeling of achievement and accomplishment filling man's heart during such new adventures. This feeling, as experienced by most of us at one time or another, can often be more satisfying than financial gain, although a harmonious combination of the two is to be desired.

Every so often we hear the public, as well as its leaders, voicing opposition to the exploration of space, claiming that it is a waste of money. It is fortunate that the world, although replete with this type of individual, has progressed into a modern society in spite of their skepticism and doubts. Ironically, those who oppose and fear progress in all fields of human endeavor are also those who are the first to indulge in the comfort of new things, once they become accustomed with the more luxurious type of life.

We must, however, not be too critical of these people who, in time, will become a part of the progress they so readily shunned.

In today's modern society, almost all technological achievements are interrelated. Thus the space program, with its specialized technology, has already contributed innumerable benefits to our society, which are often unnoticed by the average citizen. Perhaps it is because of the lack of interest regarding occurrences which do not directly affect our personal lives. To list but a few of the new benefits; the textile industry, computer sciences and application, communication, electronics, insulation, nutrition, metallurgy. All have been directly affected by the development and application of space science.

The combined effort of many industries in the United States and abroad, uniting for one common goal, was rewarded with the successful landing of a man on the Moon in 1969 by the United States. No doubt this achievement will be in the minds and hearts of men on Earth as the greatest, most daring, adventure of this civilization.

We must not stop now. The exploration of the Moon was only a preliminary one, leaving open many unanswered questions, which can only be satisfied by continuing our manned space flights to the Moon. Too many mysteries still exist on the Moon which need to be investigated. The Apollo program could be compared to the first officially recognized discovery of America by Christopher Columbus. He, too, discovered a new frontier which eventually was colonized by every country of Earth. Today man's technological achievements have opened the universe to him, and he is now capable of colonizing almost every planet through advances in technological application.

Even if the Moon has no air, although we know it does, just fifty pounds of lunar rock could supply enough oxygen to last one man twenty-four hours. Today we have completely mastered the technology necessary to establish bases on the Moon under any conditions. It is really no different than the encircling of the world under water by atomic submarines without surfacing, mastering an environment completely foreign and hostile to man.

However, we do know that the Moon supports life, although no doubt sparsely, because it is not as lush as our planet. Since man has improved upon nature and vegetation on Earth, he may also apply this knowledge to the Moon. I feel man's destiny lies in exploration and future colonization of the infinite cosmos. These new ventures will help broaden man's horizons and outlook on life. It will make him see his individual importance, but also his insignificance in this vastness of which he is but a small spark. No doubt, as it already has been shown through the favorable effects of his expanded vision, Earthman has learned to a small degree, at least, to cope with problems on this planet previously unrecognized or overlooked.

From outer space, seeing the world function under the natural law offers a revealing sight. Reducing the space budget further would have little effect on our social problems on Earth, should these funds be diverted in that direction as suggested by some skeptics. Today about forty-three percent of the national budget, at the cost of over one hundred billion dollars a year, is allocated to these social problems. Actual spending for the space budget amounts to only 3.2 billions of dollars, or 1.2 percent of the national budget. To divert these funds from the space program would be unwise indeed, because the benefits reaped from it have repaid the expenses multifold.

Spacecraft constantly serve in the fields of communications, navigation, weather observation, and environmental surveys. We can now prospect the planet Earth from outer space, using special cameras, infra-red, etc., to search out secrets hidden below the Earth's surface; discover what parts of Earth best yield crops; and later survey these crops for signs of disease and drought. Space observations and surveys have aided the forestry department, agriculture, ocean studies, and mapping the Earth as has never been done before. For instance, aerial mapping of very high terrain which had taken aircraft over twenty-five years with still much to be done, were mapped in three minutes by a manned spacecraft one hundred twenty miles up.

Although a great number of satellites were placed into orbit by NASA, for scientific purposes, the military conduct their own top secret space program. Many hundreds of secret satellites have been placed into Earth orbit to gather information concerning other countries on Earth. Space photography has been refined to the point where a person can be photographed from space. New killer satellites have made headlines. Their purpose is to destroy by laser unwanted satellites of other nations. Each nation is feverishly occupied in its attempts to gain technical superiority in space science and its application.

Manufacturing in space will permit us to produce stronger plastics and alloys, unaffected by the influence of gravity. We now speak of future factories in space which hopefully will rid the Earth of a great pollution problem. Free energy from the Sun can be utilized in space, as well as concentrated and beamed to special Earth receiving stations by microwaves. Today, some forty foreign countries are willing to share 1.5 billion dollars in this program. Many spacecraft parts are being built in Europe. We can safely say that each single penny of every tax dollar which goes into the space program has been well invested.

Recently, space minded individuals have taken up a collection of money to support NASA. The Washington Post stated on January 8, 1981, that about one hundred thousand dollars was collected to aid the budget strapped national space agency. Dr. Robert Frosch, administrator of NASA, said that this gift shows that the public may be well ahead of its leaders in recognizing the importance of space exploration. He added, "As important as the money you have raised and donated is the expression of a deep and abiding commitment by many people to a strong and ongoing space record." This money, according to NASA, will be used to analyze data from the Viking mission to Mars and to produce global maps of planet Earth. Vikings 1 and 2 went into orbit around Mars in the summer of 1976, and both dropped landers to the surface. Over fifty-two thousand pictures and mountains of data were obtained from the Viking mission. The Viking 1 lander was still operating in January of 1981, after four and one-half years on the surface of Mars. At one time over one-half of our nation was involved, directly and indirectly, in the space program. Landing a man on the Moon was a very worthwhile goal which we challenged and won. Why not go on now, to continue to explore the Moon, as we have explored the Earth, and then to go on further to the planets close to us and eventually into other solar systems?

It seems that many young people today are looking forward to meet the challenge. However, many of them show great disappointment at their inability to lend their intelligence to the diversified fields of outer space science, flight, and exploration. The new generation is waiting for that chance.

16
Beyond the Moon

This chapter does not deal with the Moon directly, but ventures farther out into our solar system. Today, despite our Mariner and Viking missions to Venus and Mars, the mystery about our neighbor planets has only widened, and most questions still remain unexplained. The most pressing question of all is, does life exist on these worlds? Many scientists have voiced their opinion that unless we send manned spacecraft to these planets and thoroughly explore them, the mystery concerning life on these worlds may never satisfactorily be explained. The late Werner Von Braun, rocket specialist for NASA, once stated that manned space flights are by far more efficient than the remote controlled devices. Man, after all, is performing his tasks in space more efficiently than any computer ever could. "Besides", Braun remarked, "Man can be mass produced by unskilled labor."

The mysteries mount because already from the early analysis of the United States Mariner and the Soviet Venera missions to Venus, many contradictory findings were reported. Since these mysteries cannot be explored by telescope as the planets are too far away, we must rely totally on data radioed back to Earth by the satellites. Over the centuries our Moon, for instance, has been the target for endless hours of telescopic observations. These observations have revealed to us that at least some unexplainable things are happening up there. The problem is, however, that even now after our Apollo landings, these mysteries still remain.

This indicates that we know what is going on, to some extent, but hesitate to talk about it.

Receiving correct information from our space probes on Venus and Mars makes it easier to conceal information, if we wish to do so. Therefore, it is for the officials to determine whether to release this truth, or untruth, over which they retain complete control. If we would live in a truthful world, it would be easy to accept all that we are told. But most of us know better. Suspecting the very real possibility of "the great cosmic cover-up" as some authors have termed it, the public needs to maintain a constant vigil on the officials and the validity of their releases. Much "between the lines" reading is required as well as an unrelenting search for contradictory statements to the press and public, in order to seize the 'wool' before it is pulled too far over the eyes of the public.

We live in a privileged country and our constitutional rights permit us to question the officials, as well as our leaders. In our country where the government is of the people, by the people, and for the people, this relationship must be maintained under all circumstances, in order that our freedom may be preserved.

Freedom alone, contrary to the belief of many, is not just the right for anyone to do as he pleases, but it also entails the duty to seek and maintain the truth about things of a political, economic, and religious nature. No doubt the technical feat of steering a remote-controlled spacecraft to the endless voids of space and locating its target with such accuracy is a great engineering undertaking. Intricate mathematical and ballistic problems must be solved in order to succeed in these missions. We know they arrived there, but is the data they send back bona fide?

The signals received here on Earth by our tracking stations were sent in a code, deciphered only by the very top scientists through sophisticated decoding equipment. The point I am trying to make is simple. While these beeps, dots, and dashes are witnessed by literally hundreds of scientists, how many of them really know what this jargon means before it is decoded? It is obvious that only a few do and we have to trust them. I recall discrepancies which arose when the United States Mariner spacecraft and the Soviet Venera spacecraft radioed back to Earth temperature differences from Venus, ranging up to 400 degrees Fahrenheit. Naturally both nations claimed technical superiority, insisting that their instruments were of superior design. Because of this conflict, secret meetings in Europe by the space experts from the United States and the USSR were held in order to coordinate their releases, as such confusion causes the public to become dissatisfied, wondering, skeptical and restless.

The soft landing devices on Venus caused much more controversy than anticipated. We were told that Venus is the Earth's sister planet, very much the same size as Earth, but that its atmospheric density is over one hundred times as dense as that of Earth, and is laden with sulfuric acid. People would have accepted that. However, when the officials stated that these spacecraft landed on Venus by parachute, this certainly stretches the imagination. The explanation is simple. It is impossible to parachute an object of this size, weight, and density to the surface of Venus through an atmosphere one hundred times as dense as Earth. That is like attempting to parachute this same device 2,000 feet down to the bottom of our sea, with pressures identical to those of the Venusian atmosphere. Even scientists at NASA confirmed this fact, indirectly, not with the planet Venus, but with Titan, Saturn's moon. The NASA press release of December 12, 1980, stated that Titan had a 300-mile thick atmosphere, hence its surface cannot be seen. The conditions there seem to be identical to those on Venus. If future spacecraft entitled the Cronos probe were to be sent to Titan to land by parachute, NASA space expert, James Murphy, indicated the parachute would not work, because the atmosphere of Titan is too dense.

If the atmosphere of Venus is really over one hundred times as dense as ours, a landing device would float to its surface by itself, like a pearl down into the bottom of a shampoo bottle. This would make a parachute landing unnecessary. Furthermore, a temperature of 800 degrees Fahrenheit produces violent thermals. I doubt seriously that even if the Venusian atmosphere were identical to ours that it would be a simple matter to land a parachute there, because of thermal activity.

When the USSR landed one of its Venera spacecraft on the surface of Venus, it transmitted some excellent photographs, depicting a bright landscape of hills and rocks, much like our deserts on Earth. This caused even greater surprise, because an atmosphere that dense should produce total darkness on the surface of Venus. How they managed to photograph this well lit landscape, emitting an abundance of sunlight, has been a continuing mystery.

This posed other questions, such as the reports of mapping the surface of Venus by radar. If this would be possible, then we should be able to map our own ocean floors by radar. However, this is not possible because on earth the water reflects the radar beams and so do water vapor clouds, which have also been detected on Venus. One would assume that with the density and consistency of water, we should instead attempt to use sonar to map the surface of Venus. From the charts recently released, the radar technique seems to work well, which raises doubts that the Venusian atmosphere is really as dense as we are being told.

Just recently released findings by the USSR, which is exhibiting much interest in Venus, revealed the discovery of electromagnetic discharges in the form of lightning flashes on that planet. Their spacecraft, Venera 11, also recorded a forceful storm ninety miles wide, with lightning discharges at the rate of twenty-five per second. United States scientists said that this was rather remarkable, because nobody expected to find lightning on Venus. Naturally, they are surprised because an atmosphere over one hundred times as dense as ours, laden with sulfuric acid, would be self-grounding, making lightning highly improbable. Does this mean now that we are fed untrue information deliberately? Or does this mean that the officials are trying to tell us something, very much like they did with the Moon? Not outright revelations, but here and there, a bit of contradiction to make us think.

There are more surprises to be found on Venus, and one of them is its cloud formations, which totally envelop the planet. According to radar observations taken in 1961, the rotation of Venus is reported to be every 243 days. One can only wonder if this is accurate. Photographs of the Venusian cloud patterns, and the behavior of their weather, at least in the upper atmosphere, is quite similar to ours. Both cloud patterns move away from the equator area toward the northern and southern hemispheres in clockwise and counterclockwise movements, and it takes them about four days to go around the planet once. One begins to wonder why these clouds behave just like those on Earth, which also takes about the same time to move around the Earth. In other words, what generates these similar atmospheric motions?

The contradictions continue, one being the importance of having all United States landing spacecraft on Venus thoroughly sterilized. This brings up the question of the necessity of sterilization in an 800 degree Fahrenheit atmosphere, which is four times as hot as boiling water. It is true that certain bacteria can survive, and even reproduce under many hostile conditions, like the cooling water surrounding nuclear reactors, in tanks of jet aircraft, or in jars of gasoline, as one scientist in Los Angeles demonstrated to me. Even below, deep in our oceans around hot volcanic geysers, certain strains of bacteria survive, as well as algae. I am certain that common bacteria, such as we are exposed to on the surface of the Earth daily, would not enjoy longevity on Venus, should it be as hot there as we have been informed.

Speaking of contamination of other planets, it has been found that micro-organisms have been traced, even to the far reaches of space, which probably were deposited there by the trail of Earth's atmosphere, or perhaps even other planets. Since these organisms seem to survive in hibernation almost indefinitely, they may in time become part of another atmosphere in another planet, attracted by its gravity, and gently flow toward its surface and multiply. If this is true, then indeed we live in a chemical universe, where one planet "pollutes" another with seeds of life. This no doubt is an interesting thought, worthwhile to consider in our quest of Nature's secrets in outer space and other worlds.

We have high temperatures in the Earth's ionosphere. About 180 miles up, where the cosmic solar rays strike the outer region of our atmosphere, a tremendous friction is generated from the disintegration of atmospheric molecules. Temperatures of up to 1800 degrees Fahrenheit have been measured there. Could it be that the high temperature readings of the planet Venus found their origin in the Venusian ionosphere as our spacecraft descended through it? This is certainly something to consider.

Another interesting explanation concerning temperatures is that the sun is positive and the planets are negative, and all are floating in a sea of electromagnetic energy. Solar rays are attracted by each planetary body differently in intensity and velocity, according to the size of the planet. If this is correct, it would explain why the temperatures in outer space are 360 degrees below zero, no matter whether it is in space, around Venus, Earth, Jupiter, Saturn, or even farther out. It would also explain why the larger planets such as Jupiter and Saturn reflect more heat. If the Sun sends out heat, then why is it 360 degrees below zero in outer space? The gravity of Jupiter and Saturn is much higher than Earth's gravity. In this case, should my ideas be correct, these larger planets would attract the solar rays with a much higher velocity and intensity than Venus and the Earth and even the Moon. In fact, cosmic ray bombardment on the Moon should only be one-sixth in intensity in this case.

On the other hand, the friction generated on Jupiter and Saturn when these rays strike their atmosphere, causes these planets to receive heat and warmth. This explains from whence their heat is generated.

According to present theories, any planet farther out than Mars is an ice world or frozen rock. This theory was shaken when our recent Voyager spacecraft discovered volcanic activity on Jupiter's moon Io. In fact, Jupiter and Saturn have been compared to individual solar systems, with many of their satellites, of which more and more are discovered each day, producing nothing but mysteries for us.

Although there remains a multitude of questions and hypotheses, the old accepted theories certainly have produced few reasonable and satisfactory explanations. Therefore, I feel the questions I am proposing deserve further open minded investigation.

The next planet I would like to mention is Mars. When the United States succeeded in the successful landing of the Viking 1 and 2 spacecraft in 1976, there was great rejoicing among the people of the Earth. This was an achievement well worthy of the celebration. After the excitement abated somewhat, certain nagging questions surfaced concerning some of the reports released to the public regarding the planet Mars. I covered these events thoroughly and in 1976, in late Autumn, I was compelled to write an article for a national magazine, entitled "Life on Mars". This article was also later reprinted in Europe and Japan. I herewith reproduce it, with only minor changes.

"For centuries man, on this earth, has wondered whether or not 'life' existed elsewhere on the distant planets that could be seen passing through the heavens at night. Mars, the fourth planet from the sun, together with Venus, our second closest neighbor, would be the most logical places to assume that there is life close to what we know it to be.

"It probably all started with the Italian astronomer, Giovanni Schiaparelli, who in 1877, reported the famous 'Canali' or canals on Mars. Only intelligent beings could have built such structures, it was suggested.

"Later, at the turn of the century, Percival Lowell, who, from his observatory in Flagstaff, Arizona in 1906, became the ranking expert on Mars' observations. He, too, reported and supported Schiaparelli's 'Canali'.

"Still later, the world renowned newscaster and actor Orson Wells succeeded in frightening millions of Americans with his famous radio broadcast of 1938, War of the World, portraying it as a real life invasion by beings from Mars landing in New Jersey.

"Decades later, during the 1960's, Soviet astronomers announced to an astonished scientific world that their close studies of the planet Mars had revealed that both moons of the Red Planet were thought to be artificial man-made satellites. Their observations, based on several very puzzling facts, led to this conclusion. Both of the Martians 'moons' were orbiting too close to the planet, only 3700 miles away. Normally they should crash into the planet in time. Also both moons reflected too much light to be natural. Probably the most puzzling fact of all was that both are orbiting the planet in a clockwise direction. All other known planetary bodies and satellites whirl in a counterclockwise direction. Even the entire Milky Way galaxy with its countless number of stars turns counterclockwise, but not the two little moons of Mars. Granted, the idea of two orbiting bodies, one five miles in diameter and the other ten miles being artificial, is a bit controversial and stretches the imagination.

"November 16, 1969, a noted space scientist and astronomer, the late Dr. Harold C. Urey, stated some things just as startling as his Soviet colleagues. Dr. Urey, speaking at the Manned Spacecraft Center in Houston, Texas, said, "We should be very careful in sending manned spacecraft to the planet Mars as the 'life' there may be hostile and could prevent the astronauts from returning to earth." Dr. Urey was a Nobel prize winner in chemistry. In the same article he also defended the space program, stating that we can afford it, for it costs only one-half of one percent of the gross national product.

"Turning the pages to 1976 and our recent Viking Missions to the Red Planet, it seems that we have certainly proven all these men wrong, or have we? It may surprise some of you, but after endless hours of study and investigation into our two missions to Mars, I must say NO, we have NOT proven these men wrong at all. In the following pages I shall endeavor to explain my findings for your own evaluation in the most logical way possible.

"The reaction of the general public can be broken down as follows: 40% were disappointed in the total negative viewpoint of the Viking mission, and 50% definitely believe that intelligent life does exist on Mars and that the officials in charge of the program are covering up for some reason, while 10% think that the Viking probes were not sent to Mars at all but rather to the Moon. All in all, there exists a great public mistrust of our officials and their ethics. Undoubtedly, some mistrust is present due to the past cover-ups and accusations that have come forth from some of our government agencies, one against the other.

"I do feel that we managed to land these two probes on the planet Mars, but that their true findings and most pictures are classified material which to this day have not been shown. My research has resulted in the following findings:

"We were told that Mars is about one-half the size of the earth, with a surface gravity of about 40% in relation to our own earth and that the atmospheric pressure is some

7.7 millibars in comparison to about one thousand millibars on earth. The Martian atmospheric density is reported to be less than 1% of that of earth. We were also told that the Martian temperatures in Fahrenheit ranged from -22 degrees below zero at early afternoon to -122 degrees below zero at night. Viking One, which landed close to the Martian equator, recorded a colder temperature than Viking Two, which touched down some one thousand miles farther north, closer to the polar caps.

"The amazed scientists discovered a 100% mistake during atmospheric measurements. The argon content of the Martian atmosphere was not 30% as they had thought but only 3%. A mistake of the same magnitude was admitted when a much higher water vapor reading was received then we had thought possible from earth measurements.

"Dr. George Sands, of Mission Control, stated, "It is obviously wetter than we anticipated. There is *ground* fog at the landing site during part of the day. Thirty microns of water have been found in the atmosphere, enough to cause not only ground fog but also frost and snow".

"I am not a scientist, but I have studied meteorology enough to be able to say that the evidence of ground fog on Mars proves that temperatures there are much warmer than we are told by the official reports. Ground fog is a product of warm moist air moving across cool land masses or water. Ground fog, as with any type of fog, is a product of temperatures above the freezing level of 32 degrees Fahrenheit.

"It is also interesting to note that evaporation clouds have been photographed at an estimated altitude of fifteen thousand feet AGL (above ground level). I can assure you that condensation clouds or any other clouds including simple ground fog cannot exist at the reported atmospheric pressure of only 7.7 millibars. Evaporation clouds on earth may reach up to forty thousand feet, but even at that altitude our atmospheric pressure is still two hundred millibars, enough to support such clouds.

"We are told that evaporation clouds exist up to fifteen thousand feet on Mars. The temperatures, therefore, must be ABOVE the freezing point of 32 degrees Fahrenheit up to at least fifteen thousand feet. When rising moist air moves upward it condenses at a given altitude and forms clouds at given altitudes depending upon the temperature. This we call the dew point level. One must note at this point that low temperatures such as the reported -122 degrees Fahrenheit on Mars may certainly exist in certain zones but not everywhere. We have recorded temperatures of -127 degrees Fahrenheit here on earth at the Antarctica Zones, and we know that life exists here on this planet.

"Regarding the Viking landers, we find some other unexplained points to ponder.

"The Viking landers were reported to have an earth weight of twelve hundred pounds. According to our reports of the Martian gravity the landers would weigh approximately four hundred eighty pounds. The parachute was fifty feet in diameter. A fifty foot parachute with a weight of four hundred eighty pounds dangling from it would slow that payload down sufficiently in the earth's atmosphere for a proper adjustment in velocity at retro-rocket firing. However, in the low density of the Martian atmosphere, as we are told (less than one percent of ours), a fifty foot parachute would have no slowing effect at all. It is even doubtful that in the legendary atmosphere there exists enough air molecules to open the chute. Calculating the size of the parachute needed in such a thin atmosphere, the canopy would have to be some seventy five hundred feet in diameter. The question then arises where would such a thing be stored and what would such a load weigh? Certainly at least two thousand pounds. It would take up about two hundred square feet of space to store it. That is more cubic space and weight than the entire lander itself. So, since they did use a fifty foot chute the air on Mars is much more dense than they tell us. I would say a density of about 40% of that of earth.

"The lander on the fifty foot chute separated at four thousand feet AGL, and activated its three descent rockets, which, like gigantic blow torches, slowed down the craft to a successful soft landing. However, the three rocket engines develop not only thousands of degrees of heat but immense thrust. These two factors not only completely sterilized the landing site before touchdown, but blew away all the soil of biological value for at least one hundred feet surrounding the lander. We should question the ability to find any signs of life in such soil. The scientists should have questioned this. Maybe they did. In the meantime, that little shovel keeps on digging and searching in that sterilized soil.

"The magazine 'Scientific American' had this to say in a recent article on Mars: 'The Martian environment is by no means so hostile as to exclude LIFE. Our hopes for obtaining a definitive answer from the Viking mission should not be too high.'

"Other interesting points are to be found. For example, sand dunes on Mars photographed by the 'orbiter' have the same height and the same dune to dune spacing as earth's sand dunes to be found in the Sangre de Christo mountains in Colorado. In a Martian atmosphere of less than one percent of ours these sand dunes could under no circumstances be there!

"It has been suggested that hurricane-like winds of two hundred m.p.h. or better are needed to move these grains of sand on Mars but up to now there has been no logical explanation as to where these two hundred m.p.h. winds come from in a total subzero environment. Again, Mars must be warmer in at least some regions to create wind of any speed in the first place. As we know, wind is created by warm air rising from the ground to be replaced by colder air masses filling in the gap. The Viking lander only recorded winds up to forty m.p.h., not two hundred. So, how did the dunes get there? Even better, how did the wind get there in an atmosphere that is only one percent of earth's and at a temperature of -120 degrees Fahrenheit?

"I think that we have to be sensible about all of this, for it can be seen that too many things just don't seem to make logical sense. Certainly if we can figure this out the scientists and others working on the project can. Some talk from both sides of the mouth does seem to be taking place.

"Viking 2 reveals that the polar caps of Mars are plain snow, just frozen water. Also, that it snows often, and the atmosphere above the poles is saturated with water vapor. Sounds good? Let us continue. A NASA article reports that the poles of Mars are all frozen water with temperatures of -90 degree Fahrenheit to -120 degrees Fahrenheit. The article continues by saying, 'The North Pole is now going through its summer, so the ice cap is about as small as it ever gets.' I would like to know how ice in subzero temperatures as reported above can *melt!!*

"Dr. Martin, who has just recently resigned his position with Pasadena Viking Control, said at the International Academy of Astronautics, 'Our biology instruments on Mars have received positive signs of LIFE in forms of biology even though we cannot find organics.' It is amazing that they have found even those little signs at such a blow-torched landing site.

"Analysis of the Martian environment has so far shown that there is carbon, nitrogen, oxygen and sufficient amounts of water vapor. Are not these the basic ingredients for LIFE?

"Quoting NASA from Pasadena, 'If we would have placed the Viking landers in our Pasadena parking lot and received the same chemical and biological readings from there as we are now receiving from Mars, we would have called it a definite sign of life.' I leave it to you to figure out what that might mean.

"I feel that so long as we are going to send probes out to other worlds with our assumptions that life is unique only to our little earth, instead of being able to see that all worlds are basically made up of the same 'stuff', we shall continue to be plagued with unyielding difficulties and insoluble questions.

"Planets do not only receive warmth from their sun in forms of friction by rays striking their atmospheres, but also by the same process, warmth from the planet is drawn out of its body, radiating and warming up the atmosphere. All planets need an atmosphere simply to equalize the pressures set up from within. No planet could exist without air, for it would disintegrate otherwise in a given time.

"The water quantity on Mars has been analyzed to be sufficient to cover their whole planet with an ocean of ONE MILE in depth, should all its water now in and under the ground be released! While the polar caps themselves show a thickness measuring one-half mile.

"Perhaps the Italian astronomer Schiaparelli's earlier reports of the Martian channels do not at all seem so impossible when they are compared with Dr. Daniel J. Milton's recent findings. Dr. Milton, a geologist with the U.S. Geological Survey, stated in 'Science Newsfront': 'We have photographed the Martian mystery channels. They resemble huge flood channels some twenty-four miles wide and several hundred miles long, shaped by sudden discharges of water that dwarf the flow of the Amazon River.'

"Finally, here is a report from the wires of the AP: 'New pictures of Mars' northern regions reveal mysterious patterns, resembling contour plowing on the planet's red surface and scientists say they cannot find a natural explanation. 'We are getting some strange things. It is very puzzling,' said Michael Carr, member of the team interpreting pictures of Mars from the Viking 2 orbiter. Carr stated that the newest pictures of the target zone showed striped patterns that resemble an aerial photograph of a farmer's field after plowing. 'The stripes are too regular to be of natural causes,' Carr stated. But what caused them? 'I really can't tell you all of the possibilities that were suggested.' Carr responded. 'But many suggestions were that it was MAN MADE.'

"I would like to point out the most important fact that the suggestion of man-made plowing by the Viking scientists was made AFTER Viking One could not find life on Mars as we were looking for it.

"To conclude this article, I would like to give credit where credit is due and report that even as we receive double talk on the extra-terrestrial findings, we have, as a civilization, gained enormous knowledge by venturing out into space. We have learned more about our earth from out there by observation and photography than is presently realized by the general public. Space satellites placed into earth orbit have revealed our global pollution problems. We have learned about the weather patterns, the ocean currents, mineral deposits, soil analysis, flood control, forestry service, and higher yield agricultural areas, both presently cultivated and those as yet unused.

"Through our earth orbiting probes we have also found that we are not always perfect. In the early days we received reports that life could not exist even on our own planet. Those probes reported back that there was not enough water vapor or oxygen to support life as we know it on Earth! Therefore we know that the probes are not always accurate. Much depends upon the pressures and amount of magnetism that surrounds the probes in space when the readings are taken.

"As it is yet to be revealed, Man's future on this earth will depend upon outer space research and exploration for it is from out there that he will be able to evaluate that small world he now calls 'home'. But one day when things become unbearable, we will be forced to venture out to find other worlds ready for inhabitation.

"Every dollar spent in this program is well spent. It can keep man busy in the peaceful way, while he is learning. The space program has all the potentials to allow man to one day to explore space and work together as brothers, so thoroughly occupied in it, that there is no time left for foolish wars that only add additional woes and miseries to mankind.

"Mankind considers himself the most intelligent creature on Earth. He will soon have the Golden Opportunity to prove it."

Bradford D. Smith, NASA scientist and head of the 1980 Voyager's photographic mission to Saturn, had this statement to make, which I feel covers or explains some of the mysteries that have baffled us about outer space. Smith stated, "With any scientific investigation of this magnitude, many of our long-standing theories—those cherished interpretations of the Universe around us, are going to become casualties."

Dr. Robert Jastrow, the founder and director of NASA's Goddard Institute for space studies, was interviewed by science reporter Marcia Golub of the Special Science Digest magazine, Spring edition of 1980. In this revealing article, titled "Life on Mars", Dr. Jastrow states very positively that life exists there. From his studies of the Viking data, there is no doubt, Jastrow admitted, that at least some form of primitive life exists on Mars.

Dr. Jastrow now teaches at both Columbia University and Dartmouth College. "But even primitive life forms such as microbes are quite complicated forms of life," Dr. Jastrow concluded, "because these would settle the question: 'Is Life common in the cosmos?' We can be sure that humanity is not alone, that planets circling other stars must be swarming with life, and that in solar systems older than ours, this life may be far more advanced than humanity on Earth."

Reporter Golub asked Dr. Jastrow this important question: "Do you think there is life on Mars? Some scientists disagree... Why?"

Dr. Jastrow answered, "My only comment is that scientific caution is fine if you spend $30.00 of your own money. But if you spend millions of dollars of somebody else's money, you have to stand the heat. Also scientists are very sensitive to being wrong."

During the Viking 1 microbe test on Mars, nutrients with radioactive carbon was the food presented to possible Martian microbes. If the microbes ate the food, they would exhale radioactive carbon dioxide, and if the Geiger counter clicked, the microbes were eating the food. The Geiger counter clicked thousands of times. While many of the Viking scientists tried to explain this positive result as a way of being merely a chemical reaction, several others, such as Dr. Jastrow, for instance, insisted that this reaction was a biological one. As a matter of fact, the Viking 2 test produced exactly the same positive reaction, as the Martian microbes ate away the radioactive carbon laden nutrients. Nevertheless, the arguments continued as to whether these tests were chemical or biological reactions.

The soil samples were stored for several months in the Viking lander storage area and the microbe test was again repeated, and this time the Geiger counter signal disappeared. Dr. Jastrow explains that if one stores living organisms in the dark, without food and water for several months, they die.

This was the convincing fact arguing for the existence of Martian microbes, as the first sign of life on Mars. Dr. Jastrow also stated that Dr. Levin, who did the microbe test, also believes that these test results prove life on Mars. But using Jastrow's own words, "Dr. Levin has been a little restrained by peer pressure from the Viking team."

Chief biologist Chuck Klein now admits that on the basis of the Viking 1 and 2 microbe tests, the conclusion would have to be drawn that metabolizing organisms were definitely present in all the samples tested. "That means life on Mars exists," Dr. Klein stated.

Dr. Jastrow concludes with these remarks: "The taxpayer got a better return on the money he invested in Mars than he realized, but nobody has told him. It has killed the Mars exploration program."

In certain scientific circles, it has been common knowledge for quite some time now, that life exists on the Moon, on Mars, and many other planets as well. Just because the general public is not aware of this fact does not make it less true. While Dr. Jastrow is a very cautious man, revealing only primitive life forms on Mars, other scientists are more outspoken.

One retired physicist with whom I had the privilege of spending an afternoon, in the summer of 1980, discussed life on other worlds, UFOs, and their propulsion methods quite openly with me. This gentleman related to me, with revealing candor, that several friends of his, all top scientists, had been taken to the Moon and Mars by the extraterrestrials. There are several secret bases here on Earth, above the 15,000 foot level in mountainous areas, where alien spacecraft land. These voyages, this scientist acknowledged to me, are not joy rides, but have an extremely valuable scientific purpose.

In addition, George Adamski reported in his book, Inside The Space Ships, that on many of his voyages into space, during the 1950's, top scientists were also taken along. Whatever these gentlemen learned from these voyages were later put into constructive use, without revealing the source of their information.

Adamski was also told by his contacts that while the air is very thin on the Moon, there are certain areas where even Earth men could walk around without a space suit and air tanks, but it would take twenty-four hours of depressurization to get their bodies acclimated to this condition. He was also told that those men from other planets visiting the Moon must experience the same procedure of depressurization.

The scientist with whom I conversed in the summer of 1980 revealed to me very much the same information. He stated that when this group of selected scientists reached the Moon, they were told by their hosts they could take a walk on the surface without space suits. Nevertheless, they were given small oxygen bottles with the explanation that they would feel very ill, very shortly, in those conditions to which they were unaccustomed. They did not go through twenty-four hours of depressurization. This group was later taken to planet Mars where they, to their surprise, found it to be inhabited with human beings. They were told that about six hundred million people live on Mars, and that the surface air pressure at sea level there was equal to a 20,000 foot altitude here on Earth. Since Mars is a bit smaller than one-half of Earth, this air pressure seemed to be sufficient enough there because of less gravitational attraction. A one hundred pound Earth person would weigh less than fifty pounds on Mars.

Even though this story sounds rather fantastic, I have no reason to disbelieve this gentleman, who struck me as a very mentally alert and honest man, still engaged in electromagnetic research in a private capacity. As a matter of fact, he too has been invited to take the same trip into outer space as his friends did some time ago. He told me that he would share all the information with me upon his return, whenever that will be.

The book, <u>Alternative 3</u>, speaks of a secret Mars mission by the U.S.A. and the U.S.S.R. in 1962. According to the authors of this book, a copy of this secret Mars tape and the special decoder were stolen from NASA in the United States, and transported to Britain via Canada. There this tape was shown to top officials and scientists in the late 70's. This tape revealed that on May 22, 1962, these two super powers, in a consolidated effort, landed a remote-controlled spacecraft on Mars, which reported a temperature and atmospheric pressure sufficient to support life as we know it. <u>Alternative 3</u> was written by three well-known British television reporters, which produced a TV program with that same title, shown by the BBC TV network in 1977, with the book following in June, 1979. The retired physicist who had presented me with the information concerning the Moon and Mars, also pointed out to me that the book <u>Alternative 3</u>, contained a vast amount of truth.

Searching for this type of truth is not an easy matter because the governments involved in such projects prefer to clamp a tight lid on their findings. However, in time, the truth will always be revealed, because only a few men can take such secrets into their graves, and sooner or later, information will leak out.

To receive the total picture of the truth, those of us who are interested in finding it must never cease to investigate every little part of it, patiently piecing together the puzzle picture until we see it clearly. It has been said that "Man know the truth and it shall make you free." The involvement of man's intellect or his mind alone is not enough, as often truth is revealed to us through intuitive feeling, or hunches, which come to us through conscious awareness.

I feel that mankind will have no chance to see the total picture of truth, unless we use both elements of his being, our minds and our conscious awareness, in harmony.

Only then we will be able to see the total picture of the truth and at the same time be capable of handling it.

Epilogue

For nearly fifty years, governmental agencies of numerous nations have collected and examined internally classified information pertaining to extraterrestrial visitations, while at the same time, continuing to avoid public disclosure relating to UFO reports. Whether masquerading under code names such as Project Sign, Grudge, Saucer, Magnet, Blue Book or the Condon Report, it is evident that there is sufficient interest and significance to these continuous sightings of extraterrestrial craft to warrant so many years of attention and concentration.

If we wished to be so naive to believe such explanations for the many unaccountable thousands of sightings as nothing more than various weather phenomena, swamp gas, plasma balls, balloons, high flying geese, reflections, ghosts, or the ranting of the mentally deranged, there would seem little value - or logic - in the continued academic study of these occurrences throughout so many decades. Naturally, when these extraterrestrial crafts are observed around the world, some with people waving from within, or venturing forth to communicate, or speeding across radar scopes at thousands of miles per hour, or performing maneuvers alongside airliners, or following maritime vessels while pulsating beneath the sea, such explanations tend to become all the more ludicrous. And even if we were to accept such absurd explanations of this phenomenon, we would still be left with approximately 27% of these sightings, which according to the United States Air Force, could not and can not be explained by any such terms.

The following brief and selected chronology of reported UFO observations is listed to help provide some insight, plus stimulate critical thinking concerning the various explanations given by Governments, the media or other sources regarding past, present or future UFO related events. For the sake of brevity, an arbitrary beginning date was selected, otherwise volumes could be filled with the many listings.

- 1619 Fluelen, Switzerland. Enormous long fiery object seen flying along a lake.
- June, 1750. Edinburgh, Scotland. Vast ball of fire moving slowly.
- October, 1755. Lisbon, Portugal. Immense bright flying globes seen many times.
- August, 1762. Basle, Switzerland. Enormous dark object, surrounded by glowing outer ring observed by pair of astronomers.
- September, 1820. Embrun, France. Wonderfully even formations of flying objects cross the town in straight lines, turn 90 degrees and then fly away in perfect formation.
- November, 1833. Niagara Falls, U.S.A. Large square luminous object seen for over an hour.
- 1838, India. Flying disc with long glowing orange appendages.
- May, 1845. Signor Capocci, of Capodimonte Observatory, Naples, observes several shining discs flying from east to west.
- June 18, 1845. Crew members of the brig Victoria

watched three luminous objects come out the sea.

- From 1869 to 1871, forty members of the British Royal Astronomical Society reported observing various geometric patterns, confirmed sightings of a moving 50 mile long opaque object, great white domes, and long bridge structures on the lunar surface.

- January, 1878. Adenison Daily News is reported to be the first newspaper to use the description "Saucer" relating to UFO reports.

- August, 1878. Professors Swift and Watson report two luminous spheres moving between Mercury and the Sun.

- May 15, 1879. Strange underwater lights were observed by the officers and crew of H.M.S. Vulture. The location of the ship at the time was in the Persian Gulf: The ship's commander noticed pulsation's of light moving at great speed beneath the water. The objects resembled giant revolving "Wheels" and traveled at far greater speeds than any device conceivable.

- July, 1880. St. Petersburg, Russia. Large circular luminous vessel followed by two smaller ones moving nimbly along a ravine. Visible for three minutes, disappearing silently.

- November, 1882. Greenwich Observatory, England. Tremendous green disc, with dark markings. Magnificent luminous mass shaped like a torpedo. Seen also in Holland and Belgium.

- February, 1884. Brussels Observatory. Extremely bright point of light on planet Venus. Nine days later it moves out from the planet traveling away in space.

- November, 1887. Huge fiery sphere rises from the sea

near Cape Race, moves against the wind, approaches the ship Siberian, then moves away. Visible for five minutes. The Captain said he has seen similar occurrences in the same area before.

- April, 1892. Large black disc slowly crosses the lunar surface, seen by Dutch Astronomer Muller.

- March, 1893. H.M.S. Caroline, between Shanghai and Japan, crew witnesses formation of discs flying slowly northwards. They pass between the ship and mountain 6000 ft. high. Observation through telescope shows them to be reddish colored, emitting trails. Seen for two hours.

- March 14, 1907. Officers of the steam ship Delta observed shafts of light, approximately 300 meters long, moving about a center like spokes around a wheel. This phenomena lasted for about 30 minutes.

- December, 1909. Boston, Mass. Luminous object seen over city. Three days later seen again over Worchester, sweeping the skies with a searchlight of tremendous power. Two hours later it returns and is seen by thousands on the streets. It hovers, heads south, then east out to sea.

- May 1909. Cardiff, England. A Cardiff man reported walking through the mountains and coming across a large cylindrical object, parked along a lonely road. Inside he saw two men, who upon seeing him, chattered excitedly in a foreign language. The next minute the machine rose silently in the air and flew away. A depression was found in the grass where he indicated the sighting.

- 1910. Longest dirigible flight recorded this year - from St. Cyr to the Eiffel Tower - A few miles. (This event was included to show the earliest recorded date of an earthly constructed object of this size to become airborne, thus negating any possibility of earlier UFO sightings being explained as dirigibles.
- January, 1912. Dr. Harris observes dark objects, poised over moon, estimates it to be at least 250 miles long.
- 1923, North Carolina. Reports of brilliant spheres or discs moving in formation or singly in the neighborhood of the Brown Mountains during a three year period. Official investigation draws no significant explanation.
- In 1943, a huge disc was observed by the crew of an American vessel beneath the waters of the Persian Gulf. The object was glowing with a soft, greenish light. The object then increased speed and accelerated away from the U.S. Naval vessel.
- 1947, Mount Rainier, Washington. Formation of silvery "Saucer" objects observed by pilot Kenneth Arnold while flying his private aircraft.
- March 1950, Denver, Colorado. A speaker at the University of Colorado addressed students concerning the existence of UFOs. Mr. Newton indicated that three saucer shaped craft had crash landed in an area several hundred miles from Denver. The military quarantined the area and removed a number of short, but definitely human, bodies. Afterwards the space crafts were removed and transported to a military installation for experimentation and examination.
- April, 1952. Haliburton, Ontario, Canada. Two silvery

objects, one directly behind the other, performing complex aerial maneuvers for five minutes.

- April, 1952. Nellis Air Force Base, near Las Vegas, Nevada. Eighteen circular, dull white objects in irregular formation, approximate altitude 12000 meters, apparent speed 1200 m.p.h.. Air Base officials stated - no balloons or aircraft reported released that day.

- April 7, 1952. LIFE Magazine ("M. Monroe Cover") begins releasing factual UFO information.

- July, 1952. Washington D.C. Numerous photographs and sightings of UFOs over the United States Capitol, White House and Pentagon for several weeks. Military radar scopes track and interceptors scramble to evaluate situation. Largest government press conference held to discredit sightings and calm population's concerns.

- November, 1952. Desert Center, California. George Adamski and six witnesses see cigar shaped object, several thousand feet long, hovering over desert. Small saucer craft lands and man walks out. Adamski and E.T. draw pictures in desert sand to converse. Space pilot leaves behind footprints containing symbolized engravings. Plaster cast made of these. Incident reported in Phoenix and California newspapers.

- February, 1954. Coniston, England. Two teenage boys photograph glowing saucer rising above valley and circle before disappearing straight up. The "Darbishire" pictures clearly show the same type craft photographed by Adamski in California several years earlier. Scientist/Engineer Leonard Cramp uses Orthographic projections to compare images within these photographs and determines them to be tangible objects of comparable dimensions. Writes excellent book titled <u>Space, Gravity and Flying Saucer</u>.

- July, 1959. Honolulu, Hawaii. Five Pan American Pilots spot an intensely bright object followed by four smaller ones in formation 1000 miles east of Hawaii. Objects intercept and accompany aircraft for over 10 seconds and within 1000 ft., then made a sharp turn and accelerated at inconceivable speed.

- August, 1959. Brisbane, Australia. Flying saucers bathed in blue light, with people on board who waved and exchanged signals, reported by university educated priest and a group of 12 other people in New Guinea. The objects hovered at varying altitudes of 450 to 2500 ft. Included were sightings spanning several days of 8 other saucer crafts and one larger cigar craft.

- May 10, 1962. Seattle Washington Newspaper. Mysterious Flying Objects Photographed by X15 Pilot Joe Walker. Five to six Disc shaped objects at an altitude of 246,700 feet. Second flight, commanded by pilot Maj. Bob White, encountered another mysterious object both seen and photographed.

- 1965, Astronauts McDivitt and White photograph several UFOs hovering within a short distance of their orbiting Gemini 4 space capsule.

- From the book <u>Our Ancestors Came From Outer Space</u> by Maurice Chatelain, a NASA scientist who helped launch the U.S. Space program. "It seems that all Apollo and Gemini flights were followed, both at a distance and sometimes also quite closely, by space vehicles of extraterrestrial origin - flying saucers, or UFO's - if you want to call them by that name. Every time it occurred, the astronauts informed Mission Control, who then ordered absolute silence."

- June 1967. The Washington Post Newspaper. UFOs High Among Thant's Worries. U.N. Secretary General U. Thant arranged to have top advocates of UFOs speak before Space committee of United Nations. Thants says he considers UFOs one of the most important problems facing the U.N.

- October, 1968. Madrid, Spain. UFO causes traffic jam in Madrid. The astronomical observatory observed the object at high power and said it gave off a blinding light. A photograph taken revealed a triangular solid and sometimes translucent object. Spanish Air Force scrambled a supersonic fighter only to be out maneuvered by the UFO.

- October, 1973. Lima, Peru. Architect and witness observe and take picture of saucer shaped UFO 50 meters away and 20 meters off the ground. The craft flew silently up the valley towards them for 30 seconds and then away. Clearly visible are portholes and is identical to Adamski type craft.

- November, 1975. Santa Cruz, California. A scientist from the University of California at Berkeley reports to symposium that Apollo 11 was followed half way to the moon by UFO and Apollo 12 was followed throughout three orbits by another UFO.

- 1976, Los Angeles, California. Astronaut Gordon Cooper quoted as saying, "Intelligent beings from other planets regularly visit our world in an effort to enter into contact with us. I have encountered various ships during my space voyages. NASA and the American government know this and posses a great deal of evidence. Nevertheless, they remain silent in order to not alarm the people."

- March, 1977. Los Angeles, California. Several witnesses report two teardrop shaped lights flying in formation and traveling at high speed above Santa Catalina Island. Witnesses state, in their opinion these vehicles exhibited positive control.

- August, 1985. Peking, China. More than 600 UFO's observed in China's skies over the preceding five years. Most recent sighting witnessed by China B747 crew above Mongolia. Described as walnut shaped, it flew along side the jumbo jet for several minutes.

- December 1989 - March 1990, Belgium. Numerous eyewitness reports of several large triangular shaped platforms maneuvering about the countryside. Entire village populations described seeing these crafts approximately 100 meters altitude. Belgian Air Force was able to confirm the positions of crafts via radar and dispatched F16 fighters to investigate. Out of nine interception attempts, six established positive contact. The targets speed varied from 50 to 1010 kts within several seconds. These events were reported worldwide, however no official explanation was ever offered.

While reports continue to surface to this day, and they certainly continue to pique our curiosity, one has to wonder how much evidence eventually becomes convincingly enough. As my father was fond of saying, "How many times does one have to witness something, film it, photograph it, examine it and rationalize it: how much evidence does one need to accumulate, before finally waking up and getting behind it? " However, as he was well aware, proof is an individual process and this book exists in order to further this means.

Yet to a certain degree, we have become too comfortably accustomed to envisioning life beyond our tiny sphere of light as something extra-ordinary. For years educational institutions, theorists, and the promoters of science fiction have perpetuated the idea that space, and the planets beyond, constitute a hostile, desolate void. This idea in turn has fostered the notion which implies that only by sheer coincidence, the earth being fortunately located just the right distance from the sun, and only by chance, just the correct combination of molecules, elements, gases and amino acids, all presumably have miraculously chanced to interact and evolve into the type of environment capable of sustaining biological life as we perceive it. However, even the most superficial examination of this very life surrounding us should challenge these age-old presumptions and dispel the notion of purposeless creation. For how can we truly rationalize and believe that the concepts supporting the evolution of life, the principles of science, nature and creation could act so erratically ... exhibiting no universal similarity?

Today, scientists are beginning to admit that the clues to the origin of life are and will be found elsewhere in the solar system, stars and galaxies. That the biological process of organic chemistry and synthesis is constantly occurring within the universe and has been raining down upon our planet since time immemorial. Recent research supports the existence of a basic chemical similarity in living things throughout the universe and the key components of all biological molecules - amino acids, which combine to form proteins, which in turn stimulate the development of the genetic materials RNA and DNA, and so on and so forth, did not appear by chance ... thus indicating life is by no means a freak accident.

When we envision the reaches of outer space, we are really contemplating the vastness of limitless cosmos containing the essence of all creation. For surrounding us out there, as well as within this world we call home, the fundamental elements of life continue to intermix, manifest and evolve in order to express their functions. Much in the same manner as we unconsciously share the compositions of our environment transported by air, earth and sea, other biological life, and the remaining assortment of organic creation ... each of our neighboring planets have shared the same source of creation some four billion years past. Plus, our planet has, and continues to be, bombarded by an assortment of organic materials, debris, and biological compositions trailed by other planets, celestial bodies and those elements permeating within the womb of space itself.

Only in recent years, have we begun to explore and unveil some of the fundamentals concerning life's Universal Principles: Nature's physical laws and relationships between gravity, mass and centrifugal forces; her constant attempt to maintain a balance of forces and expression; the rules of equal and opposite reaction, the laws of magnetism, and the fundamentals of biochemistry which produce biological life. These fundamental principles we should all be aware of, if not familiar with, and not be so eager to abandon or ignore when searching the heavens and beyond for answers.

Perhaps when we begin to realize and develop a greater understanding of who and what we are, and of how life evolves and adapts on earth, then may we begin to question some of the vivid speculation depicting extraterrestrial life as something grotesque, threatening and bizarre. Let us remember that to travel across the marvelous distances of space requires not only highly advanced and precise technologies, but also eons of development, refinement, intelligence and understanding in order to successfully accomplish this wondrous feat. And as one prominent scientist said, " When we do land on a planet somewhere, someday, do not be surprised if somebody walks up to shake your hand." The wealth of evidence would certainly indicate they have already come to shake ours long ago.

G.S.

www.gafintl-adamski.com

References (Books)

Alternative 003! .... Leslie Watkins
Avon Books, The Hearst Corporation
949 Eighth Avenue, New York, NY 10019

A Piece For A Jigsaw Puzzle .... Leonard G. Cramp
The British Book Center, Inc.
122 East 55th St., New York, NY

Colonies In Space .... T. A. Heppenheimer
Stackpole Books
P. O. Box 1831, Harrisburg, PA 17105

Flying Saucers Farewell .... George Adamski
Abelard-Schuman, Inc., New York, NY
Now—The George Adamski Foundation
P. O. Box 1722, Vista, CA 92085

*Flying Saucers
Have Landed* .... Desmond Leslie & George Adamski
The British Book Center, Inc.
420 West 45th St., New York, NY

Footprints On The Moon .... The Associated Press
American Book, Stratford Press, Inc.

Inside The Space Ships .... George Adamski
Abelard Schuman, Inc., New York, NY
Revised Edition 1981 from GAF Int'l/Adamski Foundation
P. O. Box 1722, Vista, CA 92085

Life On Mars .... David Chandler
E. P. Dutton, 2 Park Ave., New York, NY 10016

Moongate - Suppressed Findings
Of The US Space Program.................. William L. Brian, II
Published 1982
P.O. 06392, Portland, OR, USA 97206-0020

Our Ancestors
Came From Outer Space.......................... Maurice Chatelain
Dell Publishing Co., Inc. 1 Dag Hammerskjold Plaza
New York, NY 10017

Prodigal Genius
(The Life of Nikola Tesla) .... John J. O'Neill
David McKay Company, Inc.
New York, NY

Space Gravity and the Flying Saucer ...... Leonard G. Cramp
The British Book Center, Inc.
122 East 55th Street, New York, NY

Somebody Else Is On The Moon .... George Leonard
David McKay Company, Inc., New York, NY

The Principles of Ultrarelativity .... Shinichi Seike
1978 Edition, G.- Research Laboratory
P. O. Box 33, Uwajima Post Office
Uwajima - City Ehime 798 Japan

References (Magazines)

Apollo 11 On The Moon .... Look Magazine Special 1969
Look Magazine, New York, NY

Life On Mars .... Beyond Reality Magazine
Oct 1977 Edition, New York, NY

"Brookings Report"............................ Proposed Studies on
the Implications of Peaceful Space
Activities for Human Affairs"
prepared for NASA 4/18/61
HR 87 Congress, 1st Session - Report #24

*Rebellion Among
The Astronauts*........................... Astronaut, Brian O'Leary
Ladies Home Journal, Mar. 1970

*There Is A Case
For Interplanetary Saucers*....... Life Magazine, April 7, 1952

*Apollo 15 Explores The
Mountains Of The Moon*.................... National Geographic
February, 1972

National Geographic ....July, 1976

Life On Mars .... Dr. Robert Jastrow
Science Digest, Spring, 1980

*Symposium On
Unidentified Flying Objects* .....19th Congress - 2nd Session
U.S. Government Printing Office
Washington, D.C.

The Earth's Moon .... National Geographic Society

News Clippings
from Major National Daily Newspapers

New York, Washington D.C., Los Angeles
A.P. and UPI., 1969 to 1981